I0635585

The Line of Succession 6:

God Save The…?

Harry F. Rey

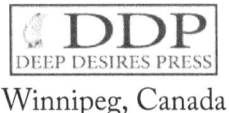

DDP
DEEP DESIRES PRESS

Winnipeg, Canada

Copyright © 2023 by Harry F. Rey
Cover design copyright © 2023 by Story Perfect Dreamscape

All characters are age 18 and over.

This is a work of fiction. Names, characters, business, places, events, and incidents are either products of the author's imagination or used in a fictitious manner. Any resemblances to actual persons, living or dead, or actual events is purely coincidental.

No part of this book may be used or reproduced in any manner without written permission from the publisher. However, brief quotations may be reproduced in the context of reviews.

Developmental editor: Craig Gibb
Proofreader: Margaret Larson

Published November 2023 by Deep Desires Press, an imprint of Story Perfect Inc.

Deep Desires Press
PO Box 51053 Tyndall Park
Winnipeg, Manitoba R2X 3B0
Canada

Visit http://www.deepdesirespress.com for more scorching hot erotica and erotic romance.

The Line of Succession 6:

God Save The…?

Chapter 1

BILL SWEATED UNDER THE TELEVISION lights. The *Britain Today* studio was a busy morass of cables and clipboards, of assistants and stars. He'd already been miked up, the thin black wires lashing him to the curved desk and the printed expanse of London washed in pastel colors as the backdrop. At any moment the news segment currently on air would finish, and Daisy Angus, the saber-toothed interviewer disguised as a sweet, perky Northern blonde, would begin her disemboweling of Bill live on *Britain Today*. An assistant producer had promised Bill water, but it had failed to materialize. Instead, headsetted assistants scurried between lumbering TV cameras, as rats might run between sleeping dragons. As soon as those cameras were turned on, it would be like waking those beasts, wondering if their mechanical jaws would breathe fire.

Bill had never been burned by journalistic fury. In fact, not very long ago, Bill had been the one to command dragon fire, burning whomever he wanted across the pages of what had once been Britain's biggest tabloid newspaper, *The*

Gazette. But the events of the last few years had raided and plundered his beloved *Gazette,* now left as a shell of its former glory. A barely literate rag of recycled viral pictures from the internet and a repository for press releases. Bill wished the powers that be had let his life's work die, instead of pulling the strings of the zombie paper like Frankenstein's Pinocchio.

The decline and fall of Bill Honnington's thirty-year tenure as editor-in-chief of *The Gazette* had begun one ordinary evening a few years back. The night before the royal twins, Prince James and Princess Alexandra (Bill cursed their names), had turned thirty. He remembered the moment with pristine clarity. Roger, his royal correspondent, had burst into his office with the scoop of the year. A rare voicemail message Roger had...*procured* from Prince James' mobile phone. A message left by one Andrew Hodes, the long-time press secretary to James during the fifteen years James was heir apparent to his late grandmother Queen Victoria II.

Bill remembered the odd grin on Roger's face. Roger had been hacking the royals' phones for years, and had written a steady stream of front-page worthy articles detailing Prince James' penchant for big-breasted models on yachts and supposed Jacuzzi sex with starlets. Roger had even found ways to download laddish pictures swapped between James and his upper-crust Eton friends. James' drinking shots from a Spanish actress' G-strung buttocks or dallying around Monaco or Barbados with his best friend Andrew, storming private beaches as if the world was their

Playboy Mansion. Yet, as Bill had learned, Prince James' Playboy life had all been a carefully crafted, and some might say overproduced, bare-faced lie.

That voicemail years ago left on James' phone by Andrew Hodes had been the chink in the armor that had changed everything. Not all at once, and not publicly either, not until James' coming out much later. But Roger and Bill knew the secrets the royals kept. They knew Prince James was hiding his sexuality and had been for years. Even as the royals defrauded the public with lies that the Swedish princess Katyn was James' girlfriend, Bill knew the truth. Even as Andrew worked for *The Gazette*, pumping out stories to support James and Katyn's so-called relationship, Bill knew the truth. Even after a terrorist attack stole Katyn's life, Bill knew the truth. Even as the police raided *The Gazette* and he'd been thrown into a cell and came face-to-face with MI5 director Lisa Mantis, Bill knew the truth.

The powers that be said Bill had committed treason. They were ready to jail him for phone hacking. But what really irked the British establishment was the simple fact Bill knew the filthy truth about the royal family. The state covering up James and Andrew's secret gay affair for God knows how long was the very least of it. The royal family had covered up a hell of a lot more than the fact their heir and now King had spent half his life as…what Bill's son Greg would call a "power bottom". Or, as Bill had joked with Greg back when the two had been speaking, Britain's Next Top Bottom.

But the TV was calling. The presenter, Daisy Angus,

was shuffling her papers, blabbing to the nation with her kitchen-table extremism. Thick black cables swung like tails. The dragons with their single eye scopes swarmed around the sweltering lair that was the *Britain Today* studio. Snapping clipboards counted down the moments until the fiery lick of live TV would scald Bill's skin. But all he could think about were the things he knew. James and Andrew were the least of it, the very least of it.

"It's been a wild ride for our beloved monarchy these last few years, in't it?" Daisy told the cameras. Bill perspired like Niagara. He'd held the evidence in his hands. The secret book by renowned Irish war reporter Liv Finnegan. "What with the canceled referendum on if we want one or t'other to be queen or king." The book that detailed in all its gruesome glory the so-called Gaveston Protocols that the security agencies, the late queen, and the government had used to blow up Prince Richard's helicopter, leaving Alexandra and James fatherless at only fifteen and thrusting James into the spotlight as heir. "Some of us are rightly saying, 'Hold up, why even bother with having a king or queen at all?'" Where was Liv Finnegan? No one had given Bill an answer, not through any of this. She'd sat in his office, and she'd sold him her book proving that Prince Richard's first wife wasn't James and Alexandra's mother, the commoner Princess Alice, but someone even more unsuitable. An undercover IRA agent turned royal mistress Calista Murphy, who had married Richard in secret and birthed the woman the world knew as nothing more than a royal cousin, Lizzie Windsor… "Joining me to discuss where the monarchy goes from here…" Where was Liv Finnegan? Would the British state really murder a journalist who had evidence the rest of the line of succession were nothing but…bastards? "Is the former editor of *The Gazette*…" Bill couldn't breathe. He was locked in a nightmare he couldn't leave. If he did, he would be killed. like Richard. Like Calista. Like Liv. "Recently ennobled by King James for his years of service to media, the Marquess of Essex, Lord William Honnington, good to have you with us."

"Good to be here, Daisy, nice to be sitting on this side of the panel for once."

"Well deserved after your years on Fleet Street, Lord Honnington. But please, tell Britain, is there a crisis in our monarchy?" Bill felt the saliva pooling in his mouth. He swallowed, and it at least quenched his dry throat.

"No, I don't think our monarchy is in crisis. But I think it's right to say we have gone through many tragedies as a nation, tragedies which have undoubtedly affected His Majesty the King, and of course her royal highness, his sister. I mean, I'm old enough to remember the horrendous night we lost Prince Richard in a helicopter crash."

"I was still in primary school."

"Well, exactly, but even more recently we had the tragic death of Princess Katyn in a car bombing. I mean, for anyone to lose a loved one that way is horrendous, but just a few months later King James, who was Prince Regent at the time, lost his beloved grandmother, Queen Victoria, who had been a rock for the family, and for this nation, for over half a century. I mean, we've all been through a collective trauma. And I wouldn't be surprised, Daisy, if we weren't all suffering a little bit, as a nation, from some post trauma."

"So, let me ask you, Lord Honnington," Bill braced himself for the sharp edge of her incisors as Daisy tapped her painted nails against her cheek, "is that the cause of the referendum debacle? Collective post-trauma?"

"I wouldn't call it a debacle, Daisy."

"Wouldn't you? Parliament passed an abdication act for James to sign. The former prime minister Zia Wajid all but pledged her allegiance to the idea of Alexandra as Queen, yet we ended up later that day with James as King."

"Yes, and that's why the royal family, in consultation with the government of the day, thought it wise to propose a referendum on who should be the next monarch."

"Which was only canceled a few weeks from the vote and after millions of taxpayer pounds was spent on setting it up."

"But you're forgetting the context, Daisy. James had just buried his beloved Katyn, the woman whom we all thought was going to be queen one day. I remember publishing those stories at *The Gazette*. It was right after such a tragedy for James to take some time out from royal duties, and naturally the question was asked if Princess Alexandra should perhaps serve as monarch instead."

"And while the king was taking this 'time out', he realized he was gay."

"I don't think it's appropriate to label His Majesty's

sexual orientation, Daisy, but he is engaged to the Duke of Cornwall, Prince Andrew, and I, for one, look forward to attending their wedding."

"Are we any closer to a date on this gay royal wedding, Lord Honnington? I mean they have been engaged for nearly a year now."

"I'm not privy to such discussions, Daisy, but I believe they want to get next month's coronation out of the way first."

"Uh huh." Daisy bit her lip and scoured the notes in front of her in that pre-gotcha moment Bill knew was coming. "I only ask you, Lord Honnington, as your son Lord Gregory is rumored to be on rather good terms with King James." Bill did not react. Not under the glare of dragon fire, at least, but the cameras raised his blood to boiling. "Partying it up with His Majesty at Windsor Castle, in Mykonos—" Daisy shot her famous sly grin that might as well have seen her turn and wink to her audience "—all the while the country is asking where exactly is the Duke of Cornwall, Andrew Hodes? I mean, the royal couple haven't been seen together in public for nearly a month while your son, Lord Honnington, appears to never be far from the King's side. Are we seeing a change of favorites, perhaps? You, yourself, very rapidly went from under arrest for illegal phone hacking to peer of the realm. I just wonder if the next time we have you on the program, we won't be calling you…well, won't be calling you Queen Mother, for want of one of your gender-neutral terms."

Bill smiled. Daisy smiled back. Between them both was

an epic war of fire and brimstone. Flaming daggers and poisoned arrows. All contained in a journalist's grin.

"It does amaze me, Daisy, the extent to which programs like yours will debase themselves for some frankly homophobic insinuation and gossip."

"Are you refusing to answer the question, Lord Honnington?"

"No, I just expected you, as the anchor of the leading breakfast television program, to ask better questions."

"Well, I'm asking this one, Lord Honnington, and if you don't know the answer, perhaps your son can ask it instead. When is King James going to have his gay wedding and will he force a split in the Church of England by insisting to marry his gay lover...or one of his lovers, at least, in a holy church?"

"It is simply not appropriate for me to engage in petty innuendo about His Majesty's private life, nor about Prince Andrew, and nor, for that matter, my son."

"Fair enough, Lord Honnington, so let me ask this, then: Princess Alexandra announced a separation from her husband Prince Faisal a few weeks ago. Since then, he's been back in Saudi Arabia with their children who are, still, second and third in line to our throne. Is she going to divorce her husband?"

"You'll have to ask her."

"Well, I am asking you as someone personally raised to the office of Marquess by the King."

"I won't be speculating on that, either."

Daisy nodded, the smile not leaving her face. Job done,

in her books. Complete meltdown avoided in Bill's mind, too. He just had to get out of the studio, find Greg, and wring his bloody neck. Daisy shuffled her papers and turned back to face the camera.

"There you have it, folks. Crisis, what crisis? So say the royals. Next up, a coronation of sodomy, so says a parish priest in Yorkshire who is going on a hunger strike in protest against the *sodom*-ation of King James. And we'll meet a wiccan high priestess who says she can cast a spell on King James and Prince Andrew and bless them with a child. We'll be back after the break."

Bill didn't wait a second. He tore up from the studio seat like the dragons in the lair had all awoken at once. He unleashed the microphone from around his neck and chest, and stormed off in the direction of the exit. The truth was, the creatures in this cavern had already had their fill of Bill. He'd been skewered and roasted. It was more fun for the tabloid beasts to play with one who used to be more powerful than them all, to toss his hide around, never quite landing a death blow so their fun could be had once again. Near the exit he saw a young assistant scurry hurriedly, she clutched a small glass bottle of soda water, patently intended for a guest other than him.

"Finally," Bill said, descending on the hapless production assistant. He snatched the bottle before she could let out a bleep. Twisting off the cap, he drunk it in front of her. The bubbles burned, but he didn't care. He'd survived a mauling. Storming through the double doors of the studio into the emptier hallway, Bill coughed away heartburn and angrily thumbed his phone. The first number was, of course, turned off, as it always was these days. Unsurprised, Bill was at least glad of the fact his new position as Marquess of Essex came with a staff and office.

The assistant, Freya, started babbling the second the call connected.

"I thought you came across very well, sir, very calm and in control of—"

"Enough!" Bill roared as he finally burst out of the TV studio and into the overcast morning. "Find my son. Now!"

Chapter 2

JAMES LAY BACK ON THE CUSHIONED pillow. Daylight streamed in from above, through Windsor Castle's ancient arrow slits now covered in glass. Still, there was always a darkness in the castle's dungeon, even after James had converted the dungeon into…well, a dungeon. He nestled into the cushioned pillow, finding some comfort in the sling. James' hands were cuffed to chains behind his head, and his feet wrapped in leather stirrups. The king was immobile, just how he liked to have sex.

Andrew had always been afraid to do these things to James. There was always an excuse; what if the public or press might see rope marks on James' arms, or what if the strange men they invited to Andrew's flat under the guise of anonymously fucking a man in a hood took liberties and tore off James' hood while he was chained up? How would they discreetly purchase the items James wanted, since ordinary ropes or cuffs would not cut it. James loved the clink of metal and the spank of leather. He was already hard with the weight of the custom-smelted collar locked into place and currently pressing into his shoulder blades. When the men who worked in Windsor Castle, from the stable hands to the footmen, were let inside the dungeon to fuck James, one after the other, the thrashing chagrin of metal chains rattling as he was pounded would very likely bring King James the Eighth to a hands-free orgasm, as he'd come to expect over these last few weeks.

James glanced to one side, where his aide Samuel—clad only in a jockstrap and leather waistcoat—prepared a small table of lubricants and poppers for the morning shift. Against the wall was the St. Andrew's cross James could also command he be lashed to, and then the myriad of shelves cluttered with instruments of torture and ecstasy. The ancient stony walls still had many of their original shackles attached. Medieval torture chamber or modern BDSM dungeon, there wasn't much of a difference.

"Are you ready, Your Majesty?" Samuel asked. A keen, kinky smile plastered on his face at ten in the morning. With a coronation to prepare for, scheduling some dungeon time had to be coordinated with various secretaries and government departments. Without any other royal stand-ins James would give permission to represent him at state functions, His Majesty's schedule was as tight as the cuffs around his wrists and ankles. *Could not the Duke of Cornwall perhaps take this audience, Your Majesty? This engagement would be perfect for Prince Andrew, should we not reach out to him? Traditionally, Your Majesty, the spouse of the monarch would…*

James rattled the sling with frustration, which Samuel took for impatience.

"Nearly ready, sir," Samuel said, stretching a cock ring around himself. "The lads are all waiting outside, they know we only have half an hour."

Another thing to blame on Andrew. They only had half an hour for the King to be secretly engaged because next on the schedule was to open some hospital clinic Andrew had made himself patron of. Andrew this, Andrew that. The whole world wanted Andrew, but Andrew didn't want them.

Andrew had always maintained that thrusting James into a shot-gun relationship with Princess Katyn had been an accident or a misunderstanding. James had thought differently. He'd always feared his lover of almost two decades would one day get bored of this secretive life, and leave James trapped in the position he'd been born in. To James, the Katyn set-up was Andrew's crowning glory of an escape plan. James remembered with piercing clarity the morning of his thirtieth birthday, when he'd been taking tea with his mother, of all things, an activity in itself as stressful as an exam. Lo and behold, Andrew Hodes, the royal press secretary, had sat on breakfast television programs and not only refuted tabloid claims that James had never had a girlfriend, claims which James was now convinced his sister Alexandra had planted, but to tell the world James *did* have a serious girlfriend and the world was on the verge of meeting her that very evening!

It boiled James' blood to think of it. Moreover, that

he'd thought they'd moved on, put it behind them, but here Andrew was again, accepting James' offer of royal titles, accepting on TV his marriage proposal, yet still for Andrew it wasn't enough. He'd got upset once again, stormed off once again, and left James quite literally in a bind. The only way for James to satisfy himself, to find five minutes in his insane life was to slip away into a dungeon, and then go off and carry out the duties which were supposed to be Andrew's as well as his own. And for what, all because James wouldn't fire Samuel? Because he was jealous of the one man James had in his life who didn't actually let him down. Did Andrew seriously expect the aging butler Charles to smuggle in a Berlin sex club's worth of equipment into Windsor Castle?

Maybe all James had wanted was the heavy weight of Andrew's body pressed next to him at night. Maybe all he'd ever dreamed of was to go about his royal life hand in hand with Andrew, not hiding his lover away from the world. Maybe the burden of half a life of secrets wasn't so easy to overcome in just a few weeks, but had Andrew really tried? Had Andrew given James a chance? The anger pulsing through him was enough to make James lose his hard-on. He needed Andrew out of his mind, and he needed a dick in his ass. No, he needed several. To be fucked until the line between pain and pleasure, reality and fantasy, was as non-existent as the current line of succession.

"Samuel, I'm ready."

• • •

James knew the first man by taste. Sweat dripped from the hairy chest of the brown-skinned footman. His cock had a familiar curve to the right that left James gasping when he slammed his weight fully inside James, as he did with every thrust as he got closer. The chains rattled with the pneumatic whacks from this barrel-chested top. Samuel was behind James, offering a hit of poppers every so often, but James was well-versed in the art of being gang-fucked. James couldn't throw his legs around the man's middle, because they were chained to the sling, but he could squeeze his thighs against thick working-man muscles. He could clamp his ass around the hefty curve of the man's uncircumcised cock, and savor the drips of sweat which dribbled from his forehead and splashed—if he was lucky— straight into James' mouth.

The man was getting close, but James wanted more. He lunged up from the sling's cushioned headrest and planted a hefty kiss on his surprised mouth. There wasn't much else for a footman to do when the king kissed him, so he kissed back. Reluctant at first, James could tell, but he eased into it. Samuel held up James' head for him as their mouths locked into a nasty smack of lips, the footman angling himself farther back to deliver a proper pounding into James, thrusting the tip of his curved dick so deeply James could feel it in his stomach.

A few slaps of their tongues later, the footman engorged himself into a full-throttle groan. James held onto his tongue as his hips whacked into an orgasmic wall. The motion of the sling shoved James' pummeled ass straight into his explosion, soaring deep inside James with ball-aching pumps he could feel. Their kiss broken, the footman withdrew himself and smirked with one corner of his mouth. He slapped the royal ass as James collapsed back onto the sling, and Samuel wafted the familiar stench of poppers under his nose. James breathed in deeply, causing the pang of deep, horny hunger to crest across his body as the next man stepped forward.

This one was a Coldstream Guard; a military man James had seen once or twice standing outside Buckingham Palace in his big bearskin hat and red and gold coat. Out of dress, he was just as imposing. Arms as thick as trunks that grabbed onto the chains as he slipped inside James. Smaller than the one before, he fucked with a smoother tone. He even caressed James' chest, gently grazing nipple in a way that had him quickly remembering whom he was fucking, before withdrawing his hands back to the chains under the watchful nod of Samuel.

James let himself settle into the rhythm of the fuck, glancing at the line of another four men standing naked in the castle dungeon, waiting to do their royal duty. The rules were clear for those stationed in the King's personal guard. Samuel vetted each and every one of them. James was pretty sure his personal secretary auditioned the men by having them fuck one of the subbier twinks of the royal household staff. They were forbidden from having sex outside of the household "bubble" and also tested for a myriad of infections every fortnight. All were asked to go on PrEP, despite there being no risk due to James' undetectable status, but the men might play with each other, too, and the system was designed to offer the King the maximum amount of pleasure, while giving those offered the honor of pleasing His Majesty a safe environment to enjoy themselves. The system seemed to be working quite well, as James' personal "bubble", vetted by Samuel, had grown from around half a dozen men when he'd first taken the throne, to well over a hundred now.

They were stationed across the royal palaces and throughout the staff. So, whether James was working at Buckingham Palace, holidaying at Balmoral, entertaining diplomats at Kensington, meeting political leaders at St. James's, or just day-to-day living at Windsor Castle, there would be a platoon of men on hand to provide His Majesty with every possible bodily desire.

The Coldstream guard panted then shouted a Northern-accented, "Oh fucking hell, man, fuck yeah," as he came inside the King. He was quickly replaced by one of James' favorites, a well-hung Scotsman with a ginger beard and Viking chest, who used a thumb and finger to spread open James' hole before slapping his girthy cock straight inside, right up to the wild bush of flame-colored pubes. But, still, it was never enough.

The sensations were all correct. Every thrust, every slam, every load brought James closer to his own spontaneous eruption. Or, at least, it used to. These days, the once common-place hands-free orgasm had become such a moving target James didn't even bother reaching for it. He just jerked off in the shower afterward while thinking about Andrew.

Andrew wasn't the most well-hung, he wasn't the thickest or lasted the longest. He didn't have the perfect body. He wasn't the tallest or the slimmest or had the most well-defined muscles. He didn't bend over backward at James' every wish and command like Samuel. Nor did he give in to James' every whim and desire. Like this sling. Like this row of vetted and vaccinated men, the very cream of Britain. But Andrew had something else none of these men had. That none of the hundreds, if not thousands, of men who had been inside James had.

James just didn't know what the hell that missing thing was.

The Scotsman finished. It could have been one minute or ten. The clinking chains and pumping thrusts all blended together in a symphony of sex that rattled the dungeon walls. There was everything in here. A torture chamber of BDSM gear; a wall of whips, a chest of collars, shelves of cock cages. Every imaginable item James had ever seen through a mobile phone screen in the darkness of an unfulfilled night. When Andrew was softly snoring beside him. In those endless, quiet hours, James had laid awake. Scrolling. Imagining. Wondering what it would be like to live in that world. Of darkened dungeons and cigar-chomping leather daddies. Dreaming of the very places he could never visit, all because of an accident of birth. He could abdicate and still he would never be let alone. Always hounded, always known.

Yes, the custom-built dungeon beneath the castle depths was fun. But it was fake. The twinky Polish cook who was now sliding his long, uncut cock inside James hadn't *chosen* to be here. He hadn't stumbled across this place of his own accord, and found James laying there, ripe for the fucking. The feeling now burning inside James, as a dick pounded at his flesh, was analogous to those scary first days of school, when James had feared the other boys only wanted to be his friend because his dad had told them to. Or more likely, they'd all been told who his dad was. This wasn't real life, only a version of it. With Andrew gone, it was all James could ever have, or ever hope for.

A crack as the dungeon door opened disturbed his thoughts and the fuck's flow. The men already spent and drinking sports drinks glanced over. The Polish man balls-deep in James stopped. James leaned up, crunching his abs while awkwardly holding onto the chains to stop from slipping away from his top. The light was blinding.

"S-sorry I'm late," a voice from the door said. Nervous. Familiar.

Samuel ran to the door like a bat out of hell, his bubble-butt ass strapped into the jock bouncing as he did. James couldn't quite see, but Samuel was speaking rapidly, if not harshly, to the figure by the door. It wasn't a cleaner or anything like that. James' eyes adjusted to the light. Someone in only underwear. Made sense. Beyond the door was a sort of changing area and locker room, along with purpose-built showers, for the men to get ready and hang up their fatigues. It reminded James of a stable. Stallions readying to pound a mare. No one got into the stables who was not invited. He looked cute, James thought. Slim and small, but inquisitive, soft-looking. Maybe even real. Walking into a top-secret orgy announcing *sorry, I'm late,* made James smile.

Soon enough, the door closed with the newcomer on the other side. Samuel scurried back. The spent men returned to their sipping sports drinks and protein shakes—just another workout for them. The Polish cook still inside James spat onto his cock and slipped back inside. James registered the depth of his cock, but was more intrigued by what Samuel had to say.

"Who was that?" James asked, looking up at Samuel who seemed on the verge of disturbed.

"Um…" He began in the typical prefix to unwanted news. "Lord Gregory Honnington, sir."

"Greg? You mean…Andrew's Greg?"

"The very same. He's on the vetted list, but I had no idea he was invited. Such a mix up, sir, please forgive me. Half of the Dragoons are away in London preparing for Trooping the Color tomorrow and he must have received a message to join us here by mistake. So sorry again, sir."

"No, no…" James said, the jackhammering thrusts becoming more annoying than horny. "No need to apologize. Um…" James reached up and tapped the top's shoulder. It broke the spell, and a question of surprise covered his sweat-drenched face. "It's all very nice and whatnot, but I just remembered I have an…engagement to get to. Isn't that right, Samuel?"

"Oh, um… yes. An engagement." Samuel checked the time on his phone on the small table of lube and poppers. The confused look on his face told James there were at least ten minutes to go of scheduled dungeon time. Samuel might be a wonder as a private secretary and procurer of unmentionables, but he was not a man who could adapt to a shifted schedule.

"Well…if you wouldn't mind," James said, as if excusing himself from an awkward conversation with an archbishop. James shooed the man off, who floated away, slightly confused. Hard, glistening cock still in hand. James rattled the chains as it took a moment for Samuel to acknowledge James wanted out. Cottoning on, he began to unbind James then helped him out of the sling. One of the men took initiative and handed James a royal velvet robe and some slippers. Slinking back a sweaty head of hair, James clothed himself as if he *wasn't* standing around half a dozen men who'd just bred his ass. James turned and nodded to them briefly, like thanking the waitstaff.

"Good show," James said to them, not oblivious to the cloddish way the situation was wrapping up, but not really caring, either. "Oh, Samuel. Ask Lord Gregory if he couldn't spare me a few minutes for a brief audience after I've hosed myself down. I'll receive him in the Orchid Room."

"Very good, Your Majesty…for any particular reason?"

"Why yes," James said, approaching the basement door. Oftentimes he would watch the men who'd just fucked him wash and dress in the newly constructed communal showers outside of the dungeon, but not today. The hospital opening he didn't care to be late to. Tomorrow's Trooping the Color ceremony didn't require much more preparation. But James was in a rush for another reason entirely. "He's the one Andrew's been fucking. I bet he knows where the bastard is."

Chapter 3

THE LONG, INTRICATELY-CARVED TABLE was set with so much fine silverware it rivaled the half an army's worth of clunking suits of armor clasping swords that besieged the dark mahogany-paneled walls. Wrought-iron candelabras hung low from the dining room's high ceiling, with more candles melted into sconces between the priceless impressionist art on the walls. Lisa Mantis, Director General of MI5, sat at one far corner of the table, the only woman among a sea of admirals and marshals and intelligence grandees drinking themselves sozzled.

The flickering candlelight bothered her. She hated these EMP-protected rooms. Entering an electronic dead zone always made her feel like a coup d'état was in progress, and she'd be gassed or poisoned or stabbed in the back somewhere between the fish course and the sorbet. God knows she'd planned enough of those "set menus" as Pudgy's MI6 called those operations.

"Not drinking, K?" Pudgy asked, refilling his own wine glass from a bottle. Lisa, or "K", eyed with suspicion. She ignored the question from "C", her Secret Intelligence Service counterpart. Also known as Sir George.

"It's barely lunchtime."

That didn't stop the other twelve "shadows" around the table having their fill of a lunchtime wine. These "shadows" were the individuals who folded into the margins of British public life, yet wielded inordinate power. All held varying titles of nobility, all except her. Sir Arthur, chief of the defense staff. Sir John, a former foreign secretary. Lord John, she should say. Two former chancellors; one a baron, one an earl. Sir Alan, a former prime minister and current lord president of the Privy Council. And Sir Peter. Queen Victoria II's former private secretary and sworn enemy of the current king. He'd managed to fall dramatically upward, newly installed as the Cabinet Secretary, in other words, the United Kingdom's shadow prime minister. The thin man with a thinner mustache practically twirled his whiskers as he sipped on port from a crystal goblet.

"Come on, K," Pudgy said again, nudging her. The room remained a clatter of good-natured conversation. She sighed, twiddling with her empty plate while the others dined on hors d'oeuvres of Caspian caviar. He lifted the bottle with an expectant, ruddy grin. "It may be a Chateau Lafite, but it's far from poison."

"Fine," she grumbled, nodding to the wine glass which he gladly glugged full. "But if masked men barge in and start shooting at us, I'm using you as a human shield."

"Fair enough. Plenty of me to go around." He tugged on his cummerbund, already stretched to oblivion. Lisa sipped the wine, channeling her ear to different snippets of conversation. Each as uninteresting as the last. Mainly about the mess the recently ousted prime minister Zia Wajid had left in her wake. And just how damned hard a job Sir Peter had in cleaning up the mess.

"I say," she overheard him chattering away, "it would be a damn sight easier to run Whitehall without those pesky politicians poking their nose in where it doesn't belong."

"Here-here!" piped up Sir Alan.

"Pudgy," Lisa said quietly, holding back an eye roll, "why exactly have I been invited to the Old Etonian buggery club's annual taxpayer-funded piss-up?"

"What?" Pudgy said, caviar smeared across his rouged cheeks. "I thought you women were always banging on about a seat at the table. Well, where are you sitting?" He grinned. The head of MI6 rather enjoyed his little wind-ups. Such as calling her up in the middle of the night and claiming a cyborg had gotten loose from a research facility in the Welsh marches, or an alien spacecraft had landed and was demanding Stonehenge be returned in its original packaging.

"How about an update on my request?"

He cleared his throat and began to speak very loudly: "I shan't be assassinating any more ex-husbands of yours, K." A few from the table glanced over with a vague smirk. Lisa plastered on a fake grin, but spoke to him quietly, and with deathly seriousness.

"Oh, Pudgy. I know your wife's internet search history.

In fact, I have it somewhere in my purse." She began to reach under the table.

"Poppycock. My wife can't use a computer. She calls up rent boys in the Yellow Pages and has them pop round to do the gutters, then force-feeds them Chelsea Buns." Pudgy was again speaking loudly, grifting a laddish joke across the table, but it wasn't landing. Lisa, however, was still in no mood, despite the wine.

"Ah, so it's you who has the username: *Grannies-Panties*?" Pudgy's face dropped. The joke wasn't funny anymore. MI6 might be the ones always running around foreign rooftops and assassinating nuclear scientists with pointy umbrellas, but K had the most dangerous weapon of all: real time access to the entire internet activity of just about everyone in the United Kingdom.

"All right, Lisa, what are you bothered about today?"

"The whereabouts of Andrew Hodes."

Lisa asked it with earnest, but in reality, she knew the answer. He was in Saudi Arabia with Faisal. Andrew had been keeping a low profile there, but he was hardly in hiding. Taking meetings and helping Faisal *build a new Saudi Arabia* or whatever the Crown Prince's new mantra was. And it seemed Andrew had quite the ear of Faisal, although that wasn't news to Lisa. This whole ruse was to test how much intelligence MI6 had on Faisal. For all the years he'd been in Britain, Faisal and his company Royal Arabian Petroleum's operations had been under Lisa's purview. And she'd penetrated his operation pretty well. Now that Faisal's operation had upped sticks and moved to

Saudi, her intelligence assets had moved with them. In the constant battle between the intelligence agencies, this gave Lisa an ace in her sleeve. Getting inside the Saudi government was notoriously hard for any foreign intelligence service to do, given how half the government was stuffed with members of the Al Saud clan. If Lisa had better intelligence in Riyadh than Pudgy, she wanted to know that for a fact.

"Oh, that old chestnut."

"Yes, Pudgy. That old chestnut. I've asked you for weeks now. I know you dismissed it as…what did you call it, a 'bum boy's tiff', but if you've not forgotten, coronation season is fast approaching, Pudgy. The press smells a scandal, and I'm not sure the monarchy can survive another one of those, do you?" She was more upset than she'd suspected, and took a long sip of wine. She knew that *he* knew something she didn't, and that was the most annoying of all.

"That's not true."

"What's not?"

"I never said 'bum boy's tiff'."

"Oh?"

"Of course not. You said, 'Prince Andrew's gone missing, and the King is busying himself with half the infantry units in the country', and I said—"

"Buggers can't be choosers," K said, rolling her eyes at his so-called wit. He offered his glass up, she reluctantly chinked it.

"But I do have a little bit of…what do they call it…tea

to spill." Pudgy's face turned redder and, well, pudgier as he drank. "It turns out those bum boys did have a tiff. On the night of their engagement, as it happens."

"I know that. Don't you know I've had Windsor Castle bugged for years?"

"Since well before your time, K. The chap before Dame Esmeralda, God rest her soul, we called Bugger-in-Chief! Can't get away with that these days."

"Couldn't get away with it then, either. But go on then, C, spill that tea."

"Who paid a visit to Andrew after their fight, but none other than Prince Faisal."

Lisa swirled the Bordeaux, thinking and sipping. If this was what Pudgy was basing his intelligence on, then Pudgy didn't have much of an operation to speak of.

"Andrew's switched sides in the past," she said. "He worked with Alexandra and Faisal shortly after James *began* his relationship with Princess Katyn." It still smarted for Lisa that the young woman, by all accounts an innocent victim in these sick royal games, had died thanks to Lisa's intelligence failures. She'd never suspected the thing police detectives always start with; that the culprit was likely known to the victim. In this case, the culprit was Lizzie. James and Alexandra's supposed cousin, but actually their older half-sister. Perhaps Pudgy didn't know Lizzie was now firmly in the pocket of Lisa Mantis.

"Maybe Andrew's turned again."

"An odd thing to do, don't you think? Trying to bring James down from the inside. If anything, Andrew's still playing both sides, perhaps he convinced Alex to withdraw from the referendum? Anyway, doesn't matter now, does it? If Alex and Faisal get divorced, they're effectively a spent force. No longer a risk to James."

"Not necessarily."

"How so?"

"Prince Andrew, Duke of Cornwall, the intended of His Majesty, has been shacked up in a Saudi palace for the last few weeks with his other royal highness, Prince Faisal bin Saud of Saudi Arabia. Once the forgotten ninth son of the Sultan, now heir apparent to the kingdom. With little miss Andrew Hodes by his side."

Lisa faked surprise. Pudgy's intelligence was simply that Andrew was there in Saudi Arabia. Lisa's intelligence was what he was doing there every day. Working with Faisal and trying, perhaps trying in vain, to get over James.

"Why? I mean…why? What do we do?"

Pudgy smiled and refilled their glasses. White-coated waiters had just stepped in to clear the caviar plates, and a brief pause to classified conversation descended across the gilded dining room. In a moment the waiters were gone. A few throats were cleared, and more wine was uncorked. Lisa sensed an anticipation to the main course. Unlikely to be a suckling pig or plump-breasted pheasant, but perhaps the reason why twelve apostles of the British state had been summoned to hear from…who?

Her self-asked question was immediately answered. Sir Peter, with a Saint-Peter-sized ego, clinked his crystal glass with a silver knife. Immediately, the room fell silent, but he continued to ding and grin like a cultist about to crucify his disciples…or ask them all to drink his poison.

"Gentlemen," Peter said, rising to his feet. He nodded at Lisa, but she sat there stony-faced. "And, of course, lady." Lisa openly rolled her eyes then hid behind her wine glass. "The conspiracy to assassinate Julius Caesar began with only two men, Cassius Longinus and, of course, Marcus Brutus. They met of an evening, not dissimilar to this, and agreed that something must be done to prevent this Caesar becoming king of the Romans."

There was a murmur of approval around the room that left Lisa shocked. As if the fathers of all these men had personally stabbed Caesar.

"On the face of it," Peter continued, gesturing with his wine glass, "our situations are slightly different. We already have a king, and, there are thirteen of us around this table, not two. Yet what so disturbed Longinus and Brutus was not so much the thought of monarchy, but the idea that Caesar would occupy that position, and form a sort of proto dictatorship of the plebs and let the state crumble into a cesspit of megalomaniacal corruption. My friends, our situations are not dissimilar at all."

The murmur of agreement grew stronger and louder. After a moment, hands were slapped on the table, bouncing the silverware in a show of force that made Lisa's skin crawl. Even Pudgy was joining in. She glared at him, and he stopped, but only to take a drink of wine.

"I spent forty years of my life by her late majesty's side." Peter flicked away a false tear, his voice trebling to a whine.

"She was petrified by what could happen to the institution she gave her life to. Succession is not an easy business, gentlemen. As you all know, we were forced by an act of treason—" Peter spat "—to activate the Gaveston Protocols once before. When it became clear that her own son, Prince Richard, had been cavorting with IRA operatives and treasonously plotting to interfere with our lawful line of succession, Queen Victoria II, God rest her soul, had no hesitation to sign the death warrant for her own son."

"Best decision we ever made," piped up Sir Arthur. Lisa felt a sickness in the pit of her stomach that the head of the British armed forces was drunkenly cheering the murder of the man who should have been his commander-in-chief. Even if the murder was "lawful".

"Unlike our Roman ancestors," Peter continued, "we have not one threat to contend with, but two. Princess Alexandra has proved herself far more of a formidable force than any of us expected. Yes, less so, now with her corrupt prime minister Zia Wajid no longer in power, and wounded, more so, with the separation from her husband, perhaps fatally, but she remains a threat, nonetheless. And that brings us to his current majesty." A rumble of disapproval rattled around the room. Lisa ignored the question popping up in her mind as if that itself constituted treason. Peter's face changed, too. From one of callous indifference to downright disgust.

"Our *king*," Peter announced to the room, turning the corner of his mouth nasty, "is a national disgrace. What homosexuals want to do in their own private time is...I suppose…tolerated these days. But for anyone in the public eye to thrust their sexual perversions in our face, not least a king who is supposed to command respect!" Peter foamed at the mouth. "Gentlemen…it's unconscionable." More agreement around the room, but Peter didn't slow down from his mutinous crescendo. "The world is a fragile place. Britain is on her own. Our monarchy is a laughingstock, and our line of succession, it's…it's…" Peter couldn't quite find the correct tone of loathing. So, Sir Arthur answered for him.

"It's being buggered into next week, that's what's what!"

The men chuckled. Lisa had had enough.

"Excuse me," she said, her sharp voice commanding the room's attention. Peter sat back down as she cut short his soliloquy. "But are we suggesting to activate the Gaveston Protocols on *both* King James and Princess Alexandra? Despite the fact the reigning monarch must sign the Protocols. And…what's that thing I'm missing…oh yeah, who the fuck takes over?"

"Well, I'm very glad you asked, K. Some of us have been discussing these ideas for a while, and we have come to the conclusion what would be best for us, excuse me, best for the country, would be a regency council."

Lisa looked around the table. There were many nods. Some seemed to have heard of this idea before, others not, but all looked in agreement. Sir Alan, the former PM who'd co-signed Prince Richard's Gaveston Protocols, took the reins.

"The regency council would give us all some breathing

space, generate some distance between the events of the last few years and this country's future. Alexandra's son Prince Hassan is what age now, ten, eleven? Parliament will of course extend his age of majority to twenty-one. It gives us a decade. We can set the country right, leave behind the bad eggs of this generation, and move forward. With any luck, Prince Hassan will be quite content to let the regency council carry out its business even after he comes of age."

"It's the best way forward," Peter said, as if convincing the others to agreement, or offering no cracks or pauses to the argument. Lisa studied the faces around the room. She could tell this was news to all but no more than three of them. Sir Peter and Sir Alan were in cahoots, she knew that much. Possibly Lord John as well, but it was obvious this was brand new information to the others. Particularly the aging Sir Arthur with his wild gray eyebrows whiskering along to the idea of a regency council.

"Once again," Lisa said, not quite believing the conspiratorial conversation occurring. "You cannot use the Gaveston Protocols on a sitting monarch! They were designed a thousand years ago to take out Piers Gaveston who was trying to get his lover, King Edward, to name his own children as heirs. It's there to protect the line of succession, not top off any monarch you don't like."

"One could argue King James' lifestyle choices have already greatly interfered with the line of succession. He will produce no lawful heir, especially given his…medical condition."

"Disgusting," Arthur grumbled. "I shook his hand with

gloves! That I burned!" The man went red under the collar. Lisa was losing patience.

"I don't care about any of that," Lisa said, "and there's no lawful reason any of you should, either. Alexandra's next in line, and her son Prince Hassan after her, as you've already acknowledged and presumably understand if you want a regency council to rule in Hassan's name." She moved to stand up. "I don't think there's any discussion to be had. There's always a line of succession, end of story." Lisa snatched her purse—empty of electronics— but Pudgy guided her back down. Peter lost all his shine and sheen; just an old, venomous snake turning his flaming attention directly on her.

"We've suffered. The country is in turmoil over who leads our most fundamental institution. James or Alexandra. This is not a simple succession crisis. In case you haven't noticed, Lisa." The room hushed and hissed at such a breach of protocol; for someone outside the intelligence community to use her own name. If he'd been a subordinate, Lisa would have been within her rights to shoot him. "We are in a civil war. Complete with subversive foreign actors and hidden agendas attempting to destabilize our country. And what does MI5 do? Grabs her purse!"

Peter was shaking. Foamy fury dripped from his lips, a few specs of which were lodged in his mustache. A quivering hand wiped them away with an embroidered napkin. But Lisa understood a bit more, helped by the accusatory looks from around the table. Even Pudgy seemed to blame her. Lisa was used to the blame for a national crisis being laid at her agency's feet. This she could handle.

"We identified the foreign threat at the earliest opportunity and have been monitoring the situation around the clock since then." The well-worn words had a calming effect on some of Peter's disciples, but not him. "The collateral damage of exposing the foreign infiltration, namely the Saudi money which brought Zia Wajid to the head of the Labour party in order to support Alexandra's claim to the throne, would have conflicted with other operational priorities."

"What priorities were those?" asked Lord John. He was a newer member of the inner circle. He didn't know what his colleagues had been up to before.

"Operation Regina," Lisa said calmly while staring at Peter, "which aimed to block James' accession to the throne in favor of his sister. An operation, I might add, which was agreed to over and above the objections of my department. Oh, and I might still have those objections somewhere in my purse, Sir Peter, if you would like to see." The gentlemen chuckled. Lisa had won them back, or at the very least, defanged them somewhat. They might even listen to her now. "In fact, we have a high value intelligence asset embedded inside Saudi Arabia right now, very, very close to the top." Pudgy gave her a sideways glance. She smiled inside.

"How close?" Sir Alan said.

"*Very* close."

"That's all well and good," Peter said, snatching back

the limelight in a desperate fight to control the conversation, "but only half the story, isn't it? What about the foreign interference on behalf of James?"

Lisa was stumped. She racked her brain, even looked at Pudgy for an answer, but he just shrugged. She shook her head.

"I wasn't aware of any foreign actors supporting James' claim."

"Oh, come on!" Peter roared. "All those gays around the world organizing on his side, marching up and down the streets waving his face on flags. Many of those groups are funded by foreign governments, I'll have you know. They've funneled millions to James' perverted campaign. Prancing up and down The Mall and showing their butt cracks on Trafalgar Square. Where's your intelligence assets there, K?"

The room fell silent for a tortuous few moments as people tried to process Peter's spitting rant. Sir Alan broke the silence.

"Are you talking about…Pride, old chap?"

"What does it matter what they call it. Let's not pretend the threats are not coming from all sides. The Saudis and the gays. Either way, this country cannot afford any more of their constant bickering and drama. Prince Hassan is a vessel—an empty one—that can be placed on a high shelf until we have straightened things out, then we can throw into him what we want. We are the regency council, gentlemen. It buys us a decade at least to return to some decorum and normality. Are we not all agreed?" There was a murmur of agreement. "Aren't we?" Peter shouted, flecks of spit dinging the silverware. The murmuring turned into a palm-slapping on the table. Each one of them agreed. Each one complicit. Lisa could not believe what she was seeing.

"No," she said, this time standing up for real. Her chair scraped and the twelve pasty white faces stared at her. "You will not assassinate the king and his sister."

"We are all agreed."

"No, we are not!" Lisa roared back. "I will not allow it and I will not carry it out." An odd silence descended from the ancient rafters. Her voice had carried upward, perhaps disturbing an unseen owl. The candelabras, their stems lost in the misty darkness, gently swung across the table. Flickering light softly illuminated the pale faces, each more serious than the last. They took no pleasure in this, Lisa could see, but their minds were sternly made up. Peter, on the other hand, was beaming.

"Your department has already proved itself incapable of an operation such as this. Nor can we afford to outsource it. MI6 will be taking this one on."

Lisa looked down at Pudgy, not letting him see the sense of betrayal stabbing through her chest. He felt it, though.

"It is better this way," Pudgy mumbled. "We can make it look like a foreign actor."

"Who? The gays?"

"You don't need to inquire about the operational details," Peter said, talking over them. "Just keep your boys off the beat and let the professionals do their work. It will be done before the coronation. We can't let *that* spectacle settle in the country's mind."

A light chatter returned. Drinks were re-poured and napkins unfurled, as if the decision to murder the king and his heir was keeping the group from their dinner. Lisa's only option was to turn and leave. But she stopped for one moment, turning back to look across the medieval table, Lisa cleared her throat, and loudly. The group stopped. Pudgy looked anxious, Peter uninterested.

"And if both James and Alexandra abdicate of their own accord?" Their curiosity was stirred.

"They never will," Peter said with a dismissive eye roll, but Sir Alan cut in.

"Hold on, old boy. What do you mean, my dear?"

Lisa bristled at the casual sexism, but let it slide with two lives on the line.

"I mean, if the King was to abdicate and his sister renounced any claim she had, perhaps at the same time, you get your regency council, don't you? The country is spared another bout of national trauma, the people don't turn their anger on their hapless government," Lisa stared sharply at several of the group, "oh, and two lives aren't cut short."

Now the murmurs were on Lisa's side. A few quiet words of approval were shared back and forth.

"Ridiculous," Peter snarled.

"I like it," Pudgy said. Under the table, he offered her a friendly pat on the back of her calf. The only part of her obscured from the other's view. She returned to her seat, squeezing his shoulder as she sat back down. Her old friend had pulled through in the end.

"Good enough for me!" Alan thundered, suddenly cheered up. The mood became infectious. From dour and depressed, now they could celebrate their power grab with a clear conscience to boot. "That, uh, thing you just said, K, about the people turning their anger on the government. Do you think they really would?"

"Oh, I think any public official who'd ever spoken critically of the royals might find themselves lynched. Especially after Liv Finnegan's book comes out." The name cut a sharp silence. They all knew of the Irish journalist who'd written the expose, and what had happened to her. Just to be sure, Lisa carried on. "You know the book I'm talking about. *The Murder of Prince Richard—A Royal Scandal.* The one that names half of you lot as signatories to Richard's death warrant. I don't imagine the public will take very kindly to politicians who murdered a father and his two children, do you?"

"It'll never come out," Peter said, but with a nervous twitch in his neck.

"It will," Lisa shot back.

"Is that a threat?"

"It's a promise."

"All right," Alan cut in, the former PM always trying to play the conciliator. "We'll cross that bridge when we come to it. We've all agreed a regency council must be established, that's for sure. We'll give Lisa a chance to talk them into abdicating, and if not...well, we've already covered that eventuality."

"Before the coronation," Peter said. "She'll never do it in less than three weeks."

"I will," Lisa said, downing her wine and standing up for the last time. "If not, I'll finish the job myself. I concur on the need for a period of stability and the regency council will offer the best chance to achieve that. But I will not allow anyone, not MI6, and especially not any of you lot, to do my job. You boys usually find a way to fuck it up."

"You don't have the capability," Peter said.

"Oh, I think you'll find I do. Just ask Grannies' Panties here." Lisa slapped Pudgy on the back. It seemed to help since he was already choking after what she'd just said. "Believe me, gentlemen, there's no need to dust out your frilly hats because there will be no coronation. I guarantee it."

Chapter 4

JAMES WRAPPED A CLEAN ROBE AROUND himself, and padded barefoot across the antique carpet of Windsor Castle's Orchid Room. It had fast become James' favorite place across all the royal residences. Set within one of the castle's turrets, great curved windows on all sides stared out onto the manicured green lawns and the triangular tips of the evergreen forest beyond. The plethora of windows gave the room a greenhouse effect that was perfect for growing orchids. So, on every conceivable surface, placed on shelves bolted into stone and all over tables across the circular room, were pots and pots of orchids. Of all different styles and colors. Some were rumored to have been around for over twenty years. The collage of white and pink and purple instead of the normal royal decor of eighteenth-century portraits gave the room a feel of a popular Instagram post in an aesthetically pleasing cafe. The beauty of the room was that it made James almost forget he was in a royal palace at all.

He sat on a firm-backed chair at his desk, a glass of freshly blended juices and superfoods sitting on one of his unopened red boxes. Government work could wait. The chance to talk to Greg was of far more value. He'd seen the kid around over the last few weeks Andrew had been away. Part of the repertoire of men who'd accompanied James on the various trips he'd taken as a "single" king. He wasn't single, but Samuel had certainly been acting that way. Maybe Andrew sensed something untoward after all.

James sipped the drink while a quiet television replayed an interview with Greg's father, Bill. That bastard newspaper man who'd spent most of the last few years doing everything in his power to bring James down. Of course, it wasn't so much *his* power. James had spoken to Bill several times since then, and the man, who was now a Marquis, had given the typical journalistic defense. He was agnostic to the content of the story. The only question being would it shift newspapers. James' private life would. Plus, he'd all but confirmed so many of the stories had been placed by his sister, and the rest of the establishment, in their various attempts to unseat James from power. "Operation Regina", it was supposedly called, a brutal about-face by the powers that be once they'd decided to write off James' right to rule. Andrew had always questioned just what had caused the sudden switch. He'd believed Alexandra and her husband, Faisal's, influence over the then prime minister had been great enough the whole tide had turned. James knew different. The establishment's switch had come the same day James had been diagnosed with HIV.

There was a knock at the door. James gulped down more juice and turned off the TV. He sucked in a deep breath and shuffled in his seat, making sure his chest was exposed just enough, and the robe loosened just enough, to entice Greg into giving up what he knew about Andrew's whereabouts. For a long time, he hadn't cared. Andrew fucking off was "the best thing that could ever happen, Your Majesty," Samuel had said so often.

"Your Majesty?" an aide said as the door creaked open. "Doctor Brian Hardy, sir."

James blinked in surprise as the tall and slender Doctor Brian walked in. A paragon of a middle-aged gay man's ability to maintain a perfect body and a full-time job counseling, testing, and treating London's gentlemen. From the king down. He walked in with a smile and his doctor's satchel. James rose to shake his hand.

"It's not been six months already, has it?"

"Not six months, no, James." The doctor was about the only man in his life who had not and would not use formalities. Brian always said they were simply doctor and patient. Not king and subject. "Time for your vaccination."

"Monkeypox again? I thought I already did those?"

"HPV—human papillomavirus."

"Ah, right." Rather sheepishly, James gathered up his robe and sat back down while Brian unfurled his case and pulled out various bits of medical equipment. "Last of three, right?"

"That's right. Now you'll be right and ready for the summer season. Every gay and bi man should get the HPV vaccine. It's a shame they only started to offer it so recently, but…" Brian unhooked a vial and syringe from the case,

"…never too late. Particularly important for people with HIV."

"And…everything is fine, right? I mean I'm still okay?" James heard the worry in his own voice. Normally he took a sedative or three before a visit with Doctor Brian, but this visit had come out of the blue. Brian smiled as he wrapped a blood pressure checker around James' upper arm.

"Of course, everything's fine. Once someone is on successful treatment for HIV and their viral load is undetectable, as yours has been since just a few weeks after you started treatment, then you stay that way. There's no reason to worry about the HIV anymore. You're undetectable, James, and that means untransmittable. No ifs, no buts. All the other bits of your health, though…"

"What?"

"Your blood pressure is a little high. And you seem tired. Can't go out in public with those bags under your eyes."

"Oh, thanks very much, doctor."

"Stressed?"

"A coronation coming up that the British state tried their best to keep me from? No, not stressed at all."

"Ha…ha." Brian unstuck the Velcro, then began to prepare the syringe. "It's very important you look after your emotional wellbeing as well as your physical, James. HIV might be nothing more than a chronic, manageable condition these days, but it's still a mindfuck. A mental health issue all on its own. You need support."

"I'm not coming to any group."

"No one's asking you to, James." Brian slid the needle into James' upper arm. He barely felt a thing. "But I did want to ask, where's Andrew at these days?"

"Honestly, Brian? Who fucking knows?"

"Did you boys have a falling out?" Brian placed a cotton ball on the injection site.

"In a manner of speaking."

"That's a shame."

"Why? Do you want a refund on your royal wedding tea towels?"

"James," Brian was already zipping up his doctor's bag, "one of the biggest mindfucks about HIV is how scared it makes other people. Even the ones guzzling down PrEP for their weekend orgy, so many of them still won't date a poz guy. It's dumb, it's stupid, but it's reality and unlikely to change."

"So, what, I should grovel to get Andrew back just because no one else will want to date me?"

"Not in the slightest. I'm just saying you two have something special. You clearly have love between you, and I know you have a lot of love to give, James. Don't throw something away until you're absolutely sure you're done with it. Yes, sometimes relationships don't work out. And sometimes that's because one or the other party wants the single life. But let's be honest, James. Your single life looks a lot different from everyone else's. And I don't think you want to go back to yachts and big-breasted models, do you?"

"Thank you, doctor, for your unsolicited advice yet again."

"That's my job," Brian said with a smile as he headed for the door. "Think about it. I have the name of a great couple's therapist I can give you. Oh, and I'll see you in a month for your sexual health check-up. I can see you've been busy entertaining the troops."

Brian marched out of the room, leaving James with a new level of shock at how he was spoken to. There wasn't much time to stay unsettled however, as the aide popped his head back through the door and announced Greg was waiting.

"Lord Honnington!" James said as Greg entered, still looking back at Brian walking away down the hallway. James stood up, causing himself to feel lightheaded after the vaccine. His robe was in a fumble as well. More flustered mother at the supermarket in her pajamas than royal in a casually revealing robe.

"Your Majesty." Greg bowed. The awkward cuteness of it made James smile.

"You don't need to touch your toes, Greg. Come in, let's sit on the couches."

James padded between the folds of orchids to a pair of settees facing each other in the center of the room. A coffee table of flowerpots between them. James curled up on one couch as Greg sat himself down on the other. James strategically peeled back his robe to reveal most of his upper thigh—and that he wasn't wearing underwear—while Greg plonked himself down in a gym tracksuit and manspread his legs.

"Coffee?" James asked.

"Sure, yeah. Thanks."

James pressed a button on the side table, and half a second later, a trolley was pushed into the room. Two white-gloved men, one of whom James knew had fucked him in the recent past, served them quickly and left. Greg and James drank their coffee and exchanged some pleasantries about the weather before James readied his forensic line of questioning.

"Y-your Majesty," Greg beat him to it. "Thank you for what you did. For my dad. I mean…he was going to prison. Probably forever." The sweetness in his eyes was overpowering. No wonder Andrew had fallen for his charm. "And being invited to hang around with you these last few weeks. I've…I've really liked it. Sorry I was late this morning. Samuel told me I shouldn't have come. Sorry if I disturbed."

"You didn't, Greg. Not at all. The more the merrier, I say." They both drank their coffee and shared a smile.

"Well, just to say, Your Majesty. Uh, sir. If there's anything I can ever do for you. Anything ever. I want you to know, I'm ready to serve."

James squinted at this eager twink. Everything about him was genuine, that was the vibe James got. His face thin and beardless. Skin unpolluted by too much drink or drugs or sun. James didn't buy a word of it.

"For how long were you fucking Andrew?" James asked the question with such a simplistic calmness it took Greg several moments to figure out what had been said. "Did you help him get rid of me?"

"Sir!"

"Did you conspire with him so he could escape? Did you help him run away once again? Are you here as his double-agent, keeping tabs on me to warn him if I get too close?" James knew he was shouting, but he didn't care. Greg took hit after hit. "Where is he, huh?" James threw his empty coffee cup across the room. It sailed past Greg's head and clattered to the ground around a tangle of orchid pots. Any more force and James would have smashed the window. Greg dropped the innocence.

"Look, me and Andrew were fucking. We were fucking for a while. But I thought you guys were done. I mean, you were with Katyn."

"That's your excuse?"

"I saw you on the TV with her like, every day. Andrew was writing stories about you in my dad's paper. I mean…what did you expect Andrew to do?"

James was taken aback. He'd expected something like *what did you expect me to do?* But that's not what Greg said. *What did you expect Andrew to do?*

"I suppose you have a point."

"When I first met you guys, you were face down on the bed with a hood over your head. I didn't really think I was getting in the middle of some kind of monogamous marriage here. Andrew gave up a lot to look after you, sir. I think he liked me because…because I was the only one who saw him for who he was. Not what he could do for me."

James stood. He didn't know what else to do. He couldn't *sit* and listen to this, so he got up and wandered to one of the windows. Hands clasped behind his back like he was on a royal walkabout, he stared out onto the castle grounds, the gardens and the flowerbeds and the forest beyond.

"Down there," James said, still not looking back, "is where Andrew and I had our engagement party. Where we told the world we loved each other." A tear pooled in James' eye. He rubbed it away, but another one came to take its place. "And now…I can't find him. I can't find him anywhere."

The tears came before James knew what he was even crying about. Loss of the past? Loss of the present? Feeling locked into yet another public relationship, or simply missing the presence of the man who had been by his side since he was fifteen years old.

James felt a hand on his back. It sparked a shock through his body. He wished it was Andrew, but knew it wasn't. He cursed the life he'd fallen into, but knew there was nothing he could do. Things had gone too far. They'd been bewitched from the beginning. That takes magic, which turns black and noxious, always.

"I lost him…" James began to say through tears. The window looked like rain splattered from the blue and white sky. Arms wrapped around James' body. More tender than an entire platoon lining up in the dungeon. That feeling was nothing compared to this. And this was nothing compared to what James had once had. "I lost him in my own fucked up way of living."

Greg's head rested between James' shoulders. It was a

small gesture. A sticking plaster. But the shadow of Andrew was soothing. Greg was the one thing removed between them.

"I know he never stopped loving you, James." The whisper of his name from the young man holding onto him sent a shock of reality, of normality, through James. He held Greg's hand, knowing it was someone else's. "You two are meant to be together."

"What makes you so sure?" James didn't say it meanly. More like asking the final question in an argument he knew he'd already lost. "I don't even know where he is."

"You're meant to be together, sir. You're the role model for…for all of us."

James turned to see Greg's face. It was young and forgettable. That's what James always remembered about him. Each time he saw Greg, it was like a surprise. An everyman symbol for everything James was not.

"When I first met you both," Greg said, thumbing an orchid branch, "you know what I thought? How jealous I was of you both."

"Jealous? But you didn't know who we were."

"I knew you were a couple. Andrew said *come and fuck my boyfriend*. Those words…they were magical. I don't know. I guess it's dumb."

"No, go on. I don't really understand. But that doesn't mean I don't want to." James wrapped his robe closer, feeling the chill from the window, but intrigued to snatch this sliver of understanding. It's the least a king should do.

"Like…you guys are together. You're together and

you're still horny and get turned on by the thought of someone else, or each other, you know? You're like…two guys. A couple of normal guys who don't run away from that inner slut we all have inside of us. You two just let it out, and let it out for each other."

"Maybe that's what destroyed us."

"Andrew said you were always doing stuff like that," Greg said.

James shrugged, struggling to remember the first time, back in the mists of their mythology, they broke the unspoken rule of monogamy. Whenever that life-changing event was, it happened a very long time ago. Greg was quiet. Carefully, he spoke again.

"Maybe it's actually what kept you together for so long. You let yourselves be normal."

"Greg, I'm a king and a slut. I'm as far from normal as can be."

Now Greg shrugged.

"I dunno, to me you're just famous. Famous and normal. For a lot of us, Your Majesty, that's the exact role model we want to look up to."

They shared a smile, but the conversation had stretched as far as it could. Further than Greg was comfortable with. More than James was. Without another word, Greg stepped across orchid blooms and end tables for the door. He stopped for a final moment, as if pondering a last thought.

"What is it, Greg?"

"If you find Andrew, please tell me."

"Oh?" Was Greg offering to snatch James' lover from out underneath him once again?

"Yeah, because I wanna slap him around the face for walking out on you, Your Majesty. Then I wanna drag him back to your side."

James smiled. He didn't know what test he'd laid out for Greg, but somehow, he'd passed it.

"Gregory, I have a little event tomorrow. Trooping the Color. One of those spectacles we're all expected to get dolled up for. It's no jaunt to Mykonos, but would you care to accompany me? Otherwise, I shall have to make conversation with the horses. Or worse, my sister."

"Um, of course, Your Majesty. Anything you want."

"Wonderful." That should rattle Andrew out of the woodwork.

Chapter 5

PRINCESS ALEXANDRA SUNK INTO A SOFT, down pillow after turning over a picture of her and her husband on the bedside table. She wasn't in her Knightsbridge home, nor the Canary Wharf penthouse Faisal had kept since his bachelor days, but in a narrow four-story house just off Finchley Road in the North of London. She'd bought it years ago, perhaps as a favor to a friend who needed some liquidity, she couldn't quite remember. For years, she'd donated the tenancy to a small women's shelter that worked exclusively with women seeking asylum who were also at risk of domestic abuse, and because of their asylum status, couldn't seek support from anywhere else. The four stories had become eight double bedrooms, plus two tatty pull-out couches downstairs, and was currently going through a top-to-bottom renovation from Alexandra's own purse. She had rented a couple of bungalows for the shelter in the meantime, but they couldn't compete with the homely-feeling safe-house; she couldn't wait to give back to them. Two of the bedrooms, the bathroom and a small kitchenette on the top floor were already complete. This is where Alexandra had taken to hiding out these days.

The beds were new, the linens fresh. The sheen of an out-the-box building had its anonymous charms. The decor; bold lines softened by pastel tones and sleek appliances screamed *new start*. The workmen—gone for the day—must've decided to do some decorating of their own, and placed a forgotten picture of the home's benefactor on the bedside table.

She'd thought about shoving the simple metal frame and the picture of two once happy people into the pine-stenched drawer before Reggie came back from the bathroom, but feared the noise would cause him to ask questions. Questions from Reggie would lead to distractions, and Alexandra couldn't afford a single one of those right now.

The white cotton duvet covered only up to her hips. She was naked both above and below. Reggie enjoyed seeing her this way. Undressed, unarmed. Faisal had been a different type of lover. He always needed "stuff" to make things work. Costumes and toys and dirty talk and role play and other unmentionable activities that made Alexandra think, what was the point in a man at all?

Before their children were born, she'd tried to play the good wife and acquiesce to some of his...habits. Despite how it made her feel, she did use to suck Faisal's dick, when he voraciously requested. It wasn't a *bad* experience, but he was large enough that her jaw would hurt uncomfortably for several days after. When he wanted to have sex, she didn't *mind* different positions, although drew the line at being asked to "climb on top and ride it like a cheap waitress at a country music bar jumping on a bucking bronco".

After Hassan and Jasmine were born, their sex life gladly took a turn for the worse. Faisal's weird requests faded away as he presumably took them elsewhere. Which was fine for Alexandra, at least for a while. After she hit her mid-twenties, with two children, a husband, but no constitutional role apart from *existing,* there was a period when she had no sex at all. Faisal made his peace with things quite quickly. She didn't ask about his habits, and he didn't tell. Once he asked her if she had a piece on the side. Not out of anger or disgust or to ask for a divorce, but because, so he'd said, he was *concerned for her wellbeing.* She'd slapped him that night. But it did make her think.

A few years back, somewhere between her busy schedule as patron and ambassador to international nonprofits from the Red Cross down, Alexandra rediscovered sex. At first it was with those international rescue types and doctors without borders who had no problem fucking a princess and never breathing another word of it again. From them grew a web of chief executives, ambassadors, even secret agents who had brought Alexandra waves of pleasure she never could have imagined with Faisal.

Truthfully, it was probably the only reason why her marriage had lasted as long as it had.

The last time she and Faisal had had sex; good, pleasurable sex, had probably been the morning of her thirtieth birthday. She'd been in a good mood that morning, a very good mood. Articles she'd spent months planting across various journalists, often via several intermediaries, about her brother James never having had a serious girlfriend finally made it onto the world's front pages. Her children had made breakfast and cards, then Faisal sent them off to school and made love to her before she went off to a Red Cross board meeting where she first remembered chatting to a hard left Labour MP, Zia Wajid, who told Alexandra she should be queen, and take the throne from her hapless brother for the good of the country and the monarchy.

Those heady days of secret lovers in the presidential suites of different cities had disappeared with her push for the throne. Mainly disappeared, and it was even harder to get back. Now she was laying on a supermarket-bought mattress on the top floor of a construction site, waiting for her divorce lawyer to finish taking his mid-evening dump so he could come and fuck her before going home to his wife and four children. Alexandra also knew the wife from the board of a vaccine distribution network for developing countries. It may be cliche to sleep with one's divorce lawyer, but it was still the best sex Alexandra remembered having in years.

"Did you speak to him?" Reggie shouted from the bathroom, steam swimming out of the door he'd opened.

"No?" she said back, still waiting on the bed. "Should I have?"

"Well, there was a counter on the custody…the Bahamas house…fourteen!"

"What? I can't hear you. Can you come out of the bathroom? Reggie?" This was why Alexandra preferred uncomplicated sex that was over in half an hour. Someone hanging around and talking about things other than what he was going to do to make her cum was *not* sexy. "Reggie?"

Finally, he emerged from the steamy bathroom. No towel, just six-foot-two of a naked Black man. He had the stomach of a forty-five-year-old, and a chest that still showed off the thick muscled torso he'd once had. Given his height, broad shoulders and bald head, Reggie always bent under doorways, so when he stood tall like now, at the foot of her bed, he towered like an onyx pillar of Hercules.

"So?" he asked, grinning. Alexandra did all she could not to sit up and stare at his cock. She couldn't see it over the curve of the duvet, but wanted nothing more than to shut him up and get fucked. She wondered if he was too conservative for a gag. "What do you think?"

"About what?"

"The Bahamas house! Their side has offered to buy your half for fourteen million. Interested?"

"Interested? What am I going to do with half a house in a tax haven? He can have it for nothing." Reggie's face turned deathly serious. "I mean, take the money, of course."

"Of course." Reggie looked relieved.

"But I don't care about any of this rubbish. I just want him to sign the damn papers already. Today, if possible."

"That…will be more tricky. The PM's office will need

to review all the details of the settlement, and then there's the matter of…"

"Of what, Reggie?"

He looked ashamed, like he'd clogged the toilet.

"Your brother will need to sign off on everything. I mean, by rights the monarch can change any part of an immediate family member's divorce proceedings. And you'll need his permission to marry again. If you two aren't on good terms, then—"

"Can we not talk about my brother?"

"Of course, ma'am."

"Can you come here, now?"

"Of course, ma'am."

As if he'd finished his billable hour and would say no more without rolling into the next, Reggie edged toward the end of the bed. Fumbling under the duvet, he clasped his mighty hand around Alex's ankle, yanking her toward himself like she weighed as much as a feather. He placed her milk white foot against his buff pec, and ran thick fingers under the inside of her calves, all the way up to the bend in her knee.

Alexandra lay back on the cotton sheets, stretching out as the familiar lick of his tongue flicked between her toes. She'd never experienced a sucked toe before Reggie. He seemed to like it, and she'd not told him no before. Now she couldn't live without it. Each one of her painted toenails knocked against the back of his teeth as he laboriously swallowed toe after toe. For Alexandra, the intense notes of a tongue and teeth nibbling her leg in the air catapulted her into the zone. Forgotten was the world outside. The only thing that mattered in her mind was the question: when was he going to move to the next foot?

In a moment, he did. Not letting go of her other leg, though, but adding it to his chest as hands stretched across her skin. The velvet touch of his palms turned her on far more than Faisal ever had. Every inch Reggie drew closer to her inner thighs lit a series of fires inside, setting off signals across her body that soon enough she was going to be entered, and owned. Reggie would be pressed on top of her, pressing her down like a slab of concrete. There was no way out but to fuck her way out; to let him claim every part of her body. To kiss her neck and slide his entire length so deep inside that she would scream across North Finchley and the neighbors would wonder who the hell was that.

Reggie climbed onto the mattress with one knee. His lips smothered the inside of her leg and she was already moaning. Alex pulled the duvet closer to her chin, covering her breasts but exposing the place she wanted him to be. Reggie grumbled. A low, hungry sound that only came from a man who had been denied what he really wanted for so long.

"Ma'am," he said, the lawyerly tone fading into a voice of need, of desperation. "Can I stop calling you ma'am?" His other knee planted onto the mattress, and Alexandra took in the full sight of his erect cock. The size of many people's forearms.

"Yes," she said, voice gasping away from her chest. "Call me what you want."

"Very good, ma'am." His tongue crawled across her thigh. The heat from his pelvis drew closer like a magnet. Soon the duvet was wrapped around her head. She couldn't bear to see what came next as her legs shook like she stood on a ship sailing into a stormy sea. "Does my little fuckpuppet want her pussy ate?"

"Mm…"

"Does she?" Reggie growled the question as he threw away completely the duvet covers. He did not dive into her, but grabbed the line between her thighs and ass and raised her *up* to him. As easy as if he was lifting a sliced open mango, and began to feast on the juice within.

Rolled back on her shoulders, Alexandra cried out into the empty room, calling into nothing and nowhere, but simply embracing the beauty of shouting about her pleasure. Reggie's lips, the same ones with which he admonished her husband's lawyers, scrambled the inside of her thighs while his tongue lapped her insides, while she felt his saliva dribble under her ass. Reggie was lost in a world of his own ecstasy, as was she. Her legs wrapped around his ears, Alexandra began to turn her Pilates body into good use. She supported her hips with her hands and slid her body upward, gently thrusting into Reggie's face while he feasted on her, so the flat of his nose pressed against her clit. He moaned as he lapped her up, a constant grumble of pleasure that vibrated through his lips into hers.

"Oh yeah, baby. Oh yeah."

A sudden terror gripped Alexandra when she opened her eyes. The image of a person standing in the background by the bedroom door, watching. She must be feeling odd. Hallucinating. She peeled her hands from supporting her waist to rub her eyes. Reggie caught her hips and pulled her closer into himself, thrusting his tongue so deeply inside she could have exploded in pleasure just then. But she had to see this hallucination wasn't real. That there wasn't actually a middle-aged woman in a raincoat with a short blonde bob standing just behind Reggie.

"Evening, ma'am," spoke a woman's voice. Alexandra screamed. She screamed so loud Reggie spun as if someone had just been shot. In surprise at the figure they could now both see very clearly, he fell off the bed and landed with a thump. Alexandra snatched up the duvet and flung it all over herself, practically hiding her face as well as her body. Lisa Mantis acted like she'd simply interrupted Alexandra taking tea. "Sorry to be a bother, but I have something rather urgent to discuss." The head of MI5's eyes flicked to Reggie, now sheepishly emerging from the floor with a comically small pillow which barely covered his enormous erection. "Don't worry, Reginald," Lisa said with the slightest smirk, "client-attorney privilege. Ma'am, I'll be downstairs when you're ready. Your builders left some choccy biscuits and an electric kettle. Tea?"

It was all Alexandra could do to nod, then wish for an instant death, as Lisa Mantis slipped out of the room as invisible as she'd come in.

Chapter 6

ANDREW HODES HAD NEVER BEEN asked his opinion as much as he had in the last few weeks. Yes, James had often inquired of him which tie would work better at a public event; one shade of black over the other, or which staged shot of him with a supermodel should be leaked to the press, one lie over the next. But Andrew had never felt those opinions really mattered. They were the inconsequential building blocks of keeping together a complicated life with the man he loved. No, the man he *thought* he loved. Love gives more than it takes, Andrew reminded himself, repeating the mantra of break-up podcasts and self-help books he'd invested all his energy in lately. Only when he wasn't spending all his waking moments reading up on all the opinions he was now expected to have.

"What do we think?" asked Paula, the city planner. The stunningly chic French woman in a breathtaking white suit commanded the attention of the dozen men around the table, half Westerners, half Saudis. The boardroom blinds were drawn, but beyond the air-conditioned walls lay the endless Arabian desert and the neon-lit city of Riyadh which sprung out of the sands like a mirage.

Their committee's decision was supposed to be a simple one. Just to decide which coast a half-trillion-dollar new city should be built, on the Persian Gulf, or the Red Sea. They'd seen the plans from every angle. The gleaming streets, the towering skyscrapers, the man-made beaches and solar-powered public transport lines. Now the questions were more esoteric. Would Saudi Arabia's existential war come from Iran in the east, or Egypt in the west? Sitting at the head of the table, Andrew kept trying to be annoyed at Faisal for putting him in the hot seat, but then again, this was exactly what Faisal had promised. Come with him to Saudi Arabia, and be a decision-maker and build a brand-new society. Have an opinion which would really matter.

"Building the new city on the western side cuts down on flight times to Europe," said one of the men from the French firm of architects.

"But the eastern coast means we can connect it to Dubai and Abu Dhabi via high-speed rail," said one of the Saudi's—all men, of course. Andrew wished it wasn't the case, but some things Faisal claimed were beyond the control of even the new Crown Prince.

"We're already twenty years behind the United Arab Emirates in cultural capital," the Frenchman answered back, "and another ten by the time this city is finished. We simply cannot compete with Dubai."

"We have no choice *but* to compete," the Saudi said.

It didn't really matter what they said, though. How

many more afternoons of debate they would get through. Everyone around the tables knew who the final decision maker would be. Everyone around the table looked at Andrew.

"It's an important question," Andrew said, bringing out his usual rehearsed lines when he felt utterly out of his depth, but didn't want to make it seem to the room he was simply taking notes for the Crown Prince. "And thank you Paula for a fascinating presentation." Andrew tried to clap, hoping to rouse the table in a round of applause that he could use as cover to finish the meeting and slip out without further explanation. The applause didn't catch on.

"Well, anyway," Andrew continued, "I think we're very close to a final decision."

"I assumed that would be today," said Paula, sharing annoyed glances with her French colleagues. "We expected final sign-off before our return to Paris."

"And you'll have that," Andrew said. She raised an eyebrow. "When's your flight?"

"Tonight."

"Ah. Okay, so let me see what I can do."

Andrew didn't dare wait another moment in the suddenly sweltering room full of burning eyes. It felt like someone had cracked open a window and the desert heat had swarmed in. He scurried out of the board room and slid the glass door firmly shut, leaving the rest of the group in limbo, but he didn't mind. He breathed a brief sigh of relief in the empty air-conditioned corridor, and wondered just how he'd ended up so far from home.

• • •

Andrew's apartment was in a different tower, but the seamless trains and elevators made the journey feel no longer than making it from one end of a mall to the other. And infinitely easier than the tube. At least everything in Riyadh was air conditioned, and spotlessly clean. In a different life he would have dismissed the penthouse apartment as soulless and metallic as the half-empty fridge full of foreign products—he still hadn't figured out the difference between what was milk and yogurt in Arabic. But that wasn't the world Andrew found himself in now. Post-it notes fluttered from the fridge as he snapped open the heavy door and pulled out a beer, one of the few benefits of being a foreigner in a strange land.

Andrew sucked down the cold comfort as he fumbled around the tiled floor for the loose notes. *I am successful. I am strong. Love does not define me. Love comes to those who love themselves.* He re-stuck the affirmations to the door, only because otherwise it would ruin the smart columns he'd placed them into before. The bathroom mirror was worse. They all fluttered to the floor every time he took a shower, which was often three times a day in this heat. The book said it was important. He forgot which book, but it was still important. The self-written avouchments of self-love covered up the spaces where magnets from weddings and polaroids of parties should go. He didn't even have a collection of bills to pay or take-out menus to hang on to.

Back in London, his apartment would still be the same as the night he left it, on Faisal's advice. The take-out menus stuck to the fridge told the story of his and James' relationship. Fried banana ice cream already melted into the Styrofoam container. That had been the night of six guys. He forgot the royal event they rushed away from, but remembered rushing into the apartment with Grindr blowing up his phone. James had been so horny that night he'd thrown on his leather hood with his suit still on. The first guy arrived so quickly; the stranger was the one to take off James' underwear while Andrew watched them fuck. *Another,* James had said once the man was done. *Another. Another. Another. Another.*

Only hunger stopped them. They'd ordered Chinese food, but had eaten the fried banana ice cream first because it was melting all over the sheets. They ate in bed.

Sorry I'm making such a mess, James had said, wiping dripping cream from his smooth chest.

You made enough of a mess before, we'll have to change these sheets anyway.

Yeah, I didn't think I'd manage to come three times. But when you shoved it in me right at the end, after they'd all finished, I couldn't help myself. You're always the best, babe. I love you, Andrew.

I love you too, James.

Andrew chewed on his bottom lip, chilled from the beer. From the panoramic window, the desert rolled on forever a thousand feet below. Had he had it all, and let it go? What had James ever done but love him and care for him and make him feel warm and welcome every day? Was living their life in secret so bad? Was Andrew living any differently now?

A knock at the door surprised him.

"Coming!" Andrew quickly placed the open beer in the sink just in case it was a Saudi at the door. "Mohan?" One of Faisal's many assistants stood at the door. He was minor Saudi royalty, but raised and educated in England, at Cambridge, no less. He'd graduated only a few years before and went straight to work under Faisal at Royal Arabian Petroleum, and was one of the many from that office who'd accompanied their boss back to Riyadh a few weeks ago. Andrew knew all this because he and Mohan had become rather close in that time.

"I'm afraid the Crown Prince will not be available for your meeting this afternoon," Mohan said in his slick English accent, the slim suit fitting like a second skin on his slender frame. Andrew gave a shrugged smile. Such was the way with Faisal. "He was delayed with an investor meeting in San Francisco, so is currently en route."

"That's all right," Andrew said. In the hierarchy of how to rebuild Saudi Arabia, meetings on Faisal's agenda took highest priority. "The French will just have to wait."

"I beg your pardon?"

"Never mind," Andrew said, coming to the rapid conclusion he would just have to decide the fate of a half trillion-dollar city by himself. "So does that mean you've got a few hours."

"Why…I believe it does." Mohan smiled back. He kept his beard trimmed close, always so determined to distinguish himself from the other Saudi men, suit included. Mohan slipped inside the apartment, quietly closing the door; the look on his face like he was doing something wrong. Or about to.

"Gin?" Andrew asked, already taking two tonics from the fridge.

"Would be lovely."

Mohan settled himself on the sofa, struggling to find the remote control among the litter of books and plastic-wrapped packs of post-it notes.

"*The Secret Rules of Getting Over a Gay Relationship*," Mohan read out the title of Andrew's latest arrival.

"It's rather good, that," Andrew replied, dropping ice into their glasses. "It's written by a lesbian, but actually a lot of the lessons surprisingly apply." Andrew handed Mohan a glass and they sat together on the couch. Mohan thumbed the pages with a dismissive smirk, the less attractive quality he'd been given by Cambridge.

"Well? What are the lessons?"

"Oh," Andrew drank deeply. "Surround yourself with friends, queer, if possible." Mohan made a face. "Go out to gay bars."

"Hmm."

"Or art galleries, vegan cafes, anywhere there might be other gay folks around, that's what she says, anyway."

"Failing that?"

"Haven't got that far yet." Andrew nearly finished the drink. Mohan flicked through to the last chunk.

"*Many have said the best way to get over a lover, is to get under another,"* Mohan read. *"For queer people, this is perhaps the most important lesson of all."*

Mohan didn't need much more of an opening to place his own half-drunk gin on top of the book, then lean in to kiss Andrew. In fact, if it was up to Mohan, they probably wouldn't talk at all. Andrew lost his worries in juniper-flavored lips, unbuttoning Mohan's tailored shirt and rubbing his hands over the Saudi's chest hair, also as tightly trimmed as his beard. In moments, Mohan was completely naked and straddling Andrew on the couch. His large brown cock, completely disproportionate to his frame, already leaking with excitement.

Andrew swirled the head around his lips, teasing his tongue through loose folds of skin while he blindly unbuckled his belt. Mohan silenced his own moan—from a lifetime of hidden lusts—as he pushed his hips all the way forward. Andrew choked a little as the trimmed scratchiness of Mohan's pubes rubbed against his nose. The thick cock all the way in his throat. Mohan tasted as he looked, clean-cut and swimming in every luxury life could imagine. The taste contrasted to James, who often tasted of sweat and lust. This was another trick Andrew had read about. Not to shy away from thoughts of an ex, but to embrace them. Contrast and compare to a current lover, picking out those flaws the ex had, and enjoying the difference. Andrew was still working on that flaw part.

"Christ almighty," Mohan moaned, the words out of place for their surroundings, but sounding perfectly normal from his upper-crust English accent. Andrew hugged

Mohan's body close to him, pressing his buttocks firmly forward, taking in all of the man's cock while Mohan fumbled for Andrew's through his underwear. As soon as Mohan's fingers found Andrew's dick, it turned hard. Andrew knew what was to come next. Sucking in a desperate breath as Mohan's wet dick slipped out of his mouth, Andrew dredged a wad of saliva onto his fingers and reached behind Mohan. He slathered some on his own dick, then found the space between Mohan's softly haired butt cheeks.

"Christ, yes," he said, sliding onto Andrew's fingers. Their gaze locked in a seedy grin. The sun shone bright through the tinted window; the air-conditioned room kept them cool. But the heat of the illegality roasted both their bloodstreams. For Andrew, just as for Mohan, this was how they'd lived their sex lives. The world had moved on. Pride marches and marriage equality, but they were still stuck in societies, in countries no less, where their entanglement meant death. Social, and actual.

Had that been the cause of Andrew bolting? The thought crept up as Mohan glided himself onto Andrew's waiting dick. The Saudi spread apart his cheeks, lowering his slender frame onto the waiting cock. Moist tip met waiting hole. They connected. Andrew breached Mohan's body, penetrating him in an act of illegal sodomy. It made him harder than he'd ever thought possible. Men age, and they worry about the inevitable time the next erection will not be as good or as strong or as long as the last. Mohan upended all of those thoughts. Or was it the crime?

With James, every single act for the vast majority of their nearly two decades together had been shrouded in secrets and lies. From that first night in the Eton dorms, both of their first times, across all those times and places, always dancing on the edge of being caught. That's why they must have first invited someone else to join them in bed, Andrew thought. The thrill of their own self destruction not quite enough. Neither of them would ever tell, but the thrill they'd started with needed to be sated. So, Andrew had spent those nights trawling the internet, or sometimes a club or a hotel bar, for a man or two or four who would come upstairs and slide his dick into a hooded stranger. Just as he was sliding into Mohan.

"Fuck, Andrew, fuck me." His words clipped, voice a whisper even though they were alone. Mohan slithered hands around his chest, gripping his nipples in involuntary acts of ecstasy. Andrew held each of his ass cheeks firmly in each hand, thrusting Mohan onto him as much as Mohan slammed himself into him.

Sweat pooled under his chin. It dribbled from his armpits and under his open shirt. Books were kicked off the table as his legs stretched out and Mohan's skinny frame bounced on Andrew's muscled thighs. Mohan leaned down, lips round and mouth open. Andrew turned away.

"Sorry," Mohan whispered, licking his lips in retreat. "I forgot."

"It's fine," Andrew said, concentrating all his thoughts on the tight ass gripped around the base of his cock. "Your hole is so fucking nice."

"It's all yours," Mohan said, redness creeping up his throat. "It's only yours." Wet lips pressed Andrew's neck. As far north as Mohan was allowed to kiss. Andrew ran his hands up the curve of his spine, smoothing soft skin and silky black hair, thrusting deeply into a hole gladly willing to receive.

"I'm so fucking close."

"I want it this time," Mohan whispered. Breaking yet another one of their rules. Andrew would not make the same mistakes of the past, diving into the kinds of sex he shouldn't. Yet here he was already, condomless inside Mohan. Doing what was wrong. "Christ, it feels so good." In Andrew's fucked up psychology, it felt so right.

"I can't," Andrew said, groaning as he came within a hair's breadth of coming. "It's wrong. I shouldn't."

"Do it," Mohan said, the devil on his tongue. "Breed me."

With a hand on either one of Mohan's hips, he held the tight body down as he thrust up, balls slapping against his ass. The moan turned to a yell and escaped loudly from his mouth as he unloaded deep inside, and then felt splash after splash from Mohan's dick shoot across his chest, his face, and drop into his open, willing mouth. Only then, once Andrew was spent and still deep inside this stranger's ass who's cum settled on his tongue, did the two men kiss.

After they showered, one, then the other, they sat in the living room in robes, on armchairs across from each other.

They drank Turkish coffee from gold and glass cups; Mohan had prepared it while Andrew had been showering. The news silently on in the background, their faces satisfied, bodies spent. For now.

"You seem to be doing better," Mohan said, crouched forward around his coffee. "Getting over him."

"Sometimes...I don't know. It's hard. But being here helps."

"Do you think about telling him? Or, you know, someone? Because, well, you know."

They glanced at the television news playing silently. Trooping the Color was coming live from London. The sun was setting in Riyadh but breaking through morning clouds in the UK, *country waits for royal appearance...* scanned across the bottom of the screen. *King James and Princess Alexandra expected shortly... Prince Andrew will not be in attendance, Buckingham Palace confirms... sources say Duke of Cornwall "doesn't want to be a distraction" before coronation.*

"Eugh," Andrew said, sipping the thick Turkish coffee.

"What? Did you not let it sit for long enough?"

"No, all this relationship stuff. I'd rather not talk about it."

"Of course. Well, I hope I am allowed to say how good you fucked me." Andrew grinned at that, then quickly unpeeled the smile from his face.

"Sorry for coming inside you. I know it's wrong."

"Don't be ridiculous." Mohan dismissed Andrew's worry with a wave. "I asked you to, plus, I've been on PrEP for years."

"Really?" That surprised Andrew. He'd been taking the drug which prevented HIV infection ever since James had been diagnosed. It surprised, if not relieved him, to know Mohan was doing the same thing. "So am I, but I brought six months of pills with me from London. Did you do the same? You can't get it here, can you?"

"No, but I switched to the injectable."

"They have that now? Even for PrEP?"

"Oh yeah, it's great. I need to get it just six times a year now. So easy. Had my clinic visit last week when I went back to London for those few days. The place on Dean Street is great. I have the cutest doctor there, Brian Hardy. He always makes a point to inject me in the exact same spot on my buttocks. What does he say...*I wouldn't want to mark your best asset.* He's a hoot. It's funny, being in his clinic is probably the only time I don't feel judged for having sex."

"I..." Andrew shrugged off feeling embarrassed. "I have him too. He's really great."

It felt so odd to Andrew, sipping coffee and comparing notes on doctors and treatments with a guy he'd just fucked. Incongruous, but also strangely normal. As if this is how gay men had been living for centuries. Forming their own networks, swapping their own stories, teaching others the way of the world. Having sex and sharing coffee.

A brutal ringtone cut through their quiet, like an alarm going off. Mohan suddenly looked worried. He didn't take his phone sitting upon a pile of self-help books, though. Instead, he bounced off the chair in his bathrobe and fished around in the breast pocket of his suit jacket. Mohan pulled out a small Nokia with a keypad, currently ringing in a violent scream. He didn't even look at Andrew, but answered and walked out of sight into a bathroom and closed a door.

Andrew sipped his coffee, not really thinking much of it. A call from Faisal, he wondered. Some conversation about an investor or a favor for some foreign ruler. Building a new state wasn't always going to be a clean task. Andrew was perfectly aware. Then the bathroom door opened again, and he heard Mohan's voice.

"You want me to tell him now? Yes. Of course, ma'am."

The *ma'am* made Andrew sit up. So British sounding. Who the hell was he talking to? A thunder erupted in Andrew's chest as Mohan reappeared, lines of concern on his face. The feeling just like the time Doctor Brian Hardy had entered James and Andrew's life. Suddenly, their private moments were not so private anymore. Hung up to be judged and treated. Was the same about to happen with Mohan? The curse of gay life writhing its death-black fingers around their thoughts. The terror gripped at Andrew's heart. Love could never come without a price.

"Andrew, I have to tell you something." Mohan's solemn face shrank even more.

"Oh, God. it wasn't your test results, was it? Because I don't know how the hell to get antibiotics here. I mean—"

"No, just listen." Mohan went back to the apartment's front door, double-checking it was locked and adding the top latch. It worried Andrew to no end that what he was about to say was somehow worse, or more dangerous, than the two of them being caught fucking in Saudi Arabia. "My name is not Mohan."

"What is it?"

"Fahrooq. But that doesn't matter. You have to listen to me. I work for MI5. That was them on the phone. It was Lisa Mantis, actually." Andrew took the news in calmly, much as he had James' HIV diagnosis. When the world seemed so big, so scary, and life destroyed the reality one hoped to live in, there was no other way to act than stoically sit and listen.

"Why are you outing yourself to me? What's happened?"

"You have to get back to London." Mohan...or *Fahrooq*, appeared more upset than Andrew. He was pacing, spinning the phone in his fingers. "It's James. He's in grave danger. She didn't say any more. Just that you have to return to London. Now."

Andrew nodded. With nothing more to be said, he sipped the coffee, wondering if it would be for the last time. The last time he would sit in this make-believe land, doing things he could not comprehend with people he would never really know. Spies and princes. There was a very good reason Andrew had not returned to London in the three weeks he had been away. He simply would not let himself. There, he didn't know who he was. He didn't know here, either, but he'd have a better chance of figuring that out four thousand miles from the man who'd swallowed up his entire existence.

They glanced at the television. The news showed

people gathering on a makeshift stand on Horse Guards Parade. The Trooping the Color was about to kick off. Marching bands in bearskin hats. Rows of soldiers on horseback. All the pomp and circumstance that obscured the true nature of power and the throne. Spies and lies and princes. Andrew watched the silent talking heads as guests appeared. One by one, people Andrew recognized like former colleagues paraded in their finery. Then James arrived. Wearing a simple suit. Likely picked out by that snake, Samuel. All James had to do was fire him, and he'd be right there by his side. All Andrew had needed was a simple demonstration of loyalty. Instead, he'd got nothing but—

"The cheek!" Andrew shouted out. Mohan jumped in worry. "How could he!"

"What? What happened?"

Andrew laughed to himself. It was, indeed, rather amusing the depths James would go to fuck with Andrew's feelings. A well-timed call to Lisa Mantis just as James took to the stage with a new friend by his side.

"That's Greg there on the TV, standing two feet behind James. Look. That little weasel-looking boy. Lord Gregory Honnington, so it is. The little shit."

"Who is that?" Mohan offered anxiously.

"Long story, but the ending is pretty simple. James is fine." Andrew gulped down more of the coffee until the thick grains at the bottom bothered his lip. He wiped it away with a hand, and stared at Mohan who was trying to square Andrew's casualness with his boss's concern. "Fancy another load?"

Chapter 7

LIZZIE WINDSOR HAD ALWAYS HATED royal events. They gave her a version of imposter syndrome she couldn't quite name. No psychologist had yet coined the right phrase to describe the feeling, nor had she ever been able to spill enough of these royal secrets to make someone understand just what she was talking about. Standing on the makeshift stage erected over Horse Guards Parade, watching endless lines of cavalry form up on a breezy London day, Lizzie was adjacent to, but separate from, the royals the world had come to see.

King James stood in the relative center in the simplest military suit he could get away with, surrounded by the latest twinks from his entourage to fill Andrew's growingly noticeable absence. A lord mayor, a lord president of the privy council, and a smattering of military officials made camp between the king and Princess Alexandra. Unlike the others, she was decidedly alone, imperious, like a statue, in a long and heavily adorned militaristic overcoat, anointed with the official ranks Alexandra held as colonel-in-chief of various regiments. She had them all on display today. Her hair was hidden under an admiral's cap, as were her intentions. Faisal was of course very much absent. The news was not new that they had separated, and he had returned to Saudi Arabia. But she didn't surround herself with anyone else. In fact, most of the two dozen dignitaries on the platform huddled several feet away. In Lizzie's other life as a roving editor of fashion magazine *Allure*, she would have written that Alexandra's outfit was "doing all of the work for her".

After the king and his sister—or heir and rival—were several other well-dressed members of the royal retinue. Guardsmen and generals, and then was Lizzie. Stood next to the railing. At the furthest end of the stage. Another child from anyone else in this line up and she'd be kicked down another place to the Gods, or the orchestra, or wherever else those who made these sorts of decisions placed the undesirables whom they must invite to any family function. Officially, Lizzie was nothing more to the royal family than a simple cousin. The supposed daughter of the brother-in-law of the late Queen Victoria II. Her place in the line of succession behind that of Alexandra's children. A royal nobody to those who mattered.

But that wasn't the truth. Lizzie had known the truth for most of the time she'd been alive, hence the inverted imposter syndrome she'd been saddled with all that time. It wasn't that Lizzie was the imposter here, but everyone else in this charade. She was the first-born child of Prince Richard, Queen Victoria II's only descendent, and the only *legitimate* child. Richard had married Lizzie's mother,

Calista Murphy, in a ceremony kept secret from the world. Did Richard's marriage to a Catholic woman without the sovereign's permission go against succession law? Absolutely. Did his second marriage to James and Alexandra's mother Alice go against every other law against bigamy? Even more so.

The Grenadier Guards below trumpeted into the first of their many songs for the parade. A death-march style rendition of *God Save the King*. It took so long for the band to bring their collective wall of sound together that most of the watching crowd—and the royals on the platform—didn't realize the national anthem was being played and was supposed to be sung until the opening chorus was halfway through and the verse had begun. Few could handle the incoherence of starting the song halfway through, so what greeted the waiting ears was a cat's chorus of a band screeching and a crowd shrieking all out of time and tune with one another.

Lizzie was at least sure the cameras did not pan wide enough to catch her smirk. More interesting was Alexandra's face. She'd started to sing, her thin lips un-pursing just enough to show the world some loose-leaf loyalty to her sovereign, but in the mess of the noisy discord, she'd stopped herself when realizing she was out of time with the music. All of the top team did. Sharing a few awkward nods and glances instead. Lizzie leaned forward to catch sight of James. He'd noticed the fuck up, and how. A whispering circle had started with his cortege, as they all searched around for the culprit.

"How about we go one more time?" a woman's quiet voice said behind Lizzie. "For the cheap seats in the back."

"Lisa."

"It's 'K' to you," the head of MI5 said, sliding alongside Lizzie, gently shoving her just that bit farther into the railing. They stared out into the sandy expanse of Horse Guards Parade as the troops began their quick march and the band found their rhythm. "How many of those men do you think the king has had fuck him?"

Lizzie turned in surprise. Lisa carried on staring, counting the regiments from behind a pair of sunglasses despite the patchy cloud.

"Oh, don't pretend you don't know what I'm talking about, Lizzie. You know as well as I do the king's an insatiable bottom."

Lizzie shrugged as they watched the parade.

"Can't say I've ever given it much thought."

"Even when you were conspiring to bring him down?"

"Clearly I'm not very good at my job." Lizzie made her annoyance known. They weren't exactly in a secure location, what with a hundred television cameras broadcasting every angle of the event. Yet Lisa Mantis seemed intent on bringing up these things Lizzie didn't care to talk about.

"Oh, I don't know about that. You managed to murder Dame Esmeralda without a trace. It's not everyone who can top off my predecessor."

Lizzie's blood turned cold.

"I served my debt to you already."

Now Lisa turned to face her, breaking the spell of the top platform all calmly watching the parade.

"Don't be so naive, Elizabeth. You should know when you're in debt to me, it's for life." She turned back to the crowd. "Anyway, don't you think his majesty would be much happier out there roaming free in the world, a bottom unburdened by the trappings of the state?"

"Is the team backing Alexandra again, then? I should have known better than MI5 sticking to a policy any longer than a season."

Lizzie watched Lisa's reaction out of the corner of her eye. A little smirk. Enough to say Lizzie was at least worth sparring over.

"I think we've found our final horse."

"Oh, do tell. Have you dug up some incontinent Hanoverian to come over in a grand reenactment of the Glorious Revolution?"

"Not quite. Someone a bit closer to home, actually. We're backing you."

Lisa said nothing else, at least not to Lizzie. She turned to her other side and began making small talk with an aging admiral. The words spun in Lizzie's head, rolling themselves over and over. She needed more information, that was the only thing Lizzie could settle on. But this was hardly the time or place to talk conspiracy. Lisa must have known that. She wanted to give a single, simple yet devastating line. They wanted her.

After several songs and several regiments had carried out their maneuvers, Lisa watched as most of those from the royal stage had been brought down for the transfer of the middling dignitaries to Buckingham Palace. Lisa eyed up the few left: the King and Lord Gregory, the twink who'd used Lizzie to sneak into the royal engagement before. She noted Alexandra, still not talking to anyone, and Lizzie. Lisa peered over railing and saw their carriages being organized down below. Three separate ones.

"One of those is for you," Lisa said. Lizzie looked surprised. She'd arrived here by taxi. "Well, you are a counselor of state. After Alexandra's children, you're the most senior royal, by law."

"And by rights."

"We all know the story, Lizzie. No need to wreck the thing before you take charge, is there?" The royals on the stage were now milling about with aides. The band had stopped playing since the action had shifted to the procession down The Mall. James was leaning against the railing at the far side, talking. Alexandra had accepted a warm drink from a flask. Aides were yelling things at other aides below. An aura of backstage after rehearsals were done took over. Lisa lit a cigarette.

"Just exactly how do you expect me to take charge?"

"That's really up to you, Lizzie."

"So, what, you're outsourcing treason now? What about the coronation?"

"Ah, good one. No, the coronation isn't happening. Actually, that's our deadline. James and Alex must be gone by then. We're going to set up a regency council under Prince Hassan, and I can see to it that you, Lizzie, will be in charge of that regency council. Just think, all the power, riches and influence of being in charge, without all that pesky administration or having to sit for portraits and see your face on stamps. Wouldn't that be grand?"

Lizzie was still trying to piece everything together. Lisa leaned over the railing to take a peek at the preparations of the horse drawn carriages down below, and tapped ash from her cigarette over the edge.

"Can you give me it straight, please? I don't know what the hell you want me to do."

"Calm down," Lisa said, still smiling. "There's cameras." She stood up and turned her back to the rapidly emptying Horse Guards Parade, and looked directly at Lizzie as she smoked. Lisa glanced to the others still on the platform. They were out of earshot, that was for sure, although the length of time Lizzie and the head of MI5 had been talking did seem to attract some attention from both James and Alexandra.

"They're looking at us," Lizzie said, also turning away.

"Let them look. Let them wonder. I tried to warn Alexandra last night, but she wasn't having it. I said there's an easy way out of this, and a hard way. Of course, she took that as a challenge." Lisa took a deep drag from the rapidly finishing cigarette. "Did you know she's fucking her divorce lawyer?"

"What are you talking about?"

"Can't blame her. He's hung like a horse thief in an old Western."

"What easy way? What hard way?"

"Oh, that. Still haven't cottoned on?" Lisa flicked her still-lit cigarette over the edge. "As I already explained, the coronation isn't happening. They've settled on a regency council until Prince Hassan comes of age. He'll be pushing thirty by the time they let him take over, knowing that lot. But at least for the next decade. You know, to provide stability."

"I don't understand."

"Okay, so a regency council is when the monarch is incapacitated or under age, and parliament appoints—"

"I know what that is!" Lizzie was getting increasingly anxious. What reason could or would she give to be annoyed talking to the head of Britain's domestic intelligence service? What would the world think?

"So, like I said, I want you, Lizzie Windsor, to be the head of that council. Queen Regent, if you like."

"You want me?"

"It's either you or Sir Peter. You know, that slimy weasel who murdered your father and mother and left you here on the sidelines of life when you should have been the one wearing the crown. You know he was the one who talked your grandmother into using the Gaveston Protocols. She just wanted to disinherit him. But Peter, oh no, he doesn't do anything by half." Lizzie didn't think there was any new information she could have been told about the death of her parents. She'd thought she'd been through every action, every possibility, every piece of the puzzle up to and including the details outlined in Liv Finnegan's book. But here was Lisa, with her tobacco breath, breathing new conspiracies into the dark abyss that was her past.

"How do I make sure it's me?" Lizzie asked quietly. She watched as Alex sipped from a flask, and James shamelessly flirted with another young aide who'd come to show him the next order of business for the day's events.

"Simple. You take control. Sir Peter has MI6 and God knows who else on his side. And they've signed Gaveston Protocols against both James and Alex."

"How? Only the monarch can—"

"Don't remind me. So, either you get both Alex and James to abdicate before the coronation—and I mean completely, irrevocably abdicate, and together, not one then the other—or, you know, do what you were planning to do all this time before. Kill them."

Lizzie sucked in a breath, stained with Lisa's perfume and the remnants of tobacco. They were ready to head down the stairway to the carriages.

"The coronation's in three weeks, I have to do this all before?"

"More like fifteen days now. So, you know, tick-tock."

A more senior aide in military uniform came up the stairs. "Your Majesty and royal highnesses, we're ready to commence the procession to the Palace. Ma'am," he gestured to Lizzie, "if you would follow me."

Lizzie was suddenly seized by the reality of the situation. Not the task ahead of her, but the outcome. Wasn't this it all? She'd wanted to burn the whole thing down, yes, and this was the final chance. If she'd become monarch in some roundabout, probably impossible way of proving her half siblings were illegitimate bastards, she'd never be able to accomplish what she'd set out to do. But as the power behind the throne, as regent for a ten-year-old boy, things could be so much different.

"Um…of course. Yes," Lizzie said, righting herself. "I'm ready."

"Hold on a moment," James said loudly from across the platform. "There you've been all this time, Lizzie, conspiring over there in the corner. You never even said hello."

"Your Majesty," the aide said as James started across the platform, "we're on a tight schedule."

"Nonsense. They won't start without us." James gleamed with a mix of desperation and hysteria. He knew that something had been happening over in Lisa and Lizzie's corner, and wanted to know.

"Can we not, James?" Alexandra said, shrinking her arms in as James barged past. "I know you aren't bothering with a change of clothes but some of us have other outfits we want to get into."

"I'm just making family conversation, aren't I?" James was now a few feet from her. Lisa had managed to disappear into the background. In fact, the spy was already halfway down the stairs. "One big happy family. So, Lizzie, what's new then, huh?" James' eyes were aflame. "What *conspiracy* are you involved in today?"

The cry of disturbed, injured horses reached Lizzie first. Then the bone-crunching crack of metal twisting, then screams and cries and the general chaos all around Horse Guards as the side of the stage that James had just been standing on collapsed in a resounding crash of broken iron and steel.

"Greg!" James screamed, galloping forward to the destroyed edge of the platform. The aide body-tackled him.

"No, Your Majesty! Stay back."

"Greg!"

A yell of shouts and screams and sudden sirens surrounded them all like a wall of noise. Another aide rushed up the creaking stairs, ready to grab Alexandra who was closest to the collapsed edge, but she avoided being snatched and rushed to the edge.

"Alex, careful!" Lizzie yelled out, jumping forward as well. Alex was bent down, reaching beyond the twisted morass of broken construction. Lizzie reached the edge and peered down, far down, into what had become a scrap heap of sharpened spokes and destroyed platforms. On the sandy ground below, soldiers rushed around, some trying to steady the bolted horses, others guiding the last remaining spectators as far away as possible as if under enemy fire.

"I've got you," Alexandra said. Lizzie suddenly saw Greg, his face shell shocked, body dangling, holding on to Alexandra for dear life. Immediately, Lizzie reached down and snatched Greg's other arm, and he gladly held on.

"We've both got you," Lizzie said. She shared a simple glance with Alex. "On three. One, two…"

"Greg!" James finally broke free and ran forward, wrapping the rescued Greg in a hug as the nervous aides did their best to shoo them away from the collapsed edge. The platform suddenly felt very unstable.

"Careful, James," Alexandra said quietly as they dusted themselves down. "The world still thinks you're engaged."

"You saved my life," Greg told them all, breathing deeply as Alexandra offered him the drink from the flask. Helicopters were now roaring overhead, and the wailing sirens made streaking tire marks across the sandy square.

"And you…" James said to Lizzie, suddenly disturbed realizing he'd been moments away from the bottom of a corrugated iron heap. "You saved mine."

Lizzie just nodded, and kept nodding, letting the shock soak in. There wasn't fifteen days. It was happening now.

Chapter 8

ANDREW'S APARTMENT HAD BECOME ground zero. Nearly two dozen people, Westerners and Saudis, crowded around the television screen in Andrew's lounge, watching the aftermath of the terrorist attack which had very nearly taken out several members of the British royals, the king included. No one in the apartment asked awkward questions. No one made reference to why Andrew's fridge was full of beer and gin. No one judged those who drank or not. Neither did anyone ask why Andrew, publicly engaged to the king who had just narrowly escaped death, was here in Saudi Arabia, and had been for long enough that he knew nearly two dozen people who felt comfortable enough to come straight to his apartment and watch the news unfold.

Thankfully, no one had found Andrew sitting alone with Mohan in their skimpy robes. No one had arrived with a question on their lips as to why they were alone together. They found Andrew dressed in gym shorts and a tank top. Mohan back in his suit. That was because Hands, the neighbor from across the hall—a German man who worked in the oil industry—banged on the door. Andrew threw on some gym clothes as Mohan ran into the bathroom to change. The TV had been on, but Andrew and Mohan had hardly been paying attention. Hans sat on the exact place they'd just been having sex not moments before, parroting a running commentary of the explosion.

In the time it took Hans to describe the collapse of the platform, that it was believed to have been caused by an explosive device, and seemed specifically targeted to go off to kill only, or mainly, James, the knocking on Andrew's door increased until it stayed open and people gathered like it was the most natural place to be. Many did offer Andrew a sympathetic pat on the shoulder, some a hug. Paula, from the firm of city planners, had arrived in a flood of tears, prostrating herself for several minutes on Andrew's behalf until he made her a drink and she quietened down.

"Must've been a radio-controlled explosion." Hans, by virtue of being first to the apartment, took on the mantle of one who knew the most about the situation, since he'd been watching the longest.

"Did you see how they saved that other guy? Princess Alexandra lunged forward to save him."

"I'm surprised the whole thing didn't come down."

"Did they only target the king?"

"They can't blame us Saudis again, surely."

"How the hell did anyone manage to plant a bomb there?"

The constant stream of speculation weighed Andrew

down. He retreated to the kitchen, facing away from the television to make another drink.

"You okay?" Mohan asked, sliding next to Andrew in the kitchen. Andrew glared at him as he dropped ice into the gin, feeling a wave of blame against this man who'd already revealed himself to be an MI5 agent called Fahrooq.

"Your timing was impeccable. Warning me James was in danger and fifteen minutes later, bang, he is?"

"You really think this is our fault?" Andrew shrugged in response. He'd dealt with more than enough of the British establishment to not trust a single one, but also to realize James had far greater enemies than Lisa Mantis.

"No…no I don't, sorry. I'm just feeling like…ugh."

Mohan gripped his shoulder.

"I get it." There was a pause, a sigh. The talking heads on the TV screen and around it filled the room with noise while Andrew would rather be alone. Truthfully, he'd rather call James. But that was his fears talking. His fears of being alone, of standing on his own two feet. It was all written down, bookmarked and highlighted among the books scattering the coffee table now used as coasters by the uninvited audience. "Can I tell you what I think?"

"Is this the official MI5 line I'll be hearing?"

"My job is to watch Faisal, not you. But, even still, watching you this last month, it's clear you love him. Very, very much. There are some people we struggle to get over because it's just hard. But other times…other times it's a struggle because we're not meant to get over them. You and James, you should be together. You should be with him."

Andrew drank deeply from the gin and tonic.

"Funny how your opinion and Lisa Mantis' opinion dovetail so well together."

"Be cynical if you want, Andrew, but I'm being serious."

"Says the spy."

"Yes. Says the spy to the prince. The prince who's in a place he doesn't belong. James did a lot for you. He came out, I mean, my God, he came out. There's a gay king sitting on the throne. He proposed to you live on television. He's fighting the church and the government to marry you. He made you a prince, he made you the Duke of Cornwall, and if I listen to the gossip around MI5, he also made your little friend Gregory Honnington and his dad nobles to stop him being dragged through the courts."

"But—"

"I know everything you're going to say, Andrew. Samuel's controlling and James only thinks of himself, but look at the big picture, Andrew. Do you want to live the rest of your life having James only in your mind, or having him in your bed, too? Because if you don't decide—" Mohan glanced at the television reshowing footage of James lunging across the raised platform just moments before it collapsed "—someone else might decide for you."

Andrew drank, annoyed Mohan was making him face the truth he'd been running from for too long. Mohan's phone rang, shocking them both.

"It's Faisal," Mohan said, answering quickly. He didn't

even get a chance to speak. Andrew heard the familiar voice through the speaker. "*Send him to me now.*"

"Prince Faisal is back," Mohan said, hanging up. "He wants to see—"

"Yeah, I got it." Andrew drained his glass. "I'll go see him now. Thanks, Fahrooq." He left the spy standing in the kitchen. No one noticed as he slipped out of his own apartment, on the way to see the most powerful man in the Middle East.

"When did you get back?" Andrew asked, making small talk that made things more awkward. Faisal was tipping papers and wires out of a briefcase on the couch, looking for something. Andrew stood to the side, playing with his fingers on a side table in the darkened penthouse. Faisal's apartment took up an entire floor of the tallest building in the Kingdom. It was a luxury befitting his rank, the blinds closed on gold, crystal, and polished mahogany furnishings.

In the quiet cool of an air-conditioned suite, Andrew immediately fell back under Faisal's scent. Rich perfume and dark skin standing out against the disinfected beige of the walls. He was not James, that much was true, but the smell had no less effect on Andrew. A taste he remembered from his Eton days, just as he knew James' taste back then.

"Found it," Faisal said, handing Andrew a small flash drive. "Two trillion dollars of investment agreements." Faisal smiled widely; his beard had grown longer since England. His hair wilder since it spent more time under a kaffiyeh. His skin more tanned. "We're going to transform this country. And it's thanks to you."

"No, it isn't," Andrew said, shrugging off the compliment.

"It is, and I want you to do more. We've got some follow-up next week with the IMF. I want you to present our democratization plan."

"You mean you want a white face to reassure the white people."

"Something wrong with that? You've been doing a good job on that front up until now." Andrew fingered the flash drive. Faisal seemed concerned, he lifted Andrew's chin with his fingers in a move that would normally have Andrew folding at the stomach, but today left his belly doing flips. "You wrote the democratization plan, Andrew. It's all you. Free elections in five years, a constitution in ten. You're changing this place for the better."

"It doesn't really feel like that, though. I mean, does it really matter whether I'm here or not?"

"Hey." Faisal held Andrew steady with a hand on his shoulder. "Is this about the attack at Horse Guards? I know you're worried, but James is fine. They'll be upping security like mad now, especially before the coronation. He's in good hands. You don't need to compromise your life, Andrew, for his."

"I know!" Andrew snapped. "I've heard what you've said a million times over. It's just…hard. I feel I should…I feel I should be there."

Andrew hung his head, shame creeping up his neck.

What was wrong with him that he had this pathological need to please his lover? If not James, then Faisal. Why could he not just say what he wanted?

Oh, Andrew realized as Faisal pulled him into a hug, it was because the wanting touch of a handsome man would lead him to do anything.

"You know what else is hard?" Faisal whispered as Andrew breathed in his lover's neck. Faisal guided Andrew's hand downward, underneath the belt of his expensive trousers, beyond the silk underwear. Andrew's knees went weak at the touch of a tussle of rough black pubes and the meat of his dick sitting calmly underneath. Faisal nuzzled his neck and the lobe of his ear, biting, chewing on the thing he owned. That thing which was Andrew.

Andrew shivered at his secret shame in the secluded lair of the Saudi Crown Prince. Since their first tryst at Eton, when Andrew had acquiesced to Faisal's demand for satisfaction in the depths of a rugby changing room, Faisal had always been at the back of his mind. Throughout those years of being with James, or watching all the others be with James, Andrew had sometimes been given over to a quiet memory of Faisal's touch.

After half a life of fugitive thoughts, these last few weeks in Riyadh had been given over to an outpouring of lust. Not as often as either of them would have liked, given the tiring schedules of building a nation anew, but when it happened, like now, Faisal ripped the very buttons from Andrew's shirt.

"My shirt," Andrew hushed as Faisal's trimmed beard scraped a trail down his neck. Faisal set the fashion, and people like Mohan followed and copied, but they never compared to the original. Andrew wanted Faisal's beard cresting down his chest, strong, hairy knuckles gripping the edges of his rib cage. If they moved another inch north, they would tickle under his armpits. Another inch south, Andrew's trousers would slide down. Faisal held him in semi-orgasmic stasis, completely at the prince's mercy as tongue and lips slipped down his navel.

"Fuck your shirt," Faisal said, now sitting on the edge of the antique chaise lounge while Andrew still stood, a now buttonless shirt billowing open. "And fuck the rest of these clothes as well."

Andrew's belt came loose with a single tug from Faisal's hand. His slacks slid down with barely a whisper from Faisal's tongue, and his body turned to flaming desire with the sight of the eager hunger with which Faisal tore off Andrew's silky boxers. Hard and helpless, Andrew stood exposed while Faisal slipped his own mighty cock from his open trousers, tugging the luscious brown skin a few times in eagerness.

"Faisal...I need...to talk to you..." The breathlessness was all-encompassing. Like a virus attacking his senses, but it was Faisal with that rare tongue of his lapping at Andrew's painfully erect dick. Andrew could almost taste the rich whiskey and cigars Faisal always smoked on his plane through his dick. "I need to talk to you about James."

Faisal didn't stop. In fact, he increased. Spinning his

tongue from just tasting Andrew, to swallowing him whole and deep. Andrew had to grip onto Faisal's shoulders, almost to pull him back from the wall of uncomfortable pleasure. Despite coming inside Mohan just an hour earlier, Andrew's body had forgotten the experience entirely. It moved with the muscle memory of Crown Prince Faisal bin Saud, sucking his cock in the inner sanctum of his high-topped palace. Only when Andrew shuddered a yelp did Faisal break free, wiping saliva from his beard.

"James is weak and pathetic." Faisal stood, anxious to get to the next part. Whatever that was to entail. "Just like his sister. That bitch wants to divorce me. She can fucking try." Faisal laughed as he threw off the rest of his clothes and stood erect, tall and powerful. "I'm going to string her along just like you're stringing along James. Let them dangle, let them suffer. The pain they've caused us. The humiliation." Faisal shook his head, the memory, the words gilding him into a rage, but a rage he was turning on Andrew. "She emasculated me for long enough, so now I'm going to fuck her brother's little top."

Andrew took in the words as a curiosity. Said across him, not to him. He was the little top in question. Did Faisal realize that? There wasn't another moment to wonder, because with a face of fury, Faisal spun Andrew around then split him over the side of the couch, throwing his face into the cushions. Faisal's mighty hands gripped each one of Andrew's ass cheeks, then the bearded face dived deep into Andrew's hole.

He was glad to have his face in the pillow. It muffled

the moans caused by Faisal's uncontrolled lapping at Andrew's insides. The tongue pushed through the barrier and sent Andrew's legs into the air, desperately seeking some dry land while Faisal unnerved him with waves of wet pleasure. Hairy cheeks rubbed hard against Andrew's smooth ones, as Faisal crammed all of his face into Andrew as he could. With every bust and push and pressure, Andrew relaxed that little bit more into Faisal, taking mind to breathe deeply, because he knew the fucking that was about to commence would be merciless.

"Faisal…" Andrew managed to gasp as the tongue-fucking let up. But what was he supposed to say now? There wasn't a way to change Faisal's mind, he didn't work like that. This wasn't a discussion or a debate. Faisal was finally acting like the ruler he'd always dreamed of being, and there was nothing that could convince him otherwise. One either bent over for Faisal, or…Andrew didn't know what the alternative would be.

The sound of spit falling onto skin was the only warning Andrew got. The head of Faisal's cock pressed into his hole, pushing down like a thumb pressing between shoulder blades. Faisal, like most men who were used to making love to women, always started too low. Andrew yelped in pain as Faisal continually thrust into the wrong place. Not even biology would stop him. Only another cry had him withdraw, spread open Andrew's ass cheeks with a thumb and finger, spit again, then try again.

Andrew felt himself fall lifeless over the couch as Faisal hit the mark and pushed inside. He willingly, desperately let himself be penetrated all the way to Faisal's teeth biting a mouthful of Andrew's shoulder.

"Fuck yeah." Faisal was verbal. "Feels good, me inside you. Yeah. Feels good." Faisal didn't ask, he told. He fucked the way he lived, comfortable with life as a hierarchy and knowing he was sitting on top. One hairy arm gripped around Andrew's neck, squeezing him tight and nearly the air out his lungs. Faisal's other arm gripped the back of the couch and began to fuck Andrew with brutal honesty.

Pleasure was still locked behind a barrier that was a good several minutes of fucking away. But this wasn't the feeling Andrew leaned into every time Faisal fucked him. It was the power play that Faisal loved. The same dynamic of flipping roles that surely kept James turning his body over to men time and time again. The powerful being overpowered. The commoners and the royals. Finding a natural order in the chaos of life's games, and slipping into the satisfaction of a place of calm serenity knowing that in life, some were born to fuck, and others born to serve them.

It took only a few more minutes, because Faisal had been away for days and Andrew's hole gripped tightly around the Crown Prince's girth, and soon the grunting became harsher. Breath quickened in Andrew's ear, their debate that wasn't rapidly coming to an end. Faisal all but encased Andrew's body, wrapping himself around him like a cloak, thrusting through pain and tightness and violating every law of the land until finally Faisal groaned with a roar that rumbled through the penthouse apartment, ending with a single drop of sweat into the crevice of Andrew's back.

Faisal slipped out and stood up. He stepped around the couch to do the thing he'd never done before being named Crown Prince. He took the final right of a top, of a king, and shoved the remnants of his erection straight into Andrew's mouth.

"That's it," he said softly. "Clean off my cock like a good little lad."

Andrew obliged like it was an order—it was—sucking off Faisal until there was nothing but thick softness. Faisal padded over to the bar, buttocks bared, and poured them both a whiskey. Andrew uncurled himself from the stretched out fetal position on the couch, and shoved his boxers back on as Faisal returned and handed him a glass. An unlit cigar sat between his lips. Faisal picked up a robe from another chair, slipped it on and took a silver gun lighter from a carved holster on the table. He lit his cigar, puffing with his robe open and cock flopping between his hairy thighs. Staring down at Andrew, he smiled with one corner of his mouth.

"What the fuck did you want to say to me earlier? Some shit about James?" Faisal flopped into the armchair. He shoved one foot onto the table, and the other straight into Andrew's lap. Andrew immediately started to rub it. He sucked in a desperate breath, intoxicated with Faisal's cigar smoke, but he was determined in his beliefs. He knew what to say, and he knew what had to be done. There was a natural order to things, and Andrew had tried for too long to deny his rightful place in that hierarchy. He was serving the wrong master. Tumbled into this submissive foot-rubber, cock-cleaner, boot-licker that wasn't really him. Andrew knew deep inside his heart which royal he was supposed to serve, and it wasn't the next sultan of Saudi Arabia.

"I think…" Andrew said, swallowing away his anxiety and turning the energy toward massaging Faisal's feet, "I think it's time for me to go home, and be with James."

Faisal sucked in the remaining drag of his cigar. He let it twist and turn around his mouth, billowing the fragrant smoke back out in circles. Then a chuckle came over him. Slow at first, but it soon built into a belly laugh.

"No," Faisal said, still smiling, but clear it might not be for long.

"No?"

Now Faisal turned serious. He stared at Andrew with the deathly look he kept for servants who displeased him.

"Next time you say something so stupid, boy, I'm stubbing this out on your little pink nipple. Now rub the other foot, and be glad I'm not making you lick them clean. For now."

Chapter 9

LIZZIE SAT IN THE MOST PRECARIOUS position of all; between two royals. James sat on one end of the long leather couch, sipping his afternoon vodka and cranberry through a straw. Alexandra was on the other end, rapidly typing on her phone. Lizzie sat between them in Buckingham Palace's map room, attempting to calm her breath.

She studied the huge, hand-stitched map hung on the wall across from her. The size was monumental. It stretched up to the ceiling, at least twenty feet high, and surely not less than fifty feet across. Across the entirety of the tapestry, a quarter of the world's surface was stitched in red. From the Canadian-American border up to the Arctic Circle. Australia and New Zealand fringing the Antarctic, some of which was obscured from view by another leather couch across the room. All of southern Africa, stretching up through Kenya to the Egyptian border, and patches on the Western coast of the continent to represent Nigeria and Sierra Leone, then across the entirety of the Indian subcontinent, stretching down through the archipelago of southeast Asia. The Empire at its height, not to mention the myriad of island nations stitched in fine detail that James was still king of today, alongside Canada, New Zealand, and Australia. Lizzie stared at the map, and it stared back. James' straw made loud noises. On either side, they were willfully oblivious to the attempted regicide which had just befallen them.

A grandfather clock ticked. Alexandra typed. James eyed up the drinks trolley for another round.

"Finally," Alexandra said as the far door opened. Lisa Mantis marched in, files under her arms and the weight of the world under her eyes. "Can we leave now?"

"Can I brief you first?" Lisa stood in front of the tapestry, but she was still dwarfed by red India.

"What was it, then?" Alexandra asked, arms folded, legs crossed, foot tapping against the leather couch. "Bad maintenance? Faulty equipment? Gust of wind?"

James snorted a small laugh. "British engineering for you."

"Actually," Lisa said, the exasperation across her face. "An improvised explosive device." She dropped the files on the couch covering the Antarctic, but held onto one. She strode across the room and handed it to James, who looked as bemused as if he'd just been given a rugby ball and told to captain a team. "And this—" James opened the folder. Lizzie leaned across to look, and Alexandra peered too. "This is the sniper we apprehended, holed up in Gwydyr House, across from Horse Guards Parade. As soon as you fell, James, he was supposed to open fire."

"On whom?" Alexandra asked, having come so far across the couch she leaned over Lizzie and snatched the folder from James' hand.

"On you, your royal highness. Our initial interrogation suggests his plan was to shoot Princess Alexandra in the head after James had died in the crush of the collapsed platform. But when James ran across at the last moment, the plan fell apart." Lizzie swallowed hard as all eyes were trained on her for a moment.

"He's not Arab," Alexandra said, studying the file. She seemed surprised. Lizzie wasn't sure if pleasantly or not. The last attack which had killed Princess Katyn had been blamed on Alexandra's Saudi in-laws, but in actual fact carried out by Lizzie's IRA allies led by Seamus. He'd been arrested after the attack, but released once Lisa Mantis understood the web which Lizzie weaved.

"No, your royal highness," Lisa said. "He's not Arab. Nor is he a terrorist. At least, not by our standards."

"Oh? Then what is he?"

"A Russian mercenary."

"Is that better?" James asked, having somehow managed to sneak himself another drink.

"No," Lisa replied. "It's much, much worse." She paced the room as the three royals watched and listened. "He's a Russian hitman for hire, which means whoever is behind this attack has the resources and connections to find this guy. And if they can buy one, they can buy another."

"He can't have been very good if he got caught,"

Alexandra said, still not seeming to take the threat as seriously as Lisa wanted them to.

"He turned himself in."

"Why on earth?"

"Like I said, soldier for hire."

James clinked the remaining ice in his glass, pondering what Lisa was saying as if it was nothing more than the details of a state banquet.

"So, we can just…pay them all more?" James said.

"I'm afraid it doesn't quite work like that, Your Majesty. The reason he turned himself in is because his fate with us is very likely a damn sight better than his fate back with his employers."

"You haven't heard James go off when someone brings him the wrong drink," Alexandra said. Even James chuckled and shrugged like it was true. Lizzie watched Lisa though, the head of MI5 not quite comprehending the relative frivolity with which the royals were treating their attempted assassination.

"I must insist," Lisa said, worry lining her face, "that you take this situation seriously."

"Oh, we are," James said, slapping his thighs as he stood up. "And I blame *her* estranged husband."

"Oh, very good, James," Alexandra shot back daggers.

"What? He's richer than you, Alex. Probably doesn't want to pay for all that couture you've become accustomed to in the divorce settlement. That was your doing, wasn't it?" James asked Lizzie. With him standing and them both still on the couch, it felt like an accusation.

"Leave her out of it," Alex snapped. "You're hardly one to judge taste. Dragging along your new little twink to public events after kicking Andrew out."

"He left me!"

"I wonder why."

"Wait," Lizzie said, catching up with the verbal volley. "Andrew left you?"

James turned sullen. He wandered over to the drinks trolley which was positioned near the double windows that looked out onto London.

"Careful by the window!" Lisa said, surging forward. James glared at her and snatched a whiskey bottle.

"Lisa," James popped the cork out, "if you think I'm going to get through a breakup and assassination attempt sober, you've pledged allegiance to the wrong monarch."

Lizzie was still trying to wrap her head around the news Andrew had left James. She'd not seen much of him in the last few weeks, but figured that was more to do with their post-engagement renaissance. She'd heard from him, though. A few messages and phone calls, but he'd never mentioned that he'd left. All the time she'd known Andrew, a decade or more, he'd been obsessed with James. More like captivated, bewitched, or, from Lizzie's point of view, kidnapped. A beautiful soul corrupted by the entice of monarchy.

All through their friendship, Lizzie reminded Andrew that James would never love him the way he deserved to be. James would never come out for him, never make a commitment to him, never place Andrew on the pedestal he deserved from his partner, from his husband. Lizzie had her own wounds to lick since the public coming out of James and engagement to Andrew. She admitted as much to Andrew that she'd not seen this coming. Pleasantly surprised, she might say. What she didn't talk about though was the cardinal rule of PR. Only admit to the potentially career-wrecking thing when there's something much more ugly to hide. She hadn't pried, but wondered.

Now for Andrew to have left? She couldn't quite hide the smile on her face. She hoped, prayed he'd run off to a big city on the other side of the world, changed his name, cut his hair, and started a brand-new life. She hoped, somehow, to never see nor hear from Andrew Hodes again. Leave James alone in his palace, with his endless men and insatiable appetite. Just let Andrew be.

James hugged the whiskey bottle, perched on the arm of the couch.

"Lisa," he said, voice croaking. Lizzie rolled her eyes at the crocodile tears. "Is there any word where he might be?"

Lisa glanced for the briefest moment at Lizzie. She wondered what the MI5 director was trying to say.

"Afraid not, Your Majesty." James was crestfallen. The pain, as fake as Lizzie might think of it, was still hard to see. He was practically whimpering. "But Your Majesty, relationships are…you know…hard. Look at your sister here, about to get divorced after over a decade with her prince charming. And Lizzie, still single and well over thirty."

"Thanks, Lisa," Lizzie said.

"Yes, thank you," Alexandra agreed. She stood now, too. "Are we done here? Our lives are in danger, you're doing your best to protect us, yadda yadda yadda. Can we go?"

"I never said that." They all looked at Lisa. "I never said we're doing our best to protect you."

"Um…why not, exactly?" James asked for them.

"Given the resources clearly available to whomever was behind the attempt on your life today," again, Lisa offered a strange glance Lizzie's way, "we are simply unprepared, and frankly under resourced, to be able to provide you with adequate protection."

"You're saying you won't protect us," James said, aghast, "because of…*budget* cuts?" Lisa shrugged in response. Alexandra took up the indigent mantle.

"Is this why you told me last night I should consider leaving?"

"She told you what?" James said, anger turning back to his sister. Lizzie watched Lisa's undisturbed face. It seemed like this was all part of a plan, and it was going well. "Lisa, you told her what?"

"I simply informed the princess there were some unspecific threats against senior royals and she should consider leaving the UK."

"Oh, and not me?"

"You have the royal protection squad, Your Majesty. Princess Alexandra doesn't." Lisa left them both dismayed. She gathered up her files, readying to leave.

"So, what are we supposed to do now?" James asked, witlessly clasping the whiskey bottle like it was love.

"My advice? Pick one of those houses you've got somewhere sunny, change your name, and hope whoever is after you only wants your titles, and not your heads, too."

"This is Faisal," James said, furious. "He's doing this so your son will take the throne and he can run everything with some self-appointed regent." James' fury was still unfurling against his sister, but it was Lisa who took the bait.

"Maybe you're right, Your Majesty, I don't know. But if that's the case, then it's a declaration of war by Saudi Arabia, and there's no way in hell this government is going to go to war with a major regional ally to protect your hides."

"So…we're on our own? That's it? Sold down the river to fend for ourselves?"

Lisa just shrugged.

"Lizzie," she said, holding the door ajar. "Shall we leave their royal highnesses to discuss their options?"

Silently, Lizzie stood. James and Alexandra were in a heads-in-their-hands phase of disbelief, so they didn't seem to care she slipped out with Lisa. The tapestry of the map, with all the places the royals might flee to, fluttered as they left.

It wasn't until they were safely out of Buckingham Palace and sitting in the back of Lisa's armored Jaguar that Lizzie said anything conspiratorial.

"Was it you, the shooter?"

"Nope," Lisa said, looking over the TV section of a tabloid. "My God, there really is nothing to watch on the telly, is there?"

The car continued to drive through central London, with Lizzie a little unsure of what was to happen now. Or where she was meant to go. Lisa turned the page.

"So, if it wasn't you…then who was it?"

"I told you, a Russian mercenary."

"Do you know who hired him?" Lisa continued to turn pages in the tabloid.

"I assume Sir Peter and MI6. Pudgy has always been on good terms with the Russians."

"Pudgy?"

"Oh, that's classified. Never mind. Anyway, Lizzie, as I told you before, there's a new order coming to Britain. A refresh from the nonsense your half-siblings have subjected us all to these last few years. I want you to come out on top, not Sir Peter and his band of reactionary pedophiles. But if you want me to help you then you need to help me first. If you can get the twins out of the picture before the coronation; by hook or by crook, then the power behind the throne is all yours, Lizzie. Oh, look what's on later, *Macbeth*. Denzel Washington? My goodness, I feel a flutter!"

"You really don't care if they live or die?" Lizzie didn't ask it with a sentimental breath, and Lisa seemed to acknowledge that. She folded the newspaper on her lap.

"The only thing I care about, Lizzie, is that I'm the one to pull the strings. Not any other agency. If your siblings decide to take the easy way out and abdicate, we can bend over backward to help. You can tell them that, I think it sounds less like a set-up if it comes from you. If they want to take the hard way...well, it's up to you, as I said."

"Up to me meaning it's really up to you, Lisa."

Lisa smiled. "Call me 'K', dear. Now, is there anything else I can help you with? Or may I drop you off, preferably at the next traffic light?"

Lizzie thought for a moment. It was real, this end of the line of James and Alexandra. It wasn't one or the other, but both, and it was coming quickly. A new order being established in front of her eyes. The only question being would Lizzie stand behind the new dynasty, or the man who murdered her parents and now was trying to murder her siblings. The car came to a stop at a busy road of traffic waiting to go green.

"Do you also know where Andrew is?"

"Of course, dear. He's in Saudi Arabia with Faisal. If you want James to fuck off with his head and balls intact, though, I'd strongly suggest getting little Andrew Hodes back on British soil."

"I agree. Now, do you have the file I asked for?"

"You're good at this game," Lisa said, looking pleasantly surprised at Lizzie's intelligent take on the situation. She gave her a rather thick manilla folder bound with string.

"Been playing it all my life, K."

"Very good. Now fuck off and take this country before someone else gets their hands on it."

Chapter 10

A SOFT DUSK HAD BROKEN OVER WIND-sor Castle as James returned, full of the anger of a summer storm. His mood not just cloudy but on the verge of a hurricane, and he took his feelings out on the handful of staff he encountered on the way to the royal apartments. James screamed to be alone at the final young aide who held the door open for him, then slammed it so hard the glass rattled in the windowpanes.

"What the heavens is going on?" Charles called out from the pantry off the kitchen. The old butler fumbled into the sitting room wearing an apron and covered in silver polish as James slumped into an arm chair and kicked off his shoes.

"Hello. I forgot you were here."

"Oh, well that's a fine way to be greeted, isn't it!" Charles harrumphed as well, chucking his silver-stained cloth onto the table and also plopping down into a chair. "If you're wanting things to smash, sir, I have a bunch more vases and such I really can't be arsed to clean."

"No. I don't wanna smash."

"*Want to,* sir, *want to.* We aren't watching one of your *music videos.* But are you all right? After this morning?"

"What do you think? And what's worse is the government don't wanna…want to help! We had a briefing from MI5 and she said they don't have the budget to protect us!"

"Oh, politics, sir, you know I can't make head nor tail of it." Charles threw up his hands in his standard response to anything mildly complicated. It always bugged the hell out of James, that the man who'd probably spent more time with James than his own mother or father, and had worked for Prince Richard before James was even born, could be so disinterested when it came to anything remotely controversial. Although, on second thought, it probably was a good way to survive the palace intrigue.

The old queen—he might as well be a palace eunuch really—shuffled back to the kitchen.

"Want some tea?" Charles called out, a familiar refrain James had heard just about every day, several times a day, for as long as he could remember.

"Fine."

"Shall I pop a bag into the pot for Andrew?"

The simple words cut James sharply. That second sentence was as widely said by Charles as the first one. Andrew liked his tea strong, so Charles always put an extra tea bag into the pot. Charles had been doing as such for nigh on fifteen years. Since that first time James had brought Andrew home at half-term.

Fifteen years ago

"Charles!" James called out, yelling through Windsor Castle's apartments. "Charles? I'm home!" James flung his satchel into a corner. He loosened his school tie now he was safely away from photographer's prying eyes, and he turned to his lover. Andrew grinned. The top button of his shirt was already undone, and James couldn't wait to spend the whole week of half term alone together, with most of their clothes off. "Jesus, why are you so fucking hot?"

James pulled Andrew into a deep, open-mouthed kiss. He ran hands through Andrew's thick black hair, so much tougher and more masculine than his own soft blond. The supple smell of slightly sweaty shirts from the car ride faded into the floral setting of Windsor's royal apartments.

"Same to you, your royal highness."

"Andrew, I told you! You don't have to call me that!" James held still on to his arms as Andrew glanced around the pristine room of antique furniture. It had been a favorite haunt of his father's, and it had taken James a year or so since his death to come back here. But he liked it. He liked the rolling lawns and green forest beyond the window. He liked hiding in the darkness of the dungeon downstairs, and imagining awful things with the relic of chains built into the stone. Most of all, he liked how close Windsor was to Eton, and how Andrew had leapt at the chance to spend half-term here with James, all alone.

"Well, I think you're sexy no matter what you're called," Andrew shied away a few strands of hair from James' face and it made his spine shiver.

"Maybe tonight," James said, starting to kiss the salty skin under Andrew's shirt collar, "you can call me that name I wanted you to."

"You sure?"

"Oh yeah. And no one's going to be around to hear us."

"What about your butler guy?" Andrew said, torn between moaning from James' kisses and glancing around for someone to burst out of the pantry or through the doors and find them in the living room.

"Don't worry about him. Once he gets into his room, he puts his opera records on and a frilly dressing gown. He's not coming out until morning."

"I just, you know, don't want him to get suspicious of us. I'm here for a whole week. What if your grandmother finds out?"

"Relax. She won't." James curved Andrew's arm around his back, and ran his hands through Andrew's hair once again. It soothed him, and they stood, holding each other, gently swaying in the comforting silence of the castle apartments. His grandmother was overseas. His sister was at boarding school in Switzerland. The only staff allowed anywhere near the royal apartments was Charles, and James knew exactly how to hide things from him. All he had to do was sneak out of the guest bedroom at seven, and into his own so Charles could come and wake him up at eight. Never a minute before.

"I can't wait to spend this week with you," Andrew said, hands running across James' back under the shirt. "I can't believe we've been boyfriends for like a year and haven't had a week together yet. I hate that we always have to hide at Eton, and I hate those weekends you have to go away."

"Not long now, though. One more term, and then we're straight off to London together."

"Oh, you know my mum and dad are getting me a flat in Shoreditch."

"Really?"

"Yeah. As soon as I turn eighteen, I'll get the keys. Don't even have to wait until I leave school. Thought it could be the perfect place for us to hide out, you know. Pretend like we're normal. Watch telly and order takeaways." A tear welled up in James' eye. Emotion overwhelmed his throat, threating to close it. His heart fluttered and he sniffed away the threat of more tears. "James, what's wrong?"

"Nothing. Nothing at all. What you said, it…it sounds fucking fantastic."

"Maybe…maybe we'll get a big chocolate Labrador and take it for walks together on Sunday afternoons in the park. We'll buy ice cream and sit on the bench and talk about people while the dog runs around and gets muddy. Then we'll go back home and watch films with our feet on the coffee table, and then we'll go to sleep together in our own little place. And in the morning, I'll make you coffee and toast, and we'll—"

James couldn't stand the dreams any longer. He snatched—no, seized—another kiss from Andrew's lips. Both tender and rough, twisted and taut. Their tongues lapped like dogs; they didn't care. They were each other's first kisses. Their first everything. First and only, that's all James wanted. Only Andrew, forever and always.

"Oh, hello," said the inquisitive voice of Charles. James froze, his mouth half open. "I don't believe we've met." James felt his heart crashing through his chest, or was it Andrew's? They parted instantly, but not fast enough. The taste of each other still on their lips as the pot-bellied butler blustered in. His eyes were on the boys, how could they not be, but he didn't offer much more than a hand to Andrew.

"Andrew. Andrew Hodes."

"A pleasure, Master Hodes. Now would you boys like some tea?"

Charles pottered around the living room, picking up their satchels and fluffing the cushions on the couch. He normally didn't do it with such force. James wanted to melt into nothingness. Charles was like his mother and father, even more so now since his father's death and his mother's decision to essentially abandon Britain for a series of foreign lovers James read about in the tabloids. Being caught by Charles was perhaps even worse than being written about in the newspapers. At least in the press one could always deny. Charles had seen everything with his own eyes.

"Um, Charles…" James trailed off. He didn't know what else to say. Andrew was slinking back, as if readying to run out the door. James could feel the sweat trickle down his spine. Charles finished fluffing the last pillow so hard the stuffing was nearly knocked out of it.

"Boys," Charles said, smoothing down his suit with a flourish that seemed to dance. Charles had always appeared to James like a tightly-wound ball of stress, but all of a sudden, his shoulders relaxed, he had a lightness about him that let his smile sing. "I'll say to you the same thing I always said to your father in the Falklands. *Homo sum humani—*"

"What did you call us?" James said, his heart spun into unknown anger. Why was Charles throwing a slur their way with a smile on his face? Andrew approached, a hand on James' back. Andrew still had the remnants of nerves across his face, but wasn't upset at what Charles was saying.

"It's Latin," Andrew said.

"Huh?"

"Oh, for heaven's sake, James! Don't you know a Latin quote when you hear it? *Homo sum humani a me nihil alienum puto.*" Charles stared at them both, searching for some glimmer of recognition. Not dissimilar to their Latin master at Eton, as it happened. James and Andrew stared blankly at each other. Just like in Latin class.

"Something about…being human?" Andrew offered.

"Oh, for crying out loud! What are they teaching you in that school? It's Terence!" More blank stares swapped between James and Andrew. But they were standing close together again. Charles was more upset at their lack of Latin knowledge than the earth-shattering kiss he'd walked in on. "Terence! The African Roman playwright? Well, anyway, the quote is: *I am human, so nothing human surprises me.*" The room stayed silent and still. Charles did seem to be waiting for something, but James had no idea what. At least the tension had broken. Charles threw up his hands in faux-despair and trundled off through the pantry to the kitchen.

"Do you boys want tea?" Charles called out. James glanced at Andrew, a look of *why not* on his face. Andrew returned it with a shrug and a nod.

"Yes, please," James shouted back.

"Master Hodes? How do you take it?"

Andrew wrapped his hands around James' back, lips ticking his neck.

"Doesn't he know you're the one taking it, James?"

Today

"Well? Shall I pop in a bag for…" Charles trailed off. The sound of an embarrassed set of China cups wafted through the pantry. James's chest was a cauldron of ire, so far from those care-free days when he'd first brought Andrew to Windsor in that wonderful week. It was a different world, a different life, but one James still longed for. The safety of a lie they could both hide behind.

"I don't want tea," James yelled back. "I'm going to the office."

James stormed from the living room and slammed closed the double doors. Charles might have yelled after him, or the glass panels might have shattered, the sounds were one and the same. But James didn't care. A whirlpool was ripping through his mind. Undercurrents of overlapping crises crashed against worried shores in his mind. An unraveling. That's what it felt like as he rioted through the empty corridors of Windsor Castle. The ropes that had been so secure, the knots which had bound the monarchy to the state, the royal family to the throne, James to Andrew, were fraying at the edges. The storms and the waves had left the sails of their ship hanging by a thread as it was cast toward the rocky shore in the dead of night.

"Samuel!" James yelled as he stormed into the Orchid Room. The normally delightful menagerie of colorful plants was suddenly a bothersome hothouse of buzzing fruit flies. "Samuel!" The desk was a mess of red boxes; government papers James always seemed to be behind on. The work of a modern king an endless pile of pointlessness. Papers upon papers for comment, for review, for signing. The decisions were never his, yet he was expected to keep abreast of all the goings on across every government department? The last few audiences with this new prime minister, Jason Keats, had been as awkward as a first date. *Anything you would like to advise me on, Your Majesty? Not really. Anything you'd like to consult me on, Prime Minister?* But the government couldn't even spring for a bloody defense of the realm? "Samuel!"

"Your Majesty," he finally burst into the room, panting.

"What the fuck's the point of having you live here if you're not around when I need you?"

"Sir, I was only—"

"Get the Prime Minister on the phone."

"Sir?"

"Did I stutter?

"No, just…what would you like to talk to him about? Nothing's on the schedule."

"I was the victim of a near assassination today, saved by

divine fucking providence. And, to be quite honest, you can tell the right honorable Mr. Keats I expected a fucking phone call to see if I'm all right!"

"Of course, sir."

James sucked in a breath that failed to calm him. He stared out the window as Samuel dialed up Number 10. James looked out across the public grounds, all the way down to Windsor town. A couple were walking a dog in the distance. A chocolate Labrador. It made him think of their own dog, Piers. The one he and Andrew had got together after his diagnosis, in those wonderful few months when they'd done nothing but walk the dog and watch TV. Every time James saw Piers now, those big eyes and floppy ears just asked *where's my other dad?*

"Yes, yes," Samuel said into the phone. "Yes, the king. Right now."

James didn't do well on his own. That much he knew about himself, and for a long time. Those times in the past he couldn't take his press secretary to some public outing or state event, James always ended up annoyed or bored or sad. Only coming back to Andrew cheered him up. Only being alone with the man he loved helped, but Andrew wasn't returning his calls. More than that, the number was disconnected, and had been since the night he'd disappeared nearly three weeks ago. Without a trace. Without a sign or a message or a—

"Sir?" Samuel said, holding the phone to his shoulder.

"What?"

"The Prime Minister is currently unavailable." James

turned his head in surprise. Pursing his lips, Samuel at least anticipated what his next question would be. "Why is the PM unavailable?" Samuel asked. He nodded into the phone. "She doesn't know, but thinks it's a diary appointment. Probably a meeting with a minister. Uh-huh, I'll ask." Samuel covered the speaker. "Do you want to leave a message, Your Majesty?"

James took a deep breath. He tried to think about what Andrew would do. It killed him to retreat into that mindset, but this was an emergency and it was the only thing that worked.

"Tell whatever bimbo receptionist is sitting on her fat ass in Number Ten that if the prime minister can't find a minute to speak to his sovereign right now, I'm dissolving Parliament and he can test his precious three-seat majority with the electorate!"

Samuel nodded, looking rather frightened. He barely had to lift the receiver to his ear.

"Did you get that?" Samuel nodded again at the "bimbo's" answer. "She'll just go get him."

James sighed with a sodden pant and fell into the chair. The day-drinking he'd indulged in earlier at Buckingham Palace hadn't done him well. He hated whiskey, another thing Andrew could've instantly reminded him of.

"Is there anything I can do for you, sir?"

"You can fuck off."

"Right away."

James snatched the receiver as Samuel gladly left the

room. It took only another second for someone on the other side to pick up.

"Your Majesty." Keats sounded breathless, like he'd been running…or fucking.

"I can't say your predecessor ever ghosted me, Mr. Keats."

"That's socialists for you, they never have very much going on apart from finding new ways to steal people's money." Keats chuckled for his own amusement. James winced. In the awkward silence that followed, the PM perhaps understood with whom he was talking. "Terrible events this morning, Your Majesty," his tone markedly changed. "Very relieved to hear you're all right, you and your sister both. Terrible, terrible."

"Yes, well *thank you* for asking…" The sarcasm soaked through the phone. "I presume there will be a full and thorough investigation?"

"I presume the same thing. But MI5 briefed you first, sir. I don't know anything more than you at this point."

"But you do know Lisa Mantis was of the opinion I am…how shall I say…not worth the expense of protecting." There was a sudden silence on the other end of the phone. A yawning quiet, a thinking of how to break bad news in the best way possible.

"I was briefed on the budgetary constraints sir, yes. The security services are dealing with so many priorities, Your Majesty, I don't think the cabinet would approve any increase at this present moment, particularly when we're having to make such drastic cuts to welfare and the health service after Zia Wajid's economic mismanagement."

"This isn't a party-political broadcast, Jason! Someone tried to kill me!"

"And while I truly sympathize with that, Your Majesty, I'd have a cabinet rebellion, not to mention a parliamentary one, if we were to propose spending any more on royal affairs in the current climate. That canceled referendum did take up quite a lot of the royal budget. Perhaps if you were to finance your own enhanced security measures—"

"You want me to pay for my own war against the Saudi's?"

"The Saudis, sir?"

"The ones behind the assassination attempt, yes. Or does a foreign power attacking the king not count as *casus belli* anymore?" James' Latin master at Eton would be proud. So would Andrew.

"Sir, I wasn't aware of any evidence linking the incident today to the Saudis. But the foreign secretary is leading a trade mission to Riyadh next month. I can have her quietly mention to the Crown Prince that we would not look kindly on any operations on our soil. But—"

"But what? You think I'm in some WhatsApp group with my brother-in-law and can tell him to knock it off?"

"Well, no, sir. Not exactly. But I mean…surely your fiancé could—" James was seized by a million questions.

"What about my fiancé?"

"Well…" He could hear Jason sweating down the line.

"I mean…not willing to pry, sir, but since Andrew is in Saudi Arabia with Prince Faisal, perhaps he could—"

James slammed down the receiver, breathing hard and fast. In any other room he'd need to throw open the windows to breathe. The one good thing about sitting in a conservatory is a hundred plants pumping in fresh oxygen. Not that it helped much. James ripped open a drawer in the desk and pulled out a pack of cigarettes. He sucked in the familiar taste of tobacco, another thing he did when Andrew wasn't around.

But he was *around*. He was around Faisal. How many betrayals did James have to stand? Setting him up with Katyn, going to work for Alexandra, and now having left him…*left him* to shack up with Faisal Ibn Saud. And to be told by the PM when Lisa Mantis clearly knew.

Fine, James thought, stubbing out the half-smoked cigarette. Very, very fine. Let Andrew live it up in Riyadh with the man who was trying to kill him. This castle was a fortress. The PM was right, he had money. He could buy an army. In fact, he had one. What did he need Andrew for when he had all the men he wanted right here.

"Samuel!" The door creaked open a moment later, as if he'd been waiting there all this time. "Call up the Coldstream Guards. I want them here."

"Did the PM—"

"I'm commander-in-chief, thank you." James flung open one of the royal boxes. "And colonel-in-chief of that particular regiment, so you can make the call, or I can find someone else who will."

"Right away, Your Majesty."

With two hands, James tore in half one file in the red box, then the next, then the next, and slammed it shut.

"Send that back to Number Ten, and round up whomever is here in Windsor right now and send them downstairs. I'll be in the dungeon."

"Do you want me to—"

"I do not. Make the calls."

Chapter 11

LIZZIE WALKED QUICKLY DOWN THE old Kent Road. South London wasn't her favorite place in the world, and she didn't care to dawdle outside for too long lest she end up assassinated for the change in her purse. She checked the address texted to her on her "other" phone, an old Nokia used exclusively for communicating with contract killers. Lizzie had quite a few numbers on there, she'd been at this for a long time. Her little black book of chaos. It was worth a smile, at least. She'd come this far. Those plans forged in the angry fire of her youth had been the anchor for her life for so long. So why did she feel so empty?

Lizzie kept a quick pace, partially to avoid the drunk staggering dangerously close to the busy road. Also, to think. The royals were so close to the end she'd dreamed of for so long. She could sit back and do nothing, and some other Russian contract killer would get them. They'd be... dead.

A wave of nausea as strong as the drink swept over her. Since when had this been all about murder? She'd wanted to cause chaos, yes. Aligned with Alexandra to bring James' secret life to light. They'd thought he'd abdicate. He was supposed to, save for Faisal's bribing of a prime minister and James and Andrew's blackmail of Zia Wajid to save his crown. She'd killed Katyn, that much was on her. Well, on Seamus, but she hadn't known he'd take it that far. It was supposed to be disruptive. To injure and frighten the young Swede back home at the height of her popularity. Instead, Princess Katyn had become a five-minute martyr, bursting briefly into the national limelight, then falling far into the forgotten realms of just another tragic celebrity death. One James had risen to new heights from. Another situation the king had managed to manipulate to his own benefit.

It wasn't Lizzie who was the death-monger. James was the family vulture, feasting off of carcasses; their father's, their grandmother's, his fake girlfriend. Lizzie was just trying to right a long-standing wrong. So why did it make her feel…protective?

The pub emerged around a corner, *Finnigan's Tool*. An old-style Irish pub. From back in the days when young people came in their tens of thousands across the Irish sea to London in search of life, freedom, opportunity, or, like her mother, national vengeance.

Lizzie had known her mother only briefly. Back then, she'd been Miss Murphy, Prince Richard's private secretary. She violently remembered being a little girl, six or seven, and being dressed by her "parents", the elderly Duke and Duchess of Windsor, for an event at the Palace. Richard had always treated her like the father she might subconsciously suspect he probably was. Richard made frequent visits to see her, once a week at least when he was in London. They played, they went for drives in his Rolls, and they cooked together. Long afternoons in the kitchen of a large flat in Kensington, away from any servants and their questioning eyes.

But Calista Murphy she'd only met a few times. On one of those occasions, when Lizzie was about twelve, someone had remarked on how similar they both looked. Flame red hair and freckles. Soft white skin and a Dubliner's smile. Lizzie didn't remember ever seeing Calista Murphy after that, but she remembered the woman's purple business suit. Her thick mobile phone. The way she commanded presence in a room, even in a palace room. And the gentle touch of her hand as it cupped her chin, smiling down from heels, telling her the dress she had on was very pretty in that Republican Irish twang.

They'd died when Lizzie was just a few weeks shy of eighteen. On the evening of her birthday, as she returned from a night out, a car stopped on the quiet road she was walking down. The engine turned off, and she gripped her keys tightly between her fingers when a man got out, carrying a package.

Elizabeth Windsor?

Stay back!

Ma'am, please. Don't be alarmed. I'm from your mother's estate. I have this for you.

She'd taken the package and shut herself up in her room. It was paperwork, mostly. Birth certificates and pensions and title deeds to a house, the one she now lived in. But among the officialdom a life—any life— accumulates, were the charred remains of what had been in Calista Murphy's bag the night they'd died—no, been murdered—in a helicopter crash. A letter, destined for the then fifteen-year-old Prince James, written by his father and telling his son in no uncertain terms that pursuing a royal life was the wrong direction, and Richard would be batting for his daughter Alexandra to succeed instead.

But that wasn't the letter that had set Lizzie's life down a different path. One that would eventually lead her to the truth, even if discovering that truth would cost yet more blood, that of Liv Finnegan, the journalist who'd pieced together the clues Lizzie had fed her.

This letter in her mother's things had been written by the late Queen, Richard's mother, Victoria II. It was opened, but untouched, and slipped into the File-o-Fax Calista carried round with her. After spending over fifteen years reading the letter over and over again, Lizzie had become convinced her father had not seen it before he died. But he could probably have guessed the contents.

Lizzie held it now, the crumpled cream paper, as she took her place at the bar inside *Finnegan's Tool* that oddly had a vibe Andrew would've loved. There were green flags of harps and Irish tricolors yes, but also rainbow banners and framed portraits of buff men dressed in leather, much like a lot of the patrons enjoying a pint of Guinness. The barman—also in a leather waistcoat, and only a waistcoat from what Lizzie could see—handed her a freshly poured pint.

"Here you are, mate. Great make up, by the way."

Lizzie followed him with indignant eyes, but the letter in her hand took back her focus.

Richard,

I read your threats and can't say I am all too pleased. Calista Murphy is not your "wife" or your "love" but an IRA agent sent to kill you, or me. Whether she's changed or just playing the long game I do not know nor care. She is to be banished from our country immediately. That you claim to have "married" her in some Popish ceremony behind my back is the cruelest trick you could play upon your mother, and I shall hear no more about it. That you fathered a secret child is bad enough. Thankfully, my cousins, the Windsors, are good people and took her in rather than drown her in a well like a bag of cats, but the fact that by your selfish actions you have illegitimized your own children and heirs is beyond reproach. And as for your little tantrum about letting Alexandra succeed before James, well…that spits in the face of God himself and I shall deign no more such nonsense. I don't care how much of a homosexual you think your son is. That's no barrier to being king, getting married, and fathering an heir and a spare!

My word, Richard, how you manage to hold your own mother in so much contempt I do not know. I shall hear no more of any such nonsense. Calista is to be banished, you are to return to your wife, Alice, and your son and heir James. Knock the buggery out of him for all I care, perhaps it will knock some sense

into you. This is your final warning, Richard. Another word of
a mess and I'll have no choice but to personally intervene to avoid
a succession crisis. And that intervention will be permanent.
Victoria II R.

"Whit you readin'?" Seamus asked, surprising her. She folded the crumpled paper back up as he slid into a stool beside her. He had fresh scratches on his shaved head, and his nose seemed bent a little differently since the last time they'd met. Men in leather grumbled in their direction, before returning to their game of darts.

"None of your business. This is the strangest Irish pub I've ever been in."

"It's a gay Irish pub, and they don't take kindly to new queens coming along without a formal introduction. Miss Paddy Whack will have your knickers." Lizzie glared at the leather men with their sharp darts. They were indeed staring at her.

"Can't you tell them I'm, you know, a woman?"

"Pfft. Think I owe you anything? You had me banged up by bloody MI5 for what you done to me."

"Done to you, Seamus? You done it yourself. I got you out."

"Aye right." Sarcasm dripped through his voice. "And you got me kicked out the sauna, too. You know I cannay go back there after you marched in wi' yer big whore heels. They shoved me on a list!"

"There aren't other places in London to have sex, Seamus?"

"I'm no talkin' about gettin' ma hole." He lowered his voice even more. "I'm talkin' about my work. That's the place people in my line o' work meet, Liz."

"So how come you're still a regular?" She slid the thick manilla folder given to her by K across the bar. "Seems like you've been a busy boy, Seamus. Carrying out hits for the Greek and Russian mafia."

Seamus ran his fingers along the folder like it was the last will and testament of Jesus Christ.

"Where did you get yer paws on this?"

"Friends in high places, Seamus, you know me. A little present for you. Everything MI5 knows or suspects about you. After reading it, seems like they don't know the half of it." They sat quietly. Lizzie drank her Guinness while Seamus shuffled through the thin sheets of fax paper, in a slight daze of awe. "I've got a job for you, Seamus."

"Lizzie, mate, I appreciate what you brung for me, but—"

Lizzie snatched the file back. Seamus was puzzled.

"One more job. Do it right, and this file is no more." His eyes flared. Hungry hands writhing over themselves as he weighed up what was on offer.

"Completely wiped?"

"Reset back to the start. I might even be able to buy you some immunity too, depending on the circumstances."

"What circumstances?"

"How well you do the job I'm about to give and you're about to accept. Now—" Lizzie finished her pint "—another drink and let's talk."

"Another round, mate," Seamus said immediately to the barman.

A taxi dropped Lizzie off at Alexandra's house. London was dark and sleeping among the white-faced terraces of Kensington. But lights were on at the princess' home. Lizzie did not approach the front steps, but took a short lane around the back, between yawning leaves of lowly trees and through cobwebbed gates.

Lizzie tapped on the backdoor, clutching her bag now empty of anything incriminating but one single letter. Alexandra opened the door wide, unsurprised to see Lizzie. She pointed to her ears which had earphones in them.

"Yes, darling, yes, I know. Mommy knows," Alexandra spoke out loud as she padded across the harlequin-patterned kitchen. Lizzie quietly opened the fridge and poured herself some white wine from the open bottle. She knew Alex would already have one. "Oh, I miss you too, sweetheart." Alexandra's voice carried from the other room. "And I'm sure daddy does, too. He's working hard, but he says he'll be seeing you the week after next, okay baby? Kisses to your sister."

Alexandra hurried back into the kitchen, earphone-less and carrying a half-full glass as Lizzie had suspected.

"How are the children?"

"Oh, you know," Alexandra said, finishing what she had in her glass then pouring herself more. They didn't even stop to clink their glasses together. Alexandra just returned to guzzling down the wine. "It's a big change for them, and I'm breaking them in slowly to the idea they won't be coming home anytime soon."

"Won't they be?" Alexandra shook her head and sighed. A stab of sadness was written across her face, as if accepting the inevitable caused unending pain.

"We can't have a custody battle over someone who is supposed to be the next king of Great Britain and also sultan of Saudi Arabia. At least not publicly. They'll stay in Saudi, I suppose, at least until Hassan is eighteen, or else those assassins manage to get James and I and he becomes king."

"And you're okay with that?" Lizzie asked, knowing she clearly wasn't.

"What can I do, Lizzie? If I want a clean divorce, or any divorce from Faisal, I had to agree to his custody. Truth be told, I'm hoping it will knock some sense into Hassan and Jasmine, and they'll grow up so removed from London and all this nonsense they'll simply go on and live their lives."

They took the bottle of wine into the living room, settling down on opposite couches while a fire crackled. They talked through the day's trauma. The attempt on James' life, what Lisa Mantis had told them, and what she hadn't. Lizzie filled in those extra details.

"MI5 are convinced," Lizzie said, "that whoever is after James is also after you, and won't stop until you're dead or gone."

"I know what was said. But I don't take kindly to threats. Never have, never will."

Lizzie sat back on the couch, shoes off and legs curled under her. She sensed the opening approach, getting across the singular message which could make everything complicated turn simple.

"You know," Lizzie said, reaching across to the coffee table and refilling both their glasses. "If something was to happen to you and James, Faisal would have no choice but to send Hassan back. Or risk holding the king hostage."

"Are you suggesting we carry out a murder-suicide pact to make that happen?"

"I'm not suggesting anything. I'm just asking, is this the life you want?"

The question hung in the air. One Lizzie had asked herself repeatedly in the last few months and weeks and hours. Lizzie knew her answer, but wondered if Alexandra had ever stopped to ask herself the same thing.

"I don't know any other life, Lizzie."

"Perhaps it's time to find a new one."

Alexandra allowed herself a moment of visible confusion while Lizzie leaned down to pick up her bag. She pulled out a crumpled letter and practically threw it across the table. With the laziness of a house cat, Alexandra picked it up. She balanced the wine between her thighs while she read.

"More proof," Lizzie said, "if you ever needed it. I still have Liv Finnegan's book that was never published, and I have this letter. All the evidence I need to prove that not only are you and James not in the line of succession, but as illegitimate children, you're not even entitled to draw a royal pension."

Alex turned a pale shade of white as she read and re-read the letter, again and again. In her grandmother's pen, signed with her name, it admitted the greatest secret imaginable. Their shared father had not lawfully married Alexandra and James' mother, because he'd already been married, to another woman, and had a child. Alexandra and James had known this since their grandmother died, but had, to their detriment, continued to act like it did not matter. That they could ignore the facts of succession and biology and the rights of succession. While the proof had not yet stared them in the face, now it was, Lizzie was making sure of that.

"Your mother was a Catholic," Alexandra said, her fists gently tightening.

"Not ideal," Lizzie shrugged, "but not a deal-breaker. More than one constitutional lawyer has pointed out to me that the ban on royals marrying Catholics has since been lifted, but the ban on illegitimate children succeeding the throne has not."

"So, you're going to court to become queen. Congratulations on being victorious in the war of succession."

"No, I don't want it." Lizzie drank from her glass; the friendly smile Alexandra had taken as fraudulent revealed to be genuine. Lizzie was giving friendly girls' night chat, not manipulative backstabbing, and it was clearly confusing Alex.

"Then what do you want?" Alexandra spoke, then the wine glass in her hand shattered into a million pieces. They both stared at the shimmering maze that fell across the table, the couch, the wooden floor, like a sudden dusting from a hailstorm. Neither had time to move though when a second sound of shattering glass shrieked from behind them both, from the window that looked out onto Kensington Street. The sound of the breaking window was muffled somewhat by the thick curtain half-closed against the darkness, but the third shot shattered their illusions entirely.

"Get down!" Lizzie screamed as a bullet fired from outside crashed into the wall behind Alexandra. Lizzie threw herself onto the glass-dusted floor, obscuring any view of Alexandra at all. The bullets kept coming. Glass kept smashing as plumes of feathers pulsed into the air from the shots fired into cushions.

Lizzie's face plastered to the patch of floor without glass, she feared to so much as raise her head to see if Alexandra was all right, let alone the chaos outside. Sirens began to screech in the distance, the noise of London breaking through the destroyed windows. Lizzie tried to shuffle under the couch, fearing a sudden swarm of armed men ready to pounce through the breach. But then she saw feet. Feet in tights that danced across the debris-strewn floor.

"Alex? What are you—"

A roar like a rocket screamed from the living room, followed by the crack of fire as chaos was returned to the outside. Alexandra was returning fire. Her feet jumped out of sight, banging onto the table and firing off another scatter shot, then straight onto the couch Lizzie had been on, feet dangling off it, close to Lizzie's face. Toes crunched as yet another burst of anger from the shotgun rioted out into the street. Lizzie ventured to look up. Alexandra was on her knees, protected by the back of the couch like she was in a fox hole. The front window was a wreck of broken glass. Out on the street, voices were shouting. People running. But the shots inside had stopped. Alexandra pumped the shotgun once more, firing out the used shell casing and letting off another counterstrike.

Outside, a man screamed and fell. A car sped away, and sirens approached from all angles.

"And stay the fuck away!" Alexandra shouted, pumping the shotgun once again but training it on an invisible figure outside. She squeezed the trigger, her face a thin line of determination, as some of the shot slapped against the remaining glass in the window. "That'll teach them."

Still cautious and holding the gun primed, Alexandra retreated from her foxhole and offered Lizzie a hand off the floor. They wiped shattered glass from themselves, blood pumping louder than the shotgun.

"Christ, Alex."

"Think I'm going to wait around for PC Plod to protect me. Speaking of."

Wailing sirens interrupted them. Men shouting, official men, yelled from the outside in.

"Is everything all right, ma'am?"

Alexandra rolled her eyes.

"What the fuck do you think?" she shouted back, and flung the shotgun on the couch. "Are you hurt?" Alexandra asked, touching Lizzie's face and the back of her head checking for blood. It took a moment for Lizzie to realize she wasn't bleeding, and shook her head. "We're unharmed," Alexandra yelled outside. "You can come in; we'll be in the kitchen." Alexandra led her through the bullet holes of the house and straight to the wine. "Drink?"

It wasn't even a question.

Chapter 12

ANDREW WONDERED TO HIMSELF HOW he'd gotten into this situation. What were the choices, the permutations of decisions and outcomes which had led him to here, dangling in Faisal's playroom, by his wrists and thighs, or was it chest and ankles? Whatever exact body part was holding Andrew up, it was the most uncomfortable he'd ever been before. And he'd been here for hours.

Andrew dangled above a floor covered in black vinyl. His naked body completely bound by thick black rope. Hands behind his back. Legs behind his back. All joints and moveable parts bound together into a thick line like a catch of the day, hanging from a heavy-duty hook in the ceiling. The rope work expertly prepared by three masked men who had not once asked for Andrew's assistance in being tied up. They did all the work for him in a way that left Andrew wondering if they weren't more used to doing this on bodies that were unconscious. For all the parts of Andrew that were tied up and inaccessible, three places remained open. His mouth, so he could scream. Not that anyone would ever hear a hundred floors up of the Kingdom Tower. His ass, which was slightly open given the angle of how his legs were tied up. He felt it every rotation, when his bare backside orbited by the air conditioning grate. And his cock and balls. They dangled loosely, gravity keeping them down.

Andrew's mind fell back to waking dreams of floating, being lifted, pirouetting naked through the air in a closed-off room. Caught in a spider's web, unable to move a single limb except look down at his flapping cock, that was somehow harder than he expected when in such a tight situation. Andrew hung calmly, only the slight strain of an otherwise secure rope as he turned, turned and turned. This was Faisal's bidding. *You'd do anything to get home to James?*

Anything.

Do exactly as I say, and I'll think about it.

After that, Faisal started to laugh. But Andrew had already agreed. Agreed to being stripped by the masked men and bound, arms and legs, and hung in this air-conditioned broom cupboard. But then the side wall started to rumble, as if being detached from the ceiling from the other side. It started to shudder then move on a railing, disappearing into the wall. Andrew was swinging in the other orbit, so he couldn't see yet, but he heard. Someone whimpering. Someone standing. Someone smiling.

By the time Andrew swung back around, he'd decided there were three figures on the other side of the fake wall. He was right. One was Faisal, topless in silk white shorts. Beside him was an older Arab man, also wearing silk white shorts but also a vest where his graying thick chest hair poked through. It took a moment for Andrew to recognize the man, Prince Nasser, Faisal's uncle and the power behind the throne for decades. But the third figure elicited a full-on cry from Andrew and sent his mind spinning.

He could have been looking in a mirror, because strung up behind Faisal and Nasser was the MI5 agent called Fahrooq, known around these parts as Mohan. Bound and hanging in the exact same situation as Andrew. *They've discovered us*, Andrew thought. One agent talking to another. In a foreign nation. This wasn't some weird sexual kink gone too far, they were about to be tortured as spies. Skinned alive. Maybe it had already happened to Mohan. He seemed out of it, hanging unconscious. A gag in his mouth, tied behind his sweaty black hair. But there was something else odd about Mohan. His cock. It didn't hang, like Andrew's. A black contraption was in the place his dick should be.

"What the fuck is that!" Andrew shouted out, flapping around in his ropes which did nothing but make him more uncomfortable.

"It's your friend, Mohan," Faisal said. Andrew studied him for any hint he knew Mohan's true identity. What would that even look like? "Oh, you mean what's around his dick?" Faisal grinned. "Like it? Just a little chastity device. You know I don't like my boys running off and playing with each other, not when there's work to be done. Didn't think I'd know what you two have been up to? Trust me, Andrew. I know everything about what you two have been doing."

Andrew noticed a silver key on a chain around Faisal's

neck. As if to prove what he was saying, Faisal swung the sleeping body of Mohan closer toward Andrew. Nasser moved out of the way as Faisal lifted the cage up. It was true, Andrew could see. A black metal device padlocked around Mohan's dick, his balls still free, but the dick physically unable to get hard. Even in his unconscious state, Mohan seemed to be surging against the constrictions.

"Why have you done this to him?"

Nasser began to laugh.

"Why?" Faisal said. "Because I own him, and I own you."

"Another one who doesn't read his contract," Nasser said. Faisal grinned.

"I don't want any part of this!" Andrew yelled, shaking the ropes again. "Let me out!"

"Shh!" Faisal snapped back. "Do you want to wake the poor guy? He's been through a hell of a time these last few hours."

"Fun for us," Nasser said.

"Oh yes, but less for him. But then again…" Faisal had something in his hand Andrew couldn't quite see. He was tossing it, like some kind of dog toy, one hand to the next. Andrew's rope was turning him away again. "Then again, lads like Mohan are trained to withstand all sorts of torture, aren't they, Andrew?" A deathly shiver ran down his spine. Of course, they knew he was a spy. What did they think of him, then? Not being able to see any of the movement behind made things a hundred times worse. His cock and ass were exposed to the Crown Prince and his torturer-in-chief. "How is my old friend Lisa Mantis?"

Andrew said nothing. He spun quicker now, being turned by Faisal who was so close Andrew could smell the cologne he remembered from their fuck earlier on. But what Andrew saw in Faisal's hand left him speechless. It wasn't a cock cage—Andrew would have chosen that in a heartbeat—but a long chain with a thick metal hoop on the end of it, like a cock ring. Faisal snapped the magnetized ring open.

"Nasser, if you wouldn't mind."

Andrew's body turned to tense shock as hands stretched his balls away from his body, almost to the point of threatening to pull them off. The next thing Andrew felt was the cold metal of the magnet snap into place, stretching his balls out. A chain swung down, nearly touching the floor and adding a considerable weight to Andrew's tied-up body.

"Ow!" Andrew said as his balls were both trapped and tugged at the same time. Next came a pair of steel nipple clamps handed to Faisal by Nasser. Andrew shook as if they were electric. They weren't, but the touch of sharp steel onto his soft pink nipples sent his body into spasms. That only made matters worse, though, as the swinging chain between his legs began to flap around like a tail, causing discomfort of too much weight on his balls. Andrew moaned, helpless, trapped, clamped.

"You've betrayed me, Andrew," Faisal said from the corner of the room, picking up a thing Andrew couldn't see.

"I'm a forgiving man, as many would agree. But that doesn't mean transgression shouldn't be met with punishment."

"What have I done?" Andrew blurted out, sweat dripping down his forehead. He tried not to move at all, because every twitch of a single muscle caused the chain to swing and yank on his already stretched out balls.

"Oh, Andrew, what haven't you done?" Faisal had a thick metal weight. It must have been a kilo at least. Nasser meanwhile was taking pictures on a mobile phone. "I gave you every opportunity, Andrew. The finest restaurants in the world." Andrew breathed solidly through his nose as Faisal bent down and reached for the chain. "Private jets, a grace-and-favor apartment." The chain clinked into the weight, brutally connected. Andrew panted louder than he ever had before. "Yet you cavort around corrupting young men who work for me then ask to go home? No, Andrew. There's no going back. That's a lesson you're here today to learn."

Faisal let the weight drop. Andrew watched it almost in slow motion. It swung rather than fell, which was almost a relief. His nipples were red and raw, and the weight kept swinging, back and forward, jerking Andrew's bound body as it did. Faisal snatched the weight again like a tether ball in a children's playground.

"Diplomatic boxes, too." Faisal held the weight high, up to his shoulder. Andrew could only whimper as the chain stretched his balls up, the heavy metal pressed hard against his dick. "You could move drugs or guns or money around the world, and no one can do anything. Unlimited power I gave you, Andrew Hodes, and this is what you want to do with it?"

"A slap in the face," Nasser agreed.

The weight dropped. Straight down, not swinging. It felt like someone had stretched Andrew's balls out then a second later crushed them between two metal baseball bats. Slowly, the metal around his skin rolled down, but somehow never stopped. Andrew swung around a new center of gravity: his balls. Saliva dripped from his listless mouth. And for the strangest reason, pre-cum leaked from his aching cock which was…rock hard?

"Oh, Andrew," Faisal said, running a finger around the head of Andrew's cock. He lifted the damp finger up and shoved it straight into Andrew's mouth, forcing him to suck on his own taste. "So predictable." Andrew sucked, and felt himself grow harder. He couldn't stop sucking on Faisal's finger. Up and down, he threw his body. Andrew tangled himself into even more knots, he was so desperate to suck Faisal's finger. Faisal began to withdraw, until only the tip of his finger was there.

"Please…" Andrew whimpered.

He looked at both men. Both grinned.

"Please what, boy?"

"Please may I worship you, sir?"

"That's more like it."

Faisal unhooked his familiar meat from the silk shorts. The smell of clean brown dick and perfectly trimmed black hair came close. He needed Faisal to come closer. To trust that Andrew's subjugation was complete.

"I'm sorry," Andrew whispered as Faisal's dick touched his lips. "I'm sorry I asked to go home. I don't know what I was thinking. My place is here. With you. Not with them."

"That's more like it. Now suck."

"I'm sorry I listened to Mohan. But I gave him nothing."

"I said suck." But Andrew didn't. The hard cock stared him in the face. Faisal's power seeping from it, demanding the attention Andrew wasn't quite giving it. Faisal tried pushing his dick between Andrew's unforgiving lips, not quite letting it in.

"I had no idea he'd been passing information to MI5 for all these years."

Faisal stopped dead. Nasser rushed forward and grabbed Andrew's hair, pulling his head back and away from Faisal's rapidly softening cock.

"What did you say?" Nasser demanded, shaking Andrew's head so hard his entire body swung on the rope. The ball chain shuddered in an excruciating swing.

"Ow! You're hurting me."

"Tell us what you know!" Nasser slapped Andrew hard across the face. He swung violently to the side, then the other side. The ball chain with him, dragging on his dick, but then quickly recentering him once again.

"Don't hit him!" Faisal shoved Nasser back. Faisal's chest beat with stress. Sweat discolored his underwear. "Andrew, tell me what you know."

"I can't really tell you very much when I'm like this, can I? And not when we're around...him."

It took a yawning effort to raise his neck up, but Faisal saw who Andrew stared at: Uncle Nasser. But Andrew was much more interested in Faisal's reaction. He did not believe for a moment these two old enemies had found some common cause. Perhaps a brief alliance, but royal dynasties were all the same. Paranoia was their life blood. Andrew had been around enough royals to know that for a fact. Faisal gave little away, but the long, lingering look the Crown Prince gave his uncle said more than Andrew needed to know.

"His name's Fahrooq," Andrew said, unprompted. "And he's not some double agent. He has a direct line to Lisa Mantis."

"I don't even know who that is!" Nasser complained, but his hands were up.

"Let me out," Andrew said, "and I'll tell you everything."

They sat in an infinity Jacuzzi in the tallest tower in the Middle East. The strong bubbles eased Andrew's aching joints but did nothing to calm his nerves. As men had come to take Andrew down from his ropes, more had come to take Nasser away. Dragged him away, kicking, screaming, and cursing. Andrew watched the water at the pool's end fall over the edge, seemingly into the endless sandy desert that stretched out into infinity beyond. Despite the powerful air conditioning, the glass roof on the highest floor was no match for the morning sun. Andrew reached behind him and took the glass of champagne and orange juice a silent servant had brought him.

Faisal had been pulling out all the stops to make things up to Andrew, although he didn't say as much. He'd been led back to his apartment in the dead of night, and hadn't seen what had befallen his place. But in the morning, it was spotless. Moreover, several boxes of designer suits and shoes had been delivered, along with a note from Faisal to join him up here, in a place Andrew had never been.

He'd been waiting for Faisal for the best part of an hour, after being shown into this private luxury spa by the myriad of servants around. They knew nothing of where the Crown Prince was, or when he was supposed to come, and Andrew had stopped asking.

He was topping up his champagne when the far door opened. Faisal came in. He was wearing a robe, but looked stressed. Andrew let the water bubble up to his chin, wondering if he should pretend to disappear. Although he'd been sitting here for long enough, he still hadn't come up with a game plan.

"I hope you don't mind we've taken your phone for testing," Faisal said as he poured champagne and orange juice for himself. His eyes were red and face looked tired, like he'd been up all night conducting a purge of his closest advisors. "Who knows what those spies put on it. It was a good thing you did, Andrew. A good thing for us."

Andrew said nothing as Faisal downed his glass in one gulp. From the back, Andrew watched as Faisal slipped off his robe, revealing his naked backside blanketed in black hair. Faisal climbed into the pool, his weighty cock briefly floating in the bubbles before he sank under the water line and swam up to Andrew. Faisal's touch made him jump and shudder, but quickly he eased into the pretense.

"I never trusted Nasser in the first place, after all those things you told me about him."

"I guess you were right," Faisal said, weaving his body between Andrew's under the water. "And I was wrong to doubt you, Andrew. Very wrong."

"You dealt with Mohan too? I mean Fahrooq."

"He will be dealt with," Faisal looked away, tracing Andrew's naked thighs. "But carefully. I can't steal too many British boys, can I?" Faisal kissed him hard. Their lips twisted for dominance, as they always did, but now it didn't feel transgressive. Now it just felt wrong. James was in danger, and so it seemed was Andrew.

"What you were doing to me when I was strung up… just a punishment, or…?"

"You're smiling. Why? Did you like it?"

"I liked you…owning me." Andrew swallowed away the rest of his dignity and launched in to Faisal's neck, kissing the wet skin and licking around his nipple. He buried his face in Faisal's armpit and wrapped arms around his wet back. "I'll do anything for you, Faisal. I always said."

"I know, my boy. And I know I failed you." They kissed again, hard and wet.

"Don't say that. It doesn't matter. You've done more for me than anyone. And I meant it that I'm sorry. I don't want to go anywhere but be here with you."

Under the water, their hands twisted across each other's bodies in a way that hadn't happened in years. For once, they were unrestrained, uninterrupted.

"This reminds me of before," Andrew said, "when we used to hang out in your private suite at the Bullman's club."

"This reminds me of another night. Our last in England at your shitty little flat in Shoreditch, when I let you have me in a way no man ever has."

Andrew detected a lie there, but he played along as Faisal straddled Andrew under the bubbling jets.

"Does the most powerful man in the world want to be taken again?" Andrew whispered, running his hands down Faisal's back, under the water line and across his hairy ass cheeks.

"I want to apologize to you, Andrew. Let me give you this."

Faisal's hand slipped beneath the water and gripped Andrew's dick. In a couple of strokes it was hard, there was nothing Andrew could do about that. Whenever he was close to a hole, he got hard. Faisal closed his eyes and breathed in deeply the way Andrew had told him weeks ago when he fucked Faisal in his flat. *Shitty* wasn't how he'd describe it. Above all else, it had been his and James' secret home for over a decade. That is something Faisal would never take away, even if he would never let him leave.

The head of Andrew's cock connected with Faisal's ass. Their hands danced under the water and between the jets. Pushing, lifting, separating.

"Breathe," Andrew whispered, licking Faisal's neck.

"Breathe and let yourself be entered. Let yourself receive me."

Andrew pushed past the barrier and into the tight hole. Faisal slid down, moaning out loud while his knees gripped Andrew's chest tightly. A jet was right underneath Andrew's balls, caressing them as Faisal let the water guide him up and down. The grip and tightness inside Faisal and the recent memory of the fucked-up scene of domination, submission and betrayal ground Andrew quickly to the edge.

Faisal was getting louder, jerking himself off just below the water, splashing Andrew in the face. Andrew thrust his head back and spread his arms across the tiles, letting the grip around the head of his cock and the water jet below his balls do all the work.

"Andrew," Faisal gasped, "give me all of it."

Cum splattered across Andrew's wet chest as Faisal unleashed, but that didn't stop him, just freed up Faisal's hands to grab Andrew's face. He tried to kiss him, but the kiss, Andrew knew, would end the fantasy. Because with his eyes closed, he could be fucking James. He could be inside the man he loved, had always loved, bringing him pleasure beyond words.

"Kiss me," Faisal begged.

But Andrew pulled away. He pushed Faisal off and he splashed into the water in surprise. His instinct was to run, but there was a charade to continue.

"Bend over here," Andrew commanded. "And…take my cock."

With Faisal bent over the side, ass pointed upward, Andrew thrust himself back inside hard. He focused only on the sway of his cock into a hole. It could be any hole. He imagined it was.

"Fill me," Faisal begged, barely audible against the splashing water. "You deserve it. You deserve everything. Breed me hard, Andrew."

The words could've been from anyone, and that's how Andrew took them. In a moment he slammed his whole body hard into Faisal and let his balls empty, pumping load after load into the Crown Prince, who furiously jerked his dick and seemed to come again.

Finally, their bodies parted. Andrew settled back into the bubbling water as Faisal dried himself off. He poured another drink, downed that, and replaced the robe.

"My chief vizier," Faisal said with a grin. "I certainly can't let you leave now knowing you can do that to me."

"Yeah?" Andrew said with a fake smile. The regret of too many wrong choices catching up to him. "You liked it?"

"I might be able to do it all day, given the chance. Perhaps your little James was on to something." Faisal laughed to himself, and thankfully turned away. In another moment he was gone, and Andrew was left alone in the bubbling water, stained by bad decisions. Stuck in a place, forced to sleep with the enemy. He finished the bottle of champagne, but it tasted bitter.

A plan, however, was forming in his mind. Faisal was right. James *was* on to something. All royals were the same, and all men who liked men, too. It might only work on a very specific subset of individuals, but Andrew knew how to manipulate a royal gay.

Chapter 13

JAMES HAD NEVER REALLY HAD MUCH OF A sense of what he was "into" sexually. It had never really come up in casual conversation. He and Andrew weren't exactly known for their good communication skills. Partly because they'd never needed to "talk" about things. Andrew had this sense of what James wanted and needed, both professionally as his press secretary, and in the bedroom.

That's why James had never doubted their connection, or their relationship, until Andrew pushed him into being publicly with Katyn. If Andrew knew him so well, then what was there to question? It had worked fine for fifteen years...until it didn't.

As James wandered through Windsor Castle toward the refreshed dungeon, he wondered why he'd not spoken about these desires, these needs to Andrew before. Was it fear? Embarrassment? Or perhaps a worry that he'd already put so much on his lover's shoulders that opening up about an interest in sadomasochism would be the straw...or chain, that snapped the camel's back.

James settled on the fact this was something new to

him, the world of whips and restraints. He undressed alone in the changing area, the heavy metal door of the Windsor dungeon closed, but waiting to welcome him into its dark embrace. If anything, these new interests developed because of being detached from Andrew in these last few years, and even when they'd come back together after James' diagnosis, they returned with stronger walls than before. In the space had opened up a well of questions. At first, they were frightening: what would James do without his lover, his best friend, his partner? But underneath those questions came answers. Answers about himself that made sense.

James loved the feeling of complete restraint, of unfettered submission, and of being completely dominated because of his power. Offering it up for someone to take away, to seize the very body of the king and, for all intents and purposes, abuse it, lit a fire inside James that continued to burn long after the first orgasm. And the second, and third, and sometimes even fourth that could be forced from James in a long session in the Windsor dungeon.

Wearing only a simple black jockstrap, James stepped into the cool, airless dungeon. A torch had already been lit on the far wall, casting a flickering orange glow that glimmered against the ancient brick walls. Atmosphere helped. There was no way Andrew's clean, modern, and somewhat sterile Shoreditch flat would suffice for the kind of submission James wanted. Even the thought of asking Andrew made him shiver. How could he put the man he loved through such things? How could he ask...yes, the man he *still* loved, to whip him across the back, flog his ass until it was red, and stamp on his cock with heavy boots, all the while men in leather laughed and smoked on cigars?

Samuel called it *Folsom in Berkshire.* In setting up the equipment for the dungeon, he and Samuel had pored over photographs and videos and even blueprints of S&M dungeons from Berlin to San Francisco. They'd watched countless hours of footage, much of it amateur and some even beyond James' taste, to understand just what it was that turned James on so much.

It's your basic leather daddy domination fetish, Samuel had said after one long evening of studying the constructions of dungeons as if they were discussing military plans. *It's pretty standard, James. Even typical of men as they get into their thirties. That's why the Folsom fairs are so popular.*

That was exactly the matter-of-factness which Andrew could never have understood. It wasn't that James didn't love Andrew. It wasn't that James didn't want to have sex with Andrew, or didn't love having sex with him. More that James had discovered another layer to himself. A deeper one, buried away and embarrassing, even scandalous in official circles, that he needed to unleash. Well, first he needed to be leashed.

James waiting barefoot and nearly naked in the chilly dungeon was part of the scene. What had happened the other morning with James in the sling off to the side had been a quick half hour distraction. Now would be something far more intense. Standing alone, facing the St. Andrew's cross he was about to be strapped to and the wall of whips and gags and instruments of sexual torture which would be unfurled upon him in the hours to come, James was as hard as he ever had been in his life.

Men's voices came from outside, beyond the door. Those initiated into the roster of men at the king's disposal were getting changed into outfits custom-made for them in the lockers. Leather chaps, leather waistcoats, heavy boots, caps and chains. The finest cigars to be placed in their leather coat pockets too. An entire production to make the scene just right.

James shivered, facing the cross, ready to be martyred. But not for too long, as the metal door behind him swung open and several sets of boots stormed into the dungeon.

"On your knees, slave."

James did exactly as he was told. The sound of leather creasing and men breathing heavily filled the dungeon as a blindfold was immediately placed over James' eyes. He shivered in anticipation, the sense of what was to come made his skin crawl with excitement. It was an odd feeling to have desires buried so deep be suddenly and immediately accessible. It had scared James at first, the things he'd written down and left in envelopes outside. The things he wanted these men to do to him. But James recalled an old saying which had rattled around his mind whenever an issue of sex came up. *No regrets.*

God knows where these desires of his had come from, or the *no regrets* attitude, but he made a mental note of how right he could be when strong, bare arms snapped a cold metal collar around his neck. It was tight, but James liked that. Alongside the shoulder-breaking feel of the metal pressing against his collar bone. His thighs ached from kneeling down, so he tried to stand.

"I said on your fucking knees, slave." The angry voice was accompanied by a boot kick in the back of his thigh. When he told these men to show no mercy, he'd meant it. James collapsed onto hard concrete as rope was quickly wrapped around his chest. Not one but several thick bounds of cotton which were wrapped and knotted by the many hands he could not see. In a matter of moments, James' hands were tied behind his back and his shoulders were immovable from the tight knots restricting his entire upper body. He was bound, blindfolded, and harder than ever before.

"Slave likes it, huh?" said another gruff voice as a boot toyed with his balls. James shivered from cold leather and boot rubber pressed against his tender skin, the anticipation of the kick that never came. "Lick it, you little bitch."

Power. That's what this kind of sex was all about. Not even sex, just the exchange of pure power. These hours he spent down in this dungeon, willingly giving up power over all facets of his body to strange men drafted in because they looked hot in leather and beards, were some of the best of James' life.

He bent over in an awkward position that stressed his back, all to lick the boot. It tasted shiny. Tasted of leather. The men shared a laugh. He heard a lighter flick as he licked, then the smell of tobacco from several cigars wafted around the closed dungeon.

"Lick this boot now, slave."

A new boot was kicked in his face. Pushed into his mouth so deep James thought he might choke. He did. The men laughed, and pushed further. Unable to move away, the boot opened his jaw wider while another's hard steel toe pressed against his balls. Tears ran down his cheeks and he hocked up so much phlegm there was a danger of drowning. But he loved the sensation. Of being used, of time when he could forget Andrew, forget his family, forget even himself and simply submit.

At the last second, the boot was pulled out of James' aching jaw. He sucked in a breath and sniffed away tears, but there was no time to rest. A cock was shoved down his throat. Gruff hands in crinkling leather yanked his head down to the stranger's balls and held it there. The dick filled his throat, lips stretched and eyes watering even more than with the boot. Waves of retching came and crashed, but James was bound. He couldn't move away even if he tried. Submission was no longer a choice.

The man let him go and James bounced back on his thighs, retching and gasping for air. It was only for a second. James couldn't see because of the blindfold but he could hear. Boots slammed on the ground, boots pushed against his sweating stomach and balls dangling between his legs, and another cock was shoved down his throat.

James estimated there were four men in total. But after an endless age of his throat being abused, it was hard to concentrate on anything but the routine of his head being held down into a hairy, sweaty crotch, while his jaw was stretched open by leather-covered fingers for a dick to be thrust inside. They were relentless, just as James wanted. He couldn't see nor touch himself, but he knew he was rock hard. Every time his mouth was passed from one man to the next, every time he wanted to collapse but was dragged up once again, brought him to the edge of ecstasy. The men seemed to notice as well.

"Time for a flogging."

James was pushed over. It took barely a feather to tip him. He crashed onto the cold, hard floor, and finally the blindfold was whipped off. Looking up, he saw only smooth leather trousers, dark hairy chests and beards in a whir of cigar smoke that enclosed their dungeon. The men were laughing with each other. They passed leather straps between them, over James laying curled on the ground with his hands tied behind his back. Leather was tied around his legs and feet so he could only move like a beached fish, struggling in one fluid motion. Something flapped overhead. The edges of a leather gag with a six-inch stubby dildo sticking out one end.

"Open up, Your Maj…" More snickering. James wondered if they loved this as well, abusing the king. Each one of the four masters had their cocks out, and each one was as hard as could be. James glanced down at his own, sticking out between the ropes and leather ties.

"He's moving away from the gag," one said.

"Cheeky slave." Leather gloved hands grabbed a fistful of James' hair as they yanked back his head. Fingers pulled his jaw apart as the dildo was stuffed in and the gag fastened around his head. It was far more uncomfortable than a dick, and it wasn't coming out any time soon. It pressed against the back of his throat so he had to continually keep his tongue relaxed to save from swallowing it. Suddenly everything was uncomfortable. The bindings hurt his feet, his shoulders were in agony from his hands tied behind his back, and his whole left side was in pain from laying awkwardly on the ground. He knew this feeling, the submissive's regret. It's where a lot of them had to give up. They'd cry out their safe word and things would be over. But for James, he knew this was where it started to get really good.

"Start with the whip."

It happened the moment the men spoke it into life, or perhaps James had moved beyond a normal perception of time. He was now firmly in submissive world. His mind twisted into the strangest place where every slap of pain became instant pleasure. And the pain came. A hard-edged whip slapped across his back, his chest, his ass, his dick even, whack after whack, lash after lash. It was then passed to the next man, who inflicted the same punishment from a different angle, then the next man, then the next, until James willingly threw himself onto his back despite his tied-up hands, just to breathe. Or tried to, through his nose.

"Dumb slave. We've not even started."

One of the leather men straddled his writhing body and showed him a stainless-steel butt plug, thicker than any of the cocks he'd sucked.

"Want this in you?"

James could only whine. He shook and groaned, but

there was no way to communicate. No way to beg for that—yes, but so much more. The man above him reached back, and without even pausing to spread James' legs, the plug invaded his body. The lubed steel slipped in with ease, but came with pain. If he'd been given a moment to take it, it would've been better. In a normal world, in a normal bedroom, James would have put his hands on the man's legs to pull back. Or he would have lunged forward and held up a finger to get one minute to breathe. But that wasn't the life of a slave. That's not what he'd begged for. That wasn't what these men had been ordered to do by James either. No mercy. No regrets.

The butt plug stole all his focus, but it soon moved to his nipples. The man straddling him tightened clamps into place. They stung. Even more when he pulled on the chain connecting them. He yanked and didn't stop even as James' eyes watered and arched his back so far up to accommodate being pulled up by his nipples. Among the pain, it was the laughing that got him the most. The sound of the men intensely enjoying every ounce of pain they inflicted.

Now came the pleasure. The excruciating pleasure. A hand wrapped around his cock. It was generously lubricated, and it teased James with expert precision. Every slither of fingers only up, never down, sent waves of shaking ecstasy through his battered body. His balls begged to release. The ache spread from his thighs up through his stomach, gripping his chest and pressing down on this throat like a hand. No, there was a hand. The man who'd been straddling him all this time, with his thick black beard and sailor's grin, played with the nipple clamp chain with one hand, and choked him with the other. And he laughed.

Whoever was playing with James' cock must have been an expert in the tantric method of edging, because James was on the constant edge of exploding. One hand, then a second, then a third, slid up his dick. Squeezing hard at the base, then releasing at the tip, just when things started to get good. A boot held down his balls, pressing them into the cold ground so he couldn't get too far. The boot would let up every few moments, just as the hand around his dick started to furiously jerk it, bringing him to the very brink before letting go just at the moment James craved. All the while the black-bearded beast didn't move from his perch on James' chest. He'd lit another cigar, puffing away while his free hand opened and closed James' throat at will.

Then things went to the next level. The combination of his entire body being bound and chained, the heavy metal collar, the dildo-gag deep in his throat, the hand around his neck, the plug in his ass and the man sitting on his chest and smoking a cigar was already enough. But the hands on his cock and the boot on his balls were more than anyone with a dick could take. The shaking became uncontrollable. The master sitting on his chest even slapped him hard to stay still, but it didn't stop. James' body was no longer his. He jerked his hips so hard he must have pulled a dozen different muscles, all in the desperate hope there was still a hand there to touch him, to bring him the release he needed so badly. But no, they'd let go, and James was coming anyway.

The ruined orgasm took over his body as it simultaneously fled from him. What he'd been on the edge of fluttered away like so much cigar smoke dissipating into the air. He was coming, and still. But it came like pissing in a sink. Different, but hardly pleasurable. A release, without the satisfaction of what he'd worked and suffered for. And he loved it. these men took everything from him. Freedom, touch, breath, and now even pleasure itself. The orgasm might've been ruined, but the deep, unguarded pleasure of the experience was lifted to even greater heights.

"Make him clean it up."

The gag was whipped off and he sucked in a desperate breath. But only for a moment. The black-bearded man on top of him climbed off, and with his boots, pushed James' sweaty body around to the mess he'd made on the floor. It was an impressive puddle, and the boot on the back of his head pushed his face straight into it.

"You're not getting up until every drop of that is off the floor, you hear? Huh?" A kick in the back of the head. "You hear!"

"Yes…master."

James did as he was told. It took five minutes, but he did it.

"Get him strapped into the fuck machine."

Like paramedics, the men practically lifted his body from the floor and onto a flat table. He wasn't untied, but simply strapped into a different set of restraints. A thick collar attached to the table was strapped across his delicate throat, while a ball gag was jammed into his mouth. Straps on his hands and across his chest immobilized his entire top half, and then came the legs. The butt plug was yanked out in a rapid motion that left him gasping. Stirrups were rolled up and his feet lifted into them. They weren't attached to the table but freewheeling, so the men had some fun stretching his legs so far he was practically doing the splits. But there was only so long James could scream before the gag forced his mouth to fill with saliva and he risked choking on his own spit.

It took a moment to remember what the point of all this was. The fuck machine. It had never been used yet. The contraption had been a late arrival to the pantheon of tools. A freestanding pneumatic machine with detachable dildos screwed onto the pulsing rod that could thrust at a speed of ten times a second.

Even stretching up as far as the bindings would let his neck go, James could only see the tip of the machine being brought onto the table between his legs. The black-bearded man stood by his head, arranging the spread of James' legs and the placing of the dildo just inside James' hole. The anticipation was agonizing. Only the tip was in, pressing just inside his hole, as if they were being kind and letting James get used to the feeling. No such luck.

They were now attaching another thing to his dick. A wrap-around silicone sock that tightened even around his semi-soft cock. A heavy magnetic, metal ring was clipped around his balls, holding them down and forcing his cock up. Of course, it was attached to another fucked-up machine which the black-bearded man ordered turned on with a wide grin. It both vibrated and slid up and down, forcing James to be hard, even if there was nothing left inside of him to give.

"Milking machine and a fuck machine? Isn't that too much?" One of the men asked. Black beard laughed in his face.

"Turn on the other one, full power."

It was instant. Thankfully, James *was* strapped in well, otherwise he would have flown off the table in a second. The pulsing pound of the fuck machine would have been welcome in this torture chamber a thousand years ago. With his balls already empty, the endless thrusts that invaded his insides mixed with the automatic jerking and vibrating on his cock brought him close to the edge once again.

He barely heard black beard tell the others to take a break. He heard the others protesting a little, because it brought him away from another yet orgasm his body could barely take.

"You sure?"

"'Course," black beard said. "Look, you can see he's enjoying it. Go, go take twenty minutes and I'll stay here. We'll fuck his used arse when you get back."

Boots slapped on the ground. A door slammed open and closed. Black beard stared down with a wide grin.

"What do you say, slave? Think you can take a bit more?"

James could only whine like a dog, the power of speech taken away. Somehow the fuck machine was turned up to a higher power. The endless pounding without even the knowledge the one doing the fucking would at some point cum himself gave a Sisyphean feel to the whole endeavor. But James did feel himself getting close again. Black beard stroked his face with leather gloves, in a strange moment of simple care. He ran gloved hands sensually across James' chest and stomach, the touch bringing James to the very edge.

"That's it, slave, let the machine do the work. Because it's not going to stop. You wanna come now?" James shook his head. "Doesn't matter, 'cause it's gonna keep going."

Another moment of powerlessness. James closed his eyes as the orgasmic feeling spread outward from his cock and hole, like a white light toward a transcendent experience he couldn't fight. An alien abduction more like. The opposite of a ruined orgasm. This one James wouldn't be able to escape, nor would he need the brief break, the cessation of touch no one with a dick could stand after coming. Again, it was not to be.

But the straps helped. The few muscles he was in control of threw themselves against the straps of the torture chamber as if it was an electric chair. A gloved hand slammed into his mouth as James cried out as best he could with a ball gag still between his teeth. The agonizing shouts muffled into the maniacal grin of the black-bearded master as the machines continued their automated torture, jerking the well-jerked cock, fucking the wrecked hole.

"You said you were at my mercy, didn't you, slave?" James nodded through the body shocks. "No one can hear you scream now." His hand hovered around James' cheek, stroking it gently, like a psychopath cuddling a kitten. "Because this is the end, Your Majesty." The man's eyes were not joking. Cold and serious. James could quite literally do nothing. Those others had been so quickly convinced to leave them alone. How had he done it?

"You fought the natural order of things, Jamie," the black-bearded embodiment of the end said softly. His leather cap like Death's hood, his hands a scythe, tightening the strap across James' throat. He could no longer swallow. "We offered you countless times to fuck off and live your perverted, twisted life away from this sacred land, but no. You had to take what didn't belong to you." James choked on the tight belt, but he knew that would not be the thing to finish him. That was going to very simply be the two gloved hands approaching his face. One pressed across his lips, pushing the ball gag deeper inside, and the other firmly pressed his nostrils together.

"No gays are allowed to do what you've done. If it was up to me, I'd have fucked you to death with a red-hot poker like old Edward I, I'm sure he would've enjoyed this, too. Both of you sick perverts. Thank Christ the Gaveston Protocols are bringing you both to an end. And there's nothing you can do about it." James tried to prove him wrong, but there was no struggle. Not while tied down and strapped in. Quite literally this assassin had the easiest job in the world. "You today, your sister tomorrow. And that's it. The dynasty that was never supposed to be, snuffed out like a light." The hands pressed down deeper. James could no longer feel the rest of his body. He could barely hear the man. "Erotic asphyxiation. How embarrassing."

With his last ounce of energy, James closed his eyes. He didn't want this man to be the last thing he saw. Instead, he saw Andrew. There was no more pain, no more struggle. No more need for air. Just Andrew's face, over and over again, for over half his life. Andrew's smile, Andrew's tears. Andrew's furrowed brow and confused face. Andrew when he couldn't understand technology. Andrew when he lifted half his lip in the middle of shared ecstasy. Andrew asleep on the pillow, face wrinkled up like a boxer dog while he watched his lover breathe through the night.

For James, the outside world was a fuzzy mess of static. One he didn't care to even watch now. Forever he would have Andrew on his mind. Andrew right here, on the pillow. The noises of beyond, of the world of the living that was no longer his. Now he could be free, forever in the well of Andrew's beauty, asleep. Waiting for him to wake up. In this pool, he would gladly drown.

Chapter 14

LISA STARED DOWN AT THE DARK, murky Thames River from "the bridge", as her office high above London was known. The MI5 watchtower in Thames House looked down on Central London, providing a moving image of the city and its twisting multitude of millions of lives within. The reinforced glass windows could survive a direct hit from a cruise missile, but not keep out the wailing drone of endless sirens.

"A double?" Pudgy asked from the drinks trolley in the corner of her office. The snap of tonic bottles being opened fizzed through the room. She barely grunted as he poured two glasses and plopped himself down onto the black leather couch. With a harassed sigh, Lisa followed.

"It's half empty," she said of the glass.

"That's a matter of perspective. Perhaps you should be looking at this glass as half full, K. This situation could work in your favor. If you let it."

Lisa glared. Darkness invaded her office from the night outside. A simple lamp offered a shattering of light that flickered like a torch, reflecting from the rain-soaked windows.

"Princess Alexandra nearly died last, Pudgy. And on my watch."

"Oh, please, it was a half-arsed attempt. A warning shot at best."

"Six armed men shooting up her house?"

"Well, she put three of them in the hospital, I think she handled herself fine. Who knew she was a dab hand with a shotgun."

"That's not the issue, Pudgy. They're coming after James and Alexandra, and making me look like a fool." Lisa drank, but it only darkened her mood. "And I was the fool to trust that Peter would give me this time to talk them into exile."

"He is giving you time," Pudgy said with a seriousness that frightened her. "He's scaring the royal twins with criminal gangs and Russian mercenaries. Far from professionals, just to prove he can target them whenever he wants. If he really wanted them dead, they'd be dead by now. Trust me, Lisa, as soon as he wants them gone, it's game over. That man learned his trade under the most ruthless operator this country has seen in a century. The late queen."

"It will be game over for me, too. Peter will pin this on MI5, I'm sure of it. I'll be their sacrificial lamb. Peter knows I know too much. He knows I don't like it, either. How exactly is that glass half full?"

Pudgy sighed and sipped into silence.

"I simply assumed you were already working the situation to your advantage. Or trying to, at least."

"Trying to is the operative word. The only leverage I have is Lizzie Windsor."

"You turned her against them?"

"Didn't take much turning, Pudgy. The only hope to save my neck from the chopping block is the woman who poisoned my predecessor. Fuck, I hate irony."

"That's the irony?" Pudgy said. "You want Lizzie Windsor to murder her half brother and sister so you can then publicly prove this... fratricidal regicide, and put Lizzie Windsor away!" Lisa drank to cover the smile creeping across her lips. "My word, you are good."

"I remember you said the same thing to me once many years ago in East Berlin. And yet here we are, some forty years later and you're still underestimating me," Lisa said with a smile.

"Lisa...what can I say."

"Nothing much. But you can hope and pray Lizzie Windsor succeeds, either by killing them or talking them into a permanent, and I mean permanent, exile. Because if I'm not the one holding the evidence, if I'm not the one briefing the PM, then Peter wins. He gets control of the young Hassan and the Regency Council, then it's curtains for us, Pudgy."

"Us, Lisa?"

"Oh yes. If I'm going down, I'm dragging you to hell with me."

Just then, the door to her office flung open like the

gates of said hell. Pudgy jumped. She supposed it didn't work that way in MI6, but Lisa waited for a full sip and swallow before turning around to the panting staffer who had thrown himself into the office.

"Alison? What's the matter?" The look on her face screamed national crisis.

"Ma'am…it's the King."

Police sirens wailed around Windsor Castle. Red, white, and blue lights scattered against the castle walls, lighting up the night sky. Several ambulances were stuck outside the castle grounds, being too big to get through the portcullis gate. Inside the grounds, police and army shoved up against each other, ruffling feathers and stepping on toes. In the fields and forests surrounding Windsor, torches danced through the darkness as search teams combed the grounds. The Coldstream Guards were milling about the road up to the castle, making a show of force with their trucks. Helicopters droned through the distance, making a show of things for the world's press now converging on the little town of Windsor.

In the Orchid Room that overlooked the chaos, the flowers would normally sleep at night. Their leaves would sink, their petals compress until the daylight came streaming through the windows in the morning. But outside, night had become something like day. The flowers had woken, James could see. He even watched one of the flowers stretch before his very eyes as helicopter lights flooded his office.

James wrapped the dressing gown tighter around his body from the chill of the outside evening, and the ongoing waves of shock the doctors had said would take time to recover from. He sipped his hot lemon and honey, but Charles didn't seem to understand James was suffering from a very different kind of sore throat.

Every siren wail and slamming door from outside reminded James of the crack of the gun which had ended his would-be assassin's life. James had heard it, like the crack of thunder that wakes one up from a nightmare, but his nightmare was still intact. He regained consciousness to the dungeon filled with perhaps fifty people in highly visibility reflective gear. Police, ambulance, coroners, and the army. They'd secured the scene and even removed the dead body from behind James, but had not untied him from the bed. They'd removed the automatic fuck machine from inside him, but only a few inches back. The contraption his dick had been stuffed into though remained wrapped around him. It was only when James came to and saw what appeared to be the fire brigade coming at him with a handheld version of the jaws of life that he decided it was better to show he was conscious and just ask to be untied. He removed the forced masturbation device all by himself.

Only after extensive examinations by the paramedics and four sets of doctors, did they finally decide James could leave. Fortunately, or not, being asphyxiated and choked to within seconds of life did not leave any lasting injuries.

Wishing oneself dead was a different matter. More so because as much as he could intellectually understand he had, by half a second, escaped death, up until then, he'd been quite enjoying himself.

"How are you feeling, Your Majesty?" Samuel had slipped inside the office without knocking. James' gaze remained fixed on the chaos outside the grounds. The normally sleepy town of Windsor looked like the site of first contact with an alien species. Spotlights and sirens.

"How goes the clean-up operation?" James asked. There was no need to say again he was fine. No one would believe it.

"Well...fortunately most of the emergency services didn't seem to understand what the, uh, dungeon was." James spurted out a surprised laugh.

"I always said the English were the most vanilla people in the world."

"Quite, Your Majesty. I spun a line to a few of the commanders and a couple of the boys in blue who seemed to know a thing or two that this was Prince Richard's *special place*. If anyone asks, Your Majesty, the working theory is that you were drugged and forced down into the dungeon to make it seem like a sexual incident."

"They're buying it?"

"They will once they see your toxicology reports."

"How are you managing that?"

"We'll figure something out with Dr. Brian. He already called me so I'm sure he'll want to help."

"Yes, I suppose he probably will. And the press?"

"They are only reporting a *serious incident*, but that you are unharmed, sir. Certainly, though, questions are being asked in the media about your safety, given the attempted assassination two days ago and the attack on Princess Alexandra's home last night."

"I would hope those questions are being asked, yes." A sudden silence descended on them. Samuel had run out of information to provide, and James had been without interest in continuing to speak for some time.

"Would you like to meet the man who saved your life?" James swirled the last of the hot lemon and honey in the china tea cup, then knocked it back as if it were vodka.

"Why not. And why don't you bring us a couple of screwdrivers for the hero and I. What's the chap's name?"

"Seamus, Your Majesty."

Samuel disappeared and James gave up his windowsill vigil. Retiring to the couch, he stretched out in the dark, mildly annoyed he'd agreed to do his royal duty and shake hands with the heroes when all he wanted to do was call Andrew.

Just as James felt his eyes flutter into much needed rest, there came a knock. Another aide brought two glasses of vodka and orange, and behind him a rather short, well-built man, still dressed in the assless leather chaps and harness from the dungeon. The aide left. Seamus stood in his spot in the shimmering lights from outside. He didn't bow nor offer a hand to shake. Just stood with his hands clasped in front of him, like a footballer waiting for a free kick. With his shaved head and bad boy smirk, he could've been one.

"Well," James said, getting up but unsure what to make of the man. "I suppose I should offer you my sincere thanks. Right place, right time and all that." He still didn't offer a hand for James to shake. But he did manage to shrug with his face, as if it had been fifty-fifty whether to shoot the assailant or James.

"Just did what they told me, didn't I?" Seamus said, his accent extremely Irish. It left James unsettled. A soldier would show far more deference than he was. James narrowed his eyes.

"How long have you been in the Coldstream Guards?"

Seamus snorted. "I ain't a soldier."

"Are you part of the household? Did Samuel vet you?"

"Listen, mate." Seamus strutted forward. James didn't know whether to recoil at the stranger approaching or the fact he'd just been called "mate". "I'm here to protect you, all right? The folks I work for, well, they say you're a bloke in some danger. And danger's my fucken' middle name."

"Who…" James gulped and clutched the loose edges of his dressing gown. "Who sent you to protect me?"

"That ain't none of your business, mate. But I'd say you're in need of some protecting."

"And they told you to dress like this? All…leathered up?"

"Nah. After I infiltrated the Castle here, some bloke saw me in the corridor and sent me down here."

So much for Samuel's vetting.

"I see. And how did you infiltrate the castle?"

Seamus grinned. The helicopter lights illuminated several missing teeth.

"Is one of them drinks for me?"

"Of course…come. Come and sit down."

James watched with delicate interest as Seamus took the invitation to sit, about the only formality he respected. Under the slim material of the leather waistcoat, there was a tattoo on his back. An epic scene of blue ink on white skin, like a Chinese vase, depicting a scene James did not understand.

"If you don't mind me asking," James said as Seamus gulped down the vodka and orange. "What is that on your back. It looks like a masterpiece."

Seamus seized the next invitation. He slipped his waistcoat off and turned around. James didn't know whether to gawk at the perfectly round set of smooth butt cheeks exposed by the leather chaps, or the oddly drawn skin-scene of an old man leading the way for others carrying a wounded child.

"Don't recognize it, Your Maj?"

"I'm afraid not."

"Bloody Sunday." Seamus said plainly, collapsing onto the couch with James' drink in hand. "When British soldiers fired on a peaceful march for civil rights. I got the names of the fourteen killed right here on the side of my chest."

"I…I don't know what to say." It was all James could say. His stock-standard response was trained into him by his father, perhaps, he couldn't quite remember. Whenever he was confronted by something unquestionably awful, and often when the cause of that awfulness had been his own family or the state they represented, there really was nothing he could say. Not constitutionally, and certainly not to bring any comfort. But this man had saved his life. This Irish nationalist who clearly believed deeply enough in his cause to tattoo one of the worst massacres of the Troubles into his skin, had been told by someone to protect James, the symbol of all Seamus hated.

But James was an adult, now. His father wasn't here to make faces for the cameras and throw around that blond charm which could disarm even the most fervent protestor. James was King, and he *could* say something.

"It was truly awful," James said to Seamus through the growing darkness. The helicopter lights were flying away. "Everything England has done to Ireland is a tragedy. I cannot pretend otherwise. I am sorry. Me, personally. I am sorry for what my ancestors did, and for what people did in their names."

The room sat in deathly silence. As if a great and powerful event had been witnessed, but only by them, and could never again be repeated.

"Thank you…Your Majesty," Seamus said in quiet acknowledgement. But James wasn't done.

"I'll visit Armagh, and Tyrone, and…and Derry. I will listen to what the people who live there tell me, and I will say the same thing that I said to you now, to them, and to anyone who will hear."

Seamus scoffed. His disbelief more than apparent.

"Let's concentrate on keeping you alive first."

"Why?" James asked with a grin. "Is someone trying to kill me? You must really respect this person who hired you to come and save me."

"I care about her a lot," Seamus said, but quickly quietened himself. He may have said too much.

"Her?" James' first thought was Lisa Mantis. But surely MI5 had better resources available than relying on outsourced Irish Republicans. Their budget cuts couldn't be that severe.

"Yeah. She's my sister. Well, half-sister. We share the same mam, me and her, but she's always been there for me, always since we learned about each other. Even after I got myself into some bother in Belfast and the like, she stepped up. She was there for me."

"And your mother? She couldn't help?"

Seamus eyes narrowed, staring deeply into James. His legs spread wide in the chaps, the front part of a jockstrap keeping things private, and oddly unsexual, James realized, despite how little either of them was wearing.

"Died in a helicopter crash about seventeen years ago. Along with your dah."

The world did not crash for James, not like it had the first time he'd heard this story. They'd been all together then. He and Alexandra and Lizzie, along with Andrew and Uncle William. The little family gathering called to finally switch off their family's matriarch. Small and lifeless, James had found the old woman. Cradled up under blankets, hooked up to a hundred beeping machines. It was a sad sight to see. Not for any sentimental or familiar bonds, for

James those had been severed forever when Queen Victoria II threatened to have Andrew murdered if he didn't marry Katyn. No, it had been sad to see anyone who had once wielded so much power over so many lives, shriveled up into nothing. Sad like the end of a great empire, perhaps even wistful for how things might have been.

That was the moment James learned the truth of his family drama. Lizzie was not the daughter of the Queen's in-laws. She was his father's daughter. His father's first born, to an Irish Republican agent sent to kill the king-to-be. Of course, Richard had charmed her, wed her, and fathered a daughter with her, a woman who already had a son, and with a well-earned grudge against the royal family.

James hadn't cared about the details then. Too wrapped up in his own issues, he hadn't bothered to understand the intricacies of a possible succession battle given he and his sister could, technically, have been born to an unlawful bigamist marriage and so be outside the line of succession. He didn't care about it then because part of him had hoped the truth would out. He would be saved from this burden. An accident of birth corrected by another accident at birth. James could have gone off to live his life with Andrew, free from the shackles of royal expectation. That wasn't why he cared now. He cared now because the man sitting across from him was not only a man who had saved his life, but who was family.

James lay awake in bed, closer to dawn than the darkness

outside suggested. The helicopters had ceased their siege on Windsor Castle. The police, ambulance, and coroner had removed their garrison also. Only the Coldstream Guards were left, pondering their existence after not one, but two, infiltrators. One who had tried to kill James, and the other who had saved his life.

Charles had offered James a cavalcade of pills to sleep, but James knew they would be useless. He didn't want to be unconscious, not after giving up control had nearly brought him to the end. Royals thought about death a lot. From the lists of their ancestors who had lived and died, to the twisted parlor game of who else had to die for them to rise up the cruelly-constructed line of succession. Not to mention the people James met in everyday life. People who ran charities for the dying. Soldiers who faced death as part of their day job. Heroes who had survived death in the attempt of saving another person's life. And James' doctor. Brian Hardy was his own hero of life. Brian Hardy kept James alive with the pills he delivered and the tests he undertook. Each visit from Dr. Brian was another stay to James' inevitable death.

The fear James had violently come to understand that evening, was not of death, but of dying without Andrew.

From his bedside drawer, he took the turned-off phone that still had Andrew's number. As King, Samuel and the regiments of aides and assistants were James' method of communication and information. He had no need for a mobile otherwise. But this was the phone he had to look out into the world from a six-inch screen in the dead of night. Where, in his time of exile, he had imagined a different life for himself, free of the burdens of kingship. Where he could just be. Where his mind wandered into Berlin dungeons and backrooms of bars. Where he browsed hook-up apps from behind an anonymous profile, just to know there was a world out there where men were not afraid to be themselves and to be with each other.

And there was Andrew's number. The one he hadn't answered in the first days of his disappearance. Now James knew Andrew was abroad, he added the country code to the saved phone number so it would connect. Laying back on his pillow, and more frightened now than he was of facing death, James pressed the fake electronic button on the phone. Clicks and rings connected through satellites and across oceans. Eventually, the phone rang. Once, twice, three times. A click. A cough.

"James," said a smooth, villainous voice. "So good of you to call."

"Faisal?"

Chapter 15

ALEXANDRA SAT ON THE EDGE OF THE motel bed, rattled. At the airport nearby, planes roared into the night sky. This anonymous room on the edge of Heathrow had been the best idea either Alex or Lizzie could come up with after yet another near-death experience at the hands of an armed gang shooting up Alexandra's front room. When Lisa Mantis had come crunching through the crime scene, her heels doing yet more damage to Alexandra's carpet, that's when she finally understood. MI5 was not here to protect the royals. Not anymore. If anything, they wanted them gone.

Lisa came with no answers, no clues, not even a hint of empathy. Alexandra watched this supposed protector survey the damage, nod to the mess outside as the police cordoned off the road, and even laugh with the situation commander. Alexandra hadn't expected Lisa to answer all her questions, but at least to pay attention to one.

"Where am I supposed to be safe now?"

"I don't know, ma'am." Came the curt response. *"Perhaps go and sun yourself on one of those islands you own?"*

That had been the only advice from MI5. Run away. Lisa had. She'd disappeared from the scene faster than the police teams had cleared up the street outside. There hadn't even been press. The news reported "an incident" outside Alexandra's home that had been "brought under control".

From the back of a taxi alongside Lizzie, they'd listened to "royal commentator" *Lord* Bill Honnington on the radio dismiss the idea the royals were somehow under threat.

"It sounds like a car crashed near her house," Bill had gaslit them live as they listened. *"I've spoken to the King. There's no reason to link this to the botched nonsense at Trooping the Color the other day. Probably a social media stunt gone wrong."*

Alexandra and Lizzie had shared a knowing look as the taxi drove them through the night, when hours before shots had been fired over their heads. There were shadows at work in the night who were out to get Alexandra, and James, and perhaps even Lizzie as well. All the while the royal mouthpieces were dismissing and obfuscating, while the only "official" advice from MI5 was to leave the country. There was a conspiracy afoot, of that Alexandra had no doubt. She just didn't understand the end goal. Until now.

The nonstop coverage from Windsor Castle while she watched, unguarded and under the radar, made it clear *this* time was supposed to be the real thing. James should have died, that was their plan. But for some reason, he'd survived, and it had been too late to call off the helicopters and the news crews, who seemed to very quickly have set themselves up across large swathes of the Windsor Estate.

James was alive, though. That much the newsreaders

were surprised about. They even wore black ties, as if having been briefed in the dressing room that solemn news would be coming from the palace tonight. Alexandra could imagine the chyrons which were supposed to be run underneath the news of James' death. *King dead…queen missing.*

Instead, the shocked faces and rolling helicopter coverage told a different story. One in which all sides were surprised to be reporting. *King James reportedly fights off assassination attempt, is injured but well. Assassin shot and killed.*

"Shocking news coming from Windsor Castle this evening," the anchor said as the helicopters continued their vigil. "We do have confirmation from the Palace that His Majesty was injured but is expected to make a full recovery. More details have emerged in the last hour that the assassin had managed to infiltrate the Coldstream Guards, and had been working at Windsor for several weeks already. Authorities still have not released his name, but sources have said the King was moments from death and was found courageously fighting off the assassin with his bare hands. Just incredible scenes we're hearing about, of course just days after an explosion at the Trooping the Color which the royal twins narrowly escaped, and a serious incident outside the home of Princess Alexandra which was first thought to be a car accident, but sources have said multiple shots were fired at her home."

No courageously fighting off assassins for me, Alexandra thought. The room was sparse. Clean, but sterile. It had been a long time since she had been in a room such as this. The odd tryst with a foreign security guard while on an international visit. Slipping into a blocked-booked hotel room, quietly judging not just everything inside it, but the life choices of the person who'd ended up in such mediocrity. She did not question such things now. Fleeing for her life had come very quickly to Alexandra, and now she found herself in such a situation, she was utterly unprepared.

The hotel room door buzzed open. Lizzie pulled back the gray sweatshirt hoody she'd hidden herself behind, and threw a supermarket bag of sustenance on the bed.

"I used the last of my cash," she said, twisting open the screw cap of cheap supermarket wine and filling two plastic cups from the bathroom. "They'll be tracking my cards." Lizzie finished the plastic cup of wine in two gulps, watching the real-life conspiracy play out on television.

"I still have Faisal's company cards. Their accounting practices are opaque, to say the least. Hard to track."

"I hope it buys us some time." The question remained, for what.

The plastic cup crinkled in Alexandra's hand. She didn't feel like drinking. Not when the window was so wide and exposed to the outside world. Visions of masked men diving through left her shivering.

"While you were out," Alexandra said quietly, eyes only on the screen. "I tried to call my children's nanny in Saudi."

"Alex!"

"*Tried* to call."

"What happened?"

"A few days ago, probably just hours prior to the explosion at Horse Guards Parade, they were taken from Riyadh—"

"Taken?"

"To a secure location. At least that's what the nanny said. She was in tears. It was sudden." Now Alexandra drank, hoping to dull the sharpness of her own words.

"Are the Saudis protecting them? Threatening them?"

"That's the thing." Alexandra held out the cup for a refill. "The nanny said they were British."

They sat quietly for a moment. The news hadn't surprised Alexandra when it had come through the nanny's tears. It was logical for anyone contemplating a shake up in the line of succession. Secure the heirs. But those heirs were her children.

"Alex," Lizzie said suddenly. "They want you dead or they want you gone. Both of you, you and James. Lisa Mantis told me so herself."

Another non-surprise.

"She told me, too."

"You can't leave by yourself. If James doesn't go too, you're still in danger."

Alexandra saw how Lizzie's lips moved. Thin and quickly. As if she'd already formed the words in her mind, and was deliberately making her mouth say them. Everything calculated, or at least that's what Lizzie liked to think about herself.

"When you light the fire, Lizzie, it's hard to see how far it can burn."

"What's that supposed to mean?"

The room was too small for a fight. It vibrated with their unspoken words, filling with gas that a single spark would ignite. Alexandra crossed her legs.

"Do you really think Sir Peter wants you to be the one running a regency council, Lizzie?"

"Lisa Mantis does."

"Lisa Mantis has been no help to you or me. She's not waging a war against the British state. She's simply running a strategic withdrawal, using you to protect herself from the fallout of James and I...exploding."

Alexandra watched Lizzie's face. It didn't remain solid and uncaring, as it so often had in the past. Her bottom lip rolled down and she nodded into the middle distance. Slowly at first, but soon her agreement was in full force.

"She sat down and told us, all three of us," Alexandra continued, "there's no more money for our protection. That's her hand. That's her warning. Our Gaveston Protocols have been signed. MI5 have already made up their minds they won't fight Sir Peter. Everything else is a question of saving face."

"But if I convince you both to flee..."

"Then you become the next target, Lizzie. You'll be isolated, and no one can fight a ghost."

"What ghost?"

"Don't you realize? We're fighting grannie. From beyond the grave. Her entire life she worked and fought and killed for an heir. And what did she get instead? Three bastard grandchildren, and no heir. We're not just enemies of the late queen, Lizzie. We're enemies of the state. And God help anyone who turns their back on the one thing this state cares about more than anything. Us bloody royals."

Alexandra found herself by the wide window, watching out for any wayward helicopters come to shoot them where they stood. Instead, there were only airplanes. Flying to and fro over Heathrow throughout the dark night made bright. She sipped the plastic cup of wine. It tasted bitter, but it also tasted real.

"What do we do now?" Lizzie asked quietly from the edge of the room. Alexandra caught a glimpse of her half-sister's reflection, mostly obscured from the television playing out the endless shock the king had survived. But this story would only end one way, Alexandra knew. Just as it had ended for their father. There was no throne to be fought over anymore, only their lives.

"Well…I'm going to get my children back."

Even the helicopters were giving James space. The spotlights were nowhere to be seen in the distance beyond his window. It was only him in the turret, sitting up in a bed which had once been occupied by Andrew, who's phone was now answered by Faisal.

"Where's Andrew?" James said into the phone, his hand shaking as he spoke. "I want to speak to Andrew."

"He's a little tied up at the moment," Faisal said, the

slickness of his voice heavy with grease and slime. Everything James had hated in the man, ever since Eton.

"He's there, with you. He is my fiancé, and I want to speak to him."

"Your fiancé?" The disdain was evident from half a world away. "Oh, I am sorry, old chap, I hadn't the foggiest idea." Faisal put on his haughty *Bright Young Things* upper class accent he'd often used around James to subtly mock him. "If I'd known, I wouldn't have dicked him so hard."

The light, tinkling laugh came through crystal clear on the phone. James took a beat. He let the words, the revelation, perhaps, wash over him. But only as an insult thrown in the heat of argument. Faisal could say what he liked. In fact, he would say whatever he wanted to hurt James. That didn't make it true. James detached from the mental image, one he'd never before thought of, let alone seen, of Andrew bottoming.

"Don't get into a dicking competition with me, Faisal. There's not one I haven't seen which hasn't later been inside me. No wonder you always changed under your towel at Eton."

It was an odd retort, James knew, but Faisal could not be left with the impression false slut-shaming Andrew would have any effect on James.

"So, you and your *fiancé* have more in common than you might think. Funny, he took my massive cock with a lot less complaining than your sister did." James said nothing. Like being yelled at by protestors, there was nothing to say. "Like I said, Your Majesty, Andrew's a little tied up at the moment, so he can't come to the phone now. But I'll be sure to pass along the message."

The phone went dead with more aggravating laughter. James sat in the electronic afterglow, conscious only of his labored breath that, only a few hours ago, had nearly been squeezed from his body. The phone buzzed a moment later. Picture after picture was coming through. All from Faisal.

James opened them, unsure what he was supposed to be looking at. A naked body, held up by ropes. His mouth stuffed, hands and feet lashed in the common way a submissive would be in a sex dungeon. In a common way James had been lashed to instruments of sublime sadomasochistic pleasure. But as he flicked through the images, his tongue stuck to the roof of his mouth. His stomach fell, and his chest imploded with the most unreal and disturbing sight of all. Andrew was the one tied up, arms and legs cuffed, mouth stuffed. What Faisal had said was true. At least on the fact he was tied up. And what was to say the rest of it wasn't true either? James had willed and wished for his best friend and lover to be by his side in these last few weeks. But who was that man? Who had Andrew become?

Twelve years ago

"I don't think this is a good idea," James said, nervously pacing every square foot of Andrew's Shoreditch apartment. "I mean, look how much work we've got to do for finals still." The stack of economics books towered over the

Styrofoam containers of old Chinese food from several days ago. James couldn't stop pacing. His hands fretting and rubbing the skin off his knuckles as if he was about to take tea with his grandmother. Andrew wasn't listening.

"What's that?" Andrew called from the bedroom. He was crashing around in there, putting away pictures and hiding any clothes which James might have been seen in recently in public.

"I said I want to talk about it for a minute. Will you stop—" fed up with being ignored, James stormed into the bedroom where Andrew was stretching out the balaclava he'd bought for this very occasion. "Can you leave that? I want to talk."

"The guy's on his way, though."

"So, we won't let him in! I want to think about this again. Once we do it, there's no going back." James didn't let go of Andrew's hand, not until it unclenched and his lover looked him in the eyes. Andrew's worried face could always melt James' heart. "Not in here, on the couch." James closed the bedroom door as they left. He didn't want a picture of what was supposed to happen in there to color anything he was about to say, or whatever answer Andrew cared to give. They sat among the stacks of university notepads textbooks, as if they were nothing more than a couple of roommates who both happened to study at the London School of Economics.

"You said this is what you wanted," Andrew opened, reaching back into the defense he'd relied on in the difficult weeks since the subject had come up.

"Andrew, we were drunk, and you asked what my biggest, sleaziest, horniest sexual fantasy was."

"And you told me. To be fucked by strangers who you don't see. Who walk in, use your hole, and walk back out again." Andrew stared at the floor, his knee jumping in the unsettling tick he displayed under immense pressure. James had seen it twice in their secret years together.

"Hey," James lifted his lover's chin. "That doesn't mean any of this has to happen. You're the one I want. Always have been. You're the only one I've had, Andrew. And I'd live the rest of my life with only you."

James stole a kiss. He tasted Andrew's reluctance, and soon he pulled away. Just as he had for weeks now.

"But...I want you to be satisfied. I want every desire in your head to happen, James. I don't want you to ever get bored of me. I don't want you to ever leave."

James hugged Andrew's soft body under a stretched T-shirt, he'd missed his beautiful skin.

"You're more likely to leave than me." He heard Andrew's tears. "Where would I go? I can't go out dating. I mean, you went and bought a fucking balaclava so no one would see. I still don't believe anyone will fall for that. I still worry...you know, the guy will whip it off me."

"I won't let that happen." Andrew had his protective face on. The one that promised so much, and bent over backward to deliver it for James. "I'll be right there. I'll throw them out if they even get close to touching your hood."

"But...do you really want to see this? Me getting...

fucked by a stranger? Neither of us have ever had anyone else. I just…I just worry what it will do to our relationship."

The quietness overcame Andrew again. A pondering silence that James knew said so much, he just didn't know what.

"I'm afraid what the alternative will do. Like you said, James…" His knee was shaking uncontrollably now. James placed a hand on it to try and settle him, but it was like trying to hold down a pneumatic drill. "We've never had anyone else. We're nearly finished university and we've got the sexual experience of our dorky mates from Eton." They both laughed. "I don't want you to ever regret a single minute of your life with me, James. I want you to have it all, and I want to be there too."

"And, you're sure? Sure you want to see this? If at any point it's too much, just say stop. Throw the guy out, Andrew. Don't hesitate for a second. I won't care."

"I think…I think it will make me feel good." Andrew's face told a different story, but James had learned to trust his lover's words. "I think it can be really fucking hot."

"You sure?"

Andrew's head was shaking. So were his knees. So was his body. He sucked in a deep breath. The doorbell rang, shaking them both into a frightened jump.

"One second!" Andrew shouted at the door. "There's only one way to find out. No regrets?"

"No regrets," James said. This kiss was not stolen, but gladly given. It could either be the last kiss of their years together, from teenagerhood to the cusp of adulthood—this night could break them—or it could be the first kiss of the rest of their lives. The man outside tapped the door again.

"I'll go," James whispered. He leapt into the dark bedroom, throwing off the tracksuit bottoms and tank top he had on. Andrew was opening the front door, and James was still dancing around the bedroom, naked and checking where the lube was.

"Hey," he heard Andrew say from outside the bedroom. "Want a beer or anything?"

God! Where was the lube? He slammed open his drawers, Andrew's drawers, the mirrored door on the wardrobe. Finally, as he heard a jacket unzip and a beer bottle being opened, he saw Andrew had placed the bottle on the chest of drawers. He tried to breathe, but it was hard. The footsteps were overwhelming. The man's voice he couldn't quite make out. The door open ajar, the fact that any moment, the world might find him here, Prince James, next in line to the throne, about to be fucked by a stranger.

James didn't waste another second. He threw on the balaclava, turning it around so the eye and mouth holes were at the back. He wanted to give no opportunity for an identity breach. They were playing with fire and gasoline, the least he could do was wear some protection to stop being burned. James climbed on the bedspread on all fours, bare ass out and waiting for whomever Andrew had invited to come.

He couldn't deny it was hot. Nor could he figure out exactly why this whole idea was such a turn-on, or why he'd admitted as much to Andrew a few drunken weeks ago.

They'd just been playing around. Watching porn after yet another university party where they'd had to pretend to be a couple of straight guys. They'd talked about who among their friends was attractive. Just guy things. Normal things two men who'd been together for more than five years ought to say to each other. But Andrew was Andrew, he believed it was his purpose on Earth to make James happy, even if James said repeatedly he didn't need someone else on staff. But here they were, soft voices talking just beyond the bedroom. Clothes being thrown over couches.

"Fuck," said a deep voice that wasn't Andrew's. It remained dark under the balaclava. Maybe the door was open, but the bedroom light wasn't on. "That's a nice cunt."

James froze in shock. He didn't know if he was more surprised by the heavy "Essex lad" accent or his ass being called a "cunt". No, not surprised. Turned on.

"It's all yours, mate," came Andrew's reply. Heavy jeans were unzipped…but what was that sound? Was Andrew *sucking* this other guy's cock? That had never been part of the discussion. Andrew had never been much of a sucker. James didn't really like receiving it. He much preferred to suck Andrew. It always felt like too much pressure to stay hard when things were reversed. James had always been clear about his position as a submissive bottom to Andrew's dominant top. Andrew wrapping his lips around James' dick was antithetical to that whole concept. Now *hearing* that very thing going on made James vibrate with fury. Maybe this had been Andrew's ruse all along. Get James into a vulnerable position where he couldn't stop things from happening, then Andrew could run wild as the slut he so clearly wanted to be. The set up was now so clear in James' mind. The underhanded motives, the casual acquiescence to James' bizarre fetish of being fucked in a blindfold. At least he was honest with Andrew about his preferences!

In the turn of a moment, the madness was replaced. A wet, sloppy cock that was decidedly *not* Andrew's pressed against James' hole. Hands which were rougher, harder, stronger, gripped his ass cheeks. A stranger's heartbeat pulsed into him, while the familiar thump of Andrew's heavy breathing came from several feet away. Not right on top of him. Like this stranger. Sliding inside. Pushing past the point of no return.

"Aw, fuck yeah, man. Take my fucking meaty cock, you little slut." James had never, *never* been spoken to like that. Nor had he ever been fucked so deep, with more to go. Nor had he ever been so turned on in his entire life. "Yeah, you like that you little cock slut, don't you? You like your boyfriend here watching while daddy owns your hole."

Boyfriend. Had they ever called each other that? Certainly no outside party ever had. No outside party even *knew.* Alexandra liked to joke about it, but she was a bitter, bookish bitch who'd never had a boyfriend herself and likely never would with her obsession over good grades despite the fact she was a senior royal. Charles only ever called them *the boys* if an external reference was required. *Boyfriends.* James liked the sound of that. Just as he liked the nasty words falling out of this rough top's mouth. Added to that the hard smack of a palm across James' bare ass cheek and the wiry, wild pubic hairs scratching him like a Brillo pad as the man continued to fuck James with every gasp and grunt in his unseen body.

"Aw, fuck yeah, man. Fucking take it. Take it. Take it." The slamming became incessant. Slaps of thigh against ass. The stranger's balls bashing James' own. The undeniable horniness of unadulterated sleaze that didn't end even as the man grabbed fistfuls of James' ass and thrust so deeply inside that James thought he might explode.

Then the panting was over. The dick loosened, and slipped out. An appreciative hand patted James' ass, much like a passer-by touching the head of a dog waiting for its owner. If James had a tail, it would be wagging.

James only let himself fall onto the bed when he heard a jacket zip up and the front door open and close.

"He's gone," Andrew said. James pulled off the hood. His lover stood there in the half-light which dripped in from the kitchen. James stood in only his boxers. His chest burned bright red, flame-licked skin creeping up to his neck, and his dick obviously still hard. Andrew looked exhausted, spent. Like he did those times they'd found themselves alone on the yacht in the middle of the Caribbean, when they could get drunk, snort a couple of lines, and fuck all night. James loved to see his spent *boyfriend* with the grin of shattered satisfaction.

"Did you cum?" James asked.

"No, did you?"

"No."

They didn't need to say any more. Their smiles said it

all. Their eyes flickered into mutual acknowledgement of what had happened, and what was to come. Just like it had all those years ago at Eton.

"Want another one?" They both said at the same time.

Today

James lay back on the bed, phone twisting in his hand as it so often had in Andrew's. The anticipation of waiting for that return message from an app Andrew had downloaded. Would they come without a face picture? Not all of them did. Some got snippy. Some engaged in endless chat that left James frustrated that Andrew had spent their increasingly precious nights alone talking to a stranger rather than paying attention to him.

You wanted this. Andrew would retort. Dismissing any attempt of James to battle away even the most futile of pursuits. So, it led them on a spiral downward. Apps were shelved for anonymous message boards. Men without pictures were invited. Men without standards. Men who only knew how to take.

James didn't know why, but he found himself scrolling through one of those websites of last resort Andrew had sometimes been forced to use when the regulars didn't answer and the apps were a bust for the night. The website required no sign up, no email address, no pictures even, just posts grouped by county. *Berkshire* was notoriously quiet. Who would bother to look for a hook up in sleepy Windsor? Not even the influx of the world's media and several regiments of the British army had brought any more action to a message board for anonymous hook ups.

There was only one new post in the last twelve hours. A strange one titled *No regrets* which had exactly one view. Most likely from the post owner. James clicked on the message for fun since sleep would not be coming.

Engaged guy. Stuck abroad. No phone. Want to come home but can't. Believe me, want to come home so badly. Missing Windsor. Missing you.

As if James needed any more convincing, the message was signed off with the Latin phrase Charles had once teased them about, but which Andrew had known.

Homo sum humani.

"Jesus, fuck," James said out loud in the darkness of his bedroom. "Andrew's being held hostage!"

Chapter 16

"HE WON'T SEE YOU," THE FIRM-NOSED secretary sitting in front of Faisal's office said to Andrew. The *Office of the Crown Prince of Saudi Arabia,* the brass-plated letters screamed in English and Arabic. The young man in a trim gray suit and high buttocks returned to bending over a printer behind his ultra-modern desk. Through the windows of this hundred-story turret, desert stretched into an endless abyss. Andrew had made it to the summit, but could not slay the last beast.

"I really just need a moment. He has my phone." Andrew said it like the situation was an honest mix-up. Perhaps they'd been playing squash and had got their bags mixed up. Andrew remembered those days of playing squash with Faisal, letting the man critique his backhand and poison his mind against James.

The slight young secretary—clearly placed in his position to merely taunt Andrew—was unmoved.

"So, go buy a new one? The second largest mall in the Middle East is down on floor one. May I point you in the direction of the elevator?"

"I know where it is, thanks. No need to escort me out."

"Oh no," the secretary said, poison on his lips. "I was only going to point."

Point he did. Directly behind Andrew, from the very place he'd come from after arguing past a dozen guards to climb his way to the top.

Andrew's fake smile turned into a snarl. It was at times like these he was grateful for never having to fight his way through gay bars. The endless torrent of judgmental looks and bitchy stares. Andrew had been the one to give those out all his life as James' press secretary. He wasn't so good at being on the receiving end of a snark.

"Piece of advice," Andrew said before taking his leave. "When he fucks you, make sure he wears a condom."

It was a mean and baseless thing to say, but Andrew did rather enjoy the look of growing horror on the secretary's face as he walked away, head held high despite going so low. But before Andrew made it to the elevator, the heavy door to Faisal's office shuddered open.

"Andrew!" Faisal said with faux surprise. "What the devil are you doing here?" Andrew played along despite practically having read the messages popping up on the secretary's watch. *No, can't see him now. Tell him to get lost.* The faux-posh accent rubbed him very much the wrong way. Faisal only spoke like the Etonian he never really was when he felt completely in his element. In control of everything and everyone around him. Which, Andrew realized, had been practically every moment since their teenage years.

Faisal didn't even invite him into the office. Andrew just followed, but not without a final sneer at the secretary, who managed to sneer back. The secretary thought he could get the last laugh.

"Don't forget your condom, Andrew," he whispered, practically whipping out a nail file as he flicked his non-existent hair.

"Don't need it darling, I'm on PrEP," Andrew shot back, and whacked the heavy door closed with his backside.

"What was that?" Faisal said, stepping behind his oversize desk. The office was grand in a refurbished Manhattan art gallery kind of way. A lot of expensive things, but nothing that could really disguise the fact Picassos were being hung in a building which had once been used for meat packing. Faisal's office was no different. Antiques stuffed into a two-year-old tower with built in air conditioning and smart windows. It struck Andrew hard just why he felt so intimidated by this place. Or by this man.

Faisal flicked on the television. The helicopters were still buzzing around Windsor Castle. More "heroics" of James were running across the bottom of the screen. Samuel was overdoing it by half. Subtle, that's what Andrew would have advised him. Let the conjecture speak for itself, and don't get too caught in a web of lies that would have people wondering just exactly how a strange man managed to get himself invited into such close quarters with the King.

"Terrible business, isn't it?" Faisal said, leaning on the edge of his giant desk. Saudi swords hung unenclosed a hand's reach from Faisal. Andrew decided to shift himself to the chintz couches in the corner. At least there was a Ming vase on the table he could hurl at the Crown Prince if they came to blows.

"I want my phone back," Andrew said calmly, smoothing down his suit as he sat. Faisal ignored him, focusing on the news.

"They're rather overdoing it with the daring feats of courage, wouldn't you say? James fighting off an intruder with his bare hands. Wrestling the man to the ground. I'll bet two guineas what those two were really up to." Faisal tried to jostle a joke out of the situation.

"I wouldn't know. You've taken my phone."

"And I dropped it in the bath, what can I say? Run along and get yourself a new one, then."

"Why won't you let me go home?"

"Home?" Faisal spat. "Home?" Shaking his head, he grabbed a whiskey decanter from the table against the back wall, but poured only one glass. "That's home? That's a fucking bomb site. Assassination central, that's what London is. Three attempts in a week! They only need to get lucky once, you know."

"I don't care. I want to leave."

"I've made this place very accommodating for you, Andrew. You don't want to see what it's like if I decide you're an uninvited guest. We can make life pretty upsetting for those who go against the royal family. And, anyway, if I send you back, what kind of host would I be? Packing you off to a warzone? No, no. I won't have your death on my conscience."

Something about the way Faisal said *death* turned Andrew's chest cold. But this was no time to retreat.

"I want to be home with my fiancé, and I would like to go now, please."

Faisal flung his glass very close to Andrew and it smashed against the wall, not two feet from where he sat. The tinkering of shattered glass echoed through the oversized office. Andrew didn't even lift his finger to wipe away the shards which dusted his trouser leg. He would not give Faisal the satisfaction of showing the slightest reaction to his tantrum.

"There is no home!" Faisal screamed out loud, his anger ringing for several surreal seconds. "Listen to me, and listen good. The British state invaded my country and seized my children. Did you know that? From right under my fucking nose. And do you know why? Does your simple, homosexual brain with nothing but dicks in it understand the significance of that? Hm? They're getting ready to kill your precious little fuck puppet. They'll force Alex out or maybe kill her as well, God knows they'd have my blessing, and set up some Regency crap and be done with all of you lot. Do you see what you've done? Ruined it. Ruined the whole fucking thing. Leave it to Alexandra and James to take a thousand-year-old monarchy and fuck it up in five minutes."

Andrew let him breathe.

"So why exactly do you want to keep me here against my own will?"

"I'm trying to protect you; don't you get that? Ever

since Eton..." Faisal was panting. Sweat prickled his face which hued with the glow of one who had said too much.

"Protect me? From the man who I spent fifteen years with, you've been trying to protect me from him?"

"You don't believe me."

"I'm not that important to you, Faisal."

"How do you know?" Something about the darkness in Faisal's eyes brought a cloud of confusion. A whispered phrase that should've been said under his breath, but came out in the open. Quietness smothered the room, like smoke from a cigar that infected every place it touched. Faisal looked down at the carpet, at his feet, at his hands clasped together between his legs as he lurked like a gargoyle against the desk. "Why did you choose him that night at Eton? Why did you pick James?"

Andrew wasn't sure he'd heard correctly. Faisal had started talking into the floor, but raised his head by the end, his face long like after tears, mourning discolored his cheeks.

"Pick James? What are you talking about? What night?"

Andrew's heart thumped in his chest. He hated dragging up their school past. He hated that he'd cheated on James with Faisal just to stop Faisal's threats of revealing their relationship. He hated how that guilt had led him to be overly keen and agree to James' desires of anonymous sex in their apartment. Most of all, Andrew hated how those paths had led them to the car crash of the last few years. James' diagnosis, Andrew's hoodwinking of Katyn,

Alexandra's putsch, Faisal's abduction. All of the blame was at his own feet, all of it driven from that one bad decision many years ago, to choose betrayal over truth in the desire to protect, but had only hurt. But, still, what night was Faisal talking about?

"It was James' birthday." Faisal began, telling himself the story more than telling Andrew. "You boys were all drinking in the common room. You hated me, or at least, they hated me. You never did, Andrew. You were always kind to me; you were always nice. Do you remember?"

"I...vaguely. I remember us talking a few times at school."

"I tried to talk to you all the time, Andrew. All the time, any time I got. And that night...I wanted you. I thought maybe after you'd had something to drink—"

"You'd take advantage of me?"

"No! Heavens, no. That we could talk, maybe even kiss. But I followed you that night through the dark corridors. I wanted to talk, but you went to *his* room. I was there. I saw it, how you two looked at each other when you went to James' room. You picked *him* over me. You picked him over anyone."

Andrew sat quietly. His mouth bone dry and heart gone from over pumping to under. All these years, Faisal had known about Andrew and James. Their secret romance since high school that he'd assumed—wrongly assumed— the world did not know. Andrew swallowed until his throat came back to life.

"You knew?"

Faisal did not respond. The answer was clear. Andrew felt his stomach turn. Alarms rang in his ears. He had to run, to flee. To where he didn't know, he didn't care. Just out of here, but that's the one thing Faisal would not let him do. As quick as the Saudi prince had shown a hint of emotion, it was snatched back. Andrew was confronted with the cold, hard edge of his captor. Slowly, Faisal smiled. He gave off nothing but manipulation. Andrew was suddenly furious with himself that he kept falling for this act.

"I knew from day one what you boys were up to." Faisal rose from his sad pose on the desk. Slipper shoes snuck across the carpet as Faisal came closer. "I knew you were fucking. And if I knew it, so did Alexandra. So did the Queen. We watched and waited as you made fools of yourselves in the press with all those girls James was linked to over the years. Right up until their thirtieth birthday, when you fell into our trap spectacularly, didn't you? Alexandra had set it well; I credit her for that. Telling the newspapers the simple truth that James had never had a serious girlfriend. And you ran around like a headless chicken, trying to prove us all wrong. We thought you'd implode, of course, we just didn't think it would go so quickly."

Evil slithered toward him. The memory of Faisal's touch on his body forced shivers down Andrew's spine. Now he was stuck with him in Riyadh while James was under threat. He would not be a victim, at least not of Faisal's anymore.

"So that's why you married Alex." Faisal stopped in his tracks. "You knew her brother was gay, so you decided you'd stick close to the family and wait it out. You told her, you fed her the information, and you set the traps so your wife would become queen." Faisal tried to let the barbs roll over his shoulders, but Andrew could see they'd landed. "The truth hurts, doesn't it, Faisal?" The Crown Prince's face fell from a great height, the pedestal smashed on the ground.

"I sent James pictures of you tied up, and how much you liked it." Andrew had suspected as much. "I tried to send him more, but he blocked your number." Faisal wandered over, thinking he'd given as good as he'd gotten, but Andrew knew when a man was lying. Faisal was not feeling as victorious as he pretended. "I know you wanted to be a queen, Andrew, but I guess you'll have to settle for being fucked by a king."

Faisal tried to stroke his cheek. Standing above Andrew who sat stone cold and silent, Faisal reached out, but Andrew's words soon stopped him.

"Oh Faisal," Andrew said, grinning for real. "Always last on everyone's list." Faisal pulled back, unsure of the situation unfolding. "We used to laugh about you, you know. James and I. We laughed about you when we were at Eton, we laughed about you afterward. And especially when you started dating Alex and became a good little Anglican boy. We laughed about you the most, then." Faisal remained deathly silent, standing in the middle of his oversized office. Andrew rose from the couch, glaring around the place with all the contempt this refurbished meat-packing plant in Hell's Kitchen deserved. "No one wanted to have a romance with you. No one wanted to fuck you. And no one wanted you as king. I only let you touch me at Eton because I was protecting James."

Faisal was shaking, Andrew could see it in his eyes. Nervous hands by his side, backing into his desk for protection.

"What about these last few years, huh? All the times we fucked in the Bullman's Club. You weren't protecting him then."

"True," Andrew shrugged. "I fucked you because I'm gay, Faisal. I am gay and—shock, horror—I liked to get fucked by guys. I can say it, Faisal, can you?" Andrew stepped forward as Faisal crashed into his desk. They were inches from each other, but Andrew wasn't finished. "I like to fuck guys, and I like to play with their cocks, even if I can't stand the guy. That's what it's like to be gay, Faisal. So, shoot me. I suppose in this country you will."

They were nose to nose for an anxious moment, both breathing heavy and hard, neither quite knowing whether a kiss or a punch would come next. Andrew didn't care for either of those outcomes. All he wanted was to never see nor think of this man again. Half a lifetime of a dull anxiety over a mistake he'd made so many years ago. Always in the back of his mind wondering what would happen if James ever found out what they'd done at Eton. All those other times since then had eclipsed that single mistake, most of all running away to Saudi Arabia and finding himself stuck here.

But something had shifted in the air. The desert wind which howled against the window roared through the silence. They were so high up nothing and no one could touch them but each other. Andrew didn't want that anymore. The storm had shifted their current, and the sand no longer obscured the structure which stood between them. Nothing but ruins. A distant memory in a dried-up oasis. Even if Andrew couldn't find his way back home, at least he could leave. On his own terms, with nothing more than a memory of a broken place, and a man there as magnetic as bones.

"I'm not letting you leave," Faisal said, but it was barely an echo. A distant whisper chased away by the desert storm.

"I don't care."

Andrew turned away from Faisal, hoping that this would be the last time. His face already being sanded down in his mind until there was nothing left but a lifeless chunk of clay. He pushed through the heavy door and ignored the desperate secretary, who rushed into Faisal's office as if the Crown Prince had been stabbed to death. Andrew took the elevator down. He walked through guarded corridors and sliding doors. Across walkways and gangways inside the crystal towers of a city that could be buried in sand by a strong wind. Andrew went all the way down to Riyadh's biggest shopping mall on the ground floor.

There he bought a new phone and sat by a bench next to a fountain. Women in black burkas and men in flowing white thawbs walked by Andrew on polished floors carrying designer bags. No one paid the westerner any attention.

Andrew powered up the phone, connected to the Wi-Fi and checked the message board where he'd left James a note before his phone had been taken.

The message had two views, and one reply.

I'm coming to rescue you.

Rex.

Chapter 17

JAMES WAS TAKING BREAKFAST IN THE SITting room. Charles had outdone himself with the spread, the butler's way of showing affection and concern. But unlike the other times when James had lost his father, lost Andrew, lost Katyn, been threatened by his grandmother, and diagnosed with an incurable condition, this morning he actually had an appetite.

James picked at the freshly-baked scones and jam from the royal estates as he scoured the morning papers full of stories about himself. He dipped buttered toast slices into runny boiled eggs as the television quietly replayed last night's events, the heroics having become even more unbelievable thanks to Samuel's unwelcome interventions. And he sipped bitter coffee from a China cup, running through ideas of how to rescue Andrew from Saudi Arabia.

"Can I get you more of anything, sir?" Charles asked, a frilly apron over his usual black suit.

"No, no. it was wonderful, old man, thank you. Come take a seat, let me pour you a coffee." Charles didn't need to be told twice. He harrumphed into an armchair as James passed him a black coffee and scone. Charles picked up a paper from the pile.

"*King Fights Off Killer*," Charles read the headline aloud. James tried to ignore the mumble of Charles reading the story to himself. He was busy poring over the articles, trying to find a single line from the government about increased security for the royals. Nothing. If only Andrew was here to leak something. "*God save the hero!*" Charles shouted out loud. James jumped. "I say, sir, it's been laid on rather thick and fast."

"Blame Samuel for that. No one thought to teach him that less is more when it comes to our sort of PR."

"If I may say, sir, if one is wanting the Duke of Cornwall to come home—"

"How do you know I want Andrew home?" But Charles only smiled in that annoying, knowing way he had.

"Let's just say if one did want the Duke home," Charles stirred his coffee, "then perhaps one should think about sending Samuel away."

James was distracted from responding when Charles took a giant bite from the scone and smacked his lips.

"How do you still chew like a horse?"

The sitting room door opening surprised them both.

"Speak of the devil!" Charles said while chewing. Samuel stood there, wringing his hands as he often did these days. Perhaps Charles was right. It wasn't just for Andrew's benefit, either. The job of the king's right-hand man seemed to have somewhat destroyed Samuel.

"Your Majesty, there's been a call from the government."

"Finally! Maybe the PM can hold back his Cheshire cat grin for five minutes and recognize we're in a national crisis. What do they want?"

"Um…nothing like that, sorry. Princess Alexandra was stopped at Heathrow airport. She was trying to board a plane for Riyadh."

"What, did they arrest her?"

"Oh no, nothing like that. I mean she was escorted away by the police, but the reports are she was very cooperative. Apparently, senior royals require the king's prior permission to travel abroad."

"Is that so?"

"Oh yes," Charles answered. "Your grandmother signed an annual waiver for you, though. I don't think she was too worried about you meeting foreign dignitaries on an unsanctioned state visit. No offense, sir."

"Oh…no. None taken." James sat quietly for a moment, letting an idea simmer in his mind. "Samuel, find out where Princess Alexandra is right now."

"Oh, they told me. She's staying at a motel near Heathrow."

"Motel!" Charles shouted, flecks of scone spitting out his mouth. "My God, she really is on the run."

"Charles, would you be a dear and pack me a flight bag? I'd like a word with Samuel."

"Of course, Your Majesty."

Charles withered away, leaving Samuel alone and looking awkward.

"Samuel, I've decided to go and bring Andrew home from Saudi Arabia."

"Oh? How are you going to do that, sir?"

"I haven't quite got all the details figured out yet, but I imagine my turning up there on, what did Charles call it, an unsanctioned state visit might help grease the wheels. And, well, you've been a great help these last few years, and a great friend. But when I get back, please don't be here. Transfer yourself anywhere you'd like. I'll sign the orders, but just not anywhere we can bump into you."

James was expecting shouts or tears, but not a massive smile. Samuel let out a huge sigh of relief. The lines on his face disappeared and his shoulders relaxed like he'd just had his dreams made true.

"Oh, thank you, sir. Thank you."

"I didn't expect you to be so relieved. But glad I could help."

"It's been a pleasure working with you, sir, don't get me wrong, I just never wanted this job."

"Really? Then why did you take it?"

"Well, I was told to."

"By whom?"

"Sir Peter and MI5." James stared back with surprise. Samuel leaned against the wall like he'd been completely relieved of duty, and they had instantly become mates. "Yeah, they told me to bring a sample of your semen. Sir Peter said I was the best bugger for the job. Cheeky git. But

I stopped sending them any information about you as soon as the queen died, honest. 'Course, Charles said he'd murder me if I did, but I was on your side, sir. I swear."

"Uh huh…" James's head spun like he'd had a good night out, not an overwhelming morning. "Why, exactly, did they want my semen?" He recalled an odd blow job from Samuel in the car. James thought he'd spat the load onto the floor, but had been unable to spot any evidence. James' stunned silence had apparently given Samuel license to pick up his own scone from the breakfast spread. He ate it like an apple.

"They had some crazy scheme to impregnate Princess Katyn."

"Huh."

"I wonder why it didn't work. But they never asked again. Although, if you don't mind me saying, sir…" He chewed loudly.

"Oh, Samuel, I'm not sure there's much want for airs and graces anymore."

"Well, after all that happened, that's when they turned on you, sir. Sir Peter and MI5. They shifted allegiance to your sister like the next day."

"All right, thank you, Samuel." James stood up quickly and readied to leave. Samuel apologized with his eyes that he'd said something wrong. At least James could see the anguish he'd been expecting with the end of an era. He hoped never again to see those sorrowful eyes and the backstabbing brain behind them.

• • •

"So, this is an airport motel?" James asked Charles as they walked into the luminous lobby. "There's a lot of luggage around, have they run out of rooms?"

"Sir, I am not a PR man," Charles said, nervously glancing back outside for the police escort to inevitably catch up to them. "But I think whilst in public, you should shut your mouth." They'd fled Windsor Castle, there was no other word for it. Ironically, the fact the place was still crawling with soldiers and police now examining the castle inch by inch made it pretty simple for Charles to take a royal four wheel drive out of the grounds with only a cursory nod from the police who were fully focused on making sure no one got in. That James had been laying down in the backseat with a blanket over his face was underhanded, but effective, nonetheless.

Charles had insisted on something like a disguise for James. The closest thing at hand before they'd fled was a leather cap from the collection of BDSM outfits, and a flowery silk scarf Charles had tied around James' neck in the style of a puffy ascot he could bury his face in if someone walked too close.

"I look like a leather daddy Madame Butterfly in this get up," James said, fiddling with the scarf.

"Don't tease me," Charles snapped. He never enjoyed being snatched out of his comfort zone. "I'm waiting for *someone* to at least confirm what floor Alex is on. Unless you prefer to run from room to room through this establishment yelling her name?"

"I'd rather not."

A family passed them by while they stood in the middle of the lobby. Only the children shot James a narrow-eyed glance. Out of instinct, he waved at them. Charles slapped his hand back down, and the family went on its way without a second thought. It struck James just how isolated he suddenly was. No entourage. No advance team. No royal protection officers. Even those nights at Andrew's flat had been watched over by an unmarked police car across the road. He felt like a tiger that had wandered loose from the zoo. In a strange new world of freedom, but in a land that did not feel his own. His homeland was Andrew, and he would stalk the nights and hide in the days to get him back home.

"Third floor, let's go."

They walked quickly, James' heart suddenly making itself known. How could he be sure danger didn't lurk around this corner, either. He hadn't tried to speak to his sister, figuring she would smack him down and the slightest suggestion of working together. This could be another trap.

Charles knocked on the door. Footsteps dimmed the light, a pause while whomever was behind it peered at them both through the peephole.

"Who is it?" asked a voice from deep inside the room. Alexandra perhaps?

"I think it's Charles from James' staff. And his driver." That sounded like Lizzie. So those two really had ganged up against him. The door flew open nonetheless, and James barged in, unraveling his scarf.

"Driver, am I? Driven all the way here to save your

backside." Alexandra was perched on a motel chair dressed in her serious princess garb, a flight bag beside her. Her eyes were red. "Jesus, Alex, you look like Jackie Kennedy at her husband's funeral, what's with the tears?" She shrugged in response, but snatched a tissue. Lizzie slid between them.

"Why don't you sit down, James."

"Why? So, you can offer me a poisoned drink? The legionella in the travel kettle will probably do the job for you."

"James—"

"I've had enough attempts on my life, thank you. I don't even know why I came here."

"Sit down!" Charles yelled, surprising them all. James did as he was told.

"And I know there's been attempts on your life, James," Lizzie continued. "That's why I sent Seamus to look after you."

"I know. I know you did. And thank you. To both you and your brother. I'm here in peace. Honestly, Alex, I am. I think we can see we're in this together." There was a moment of acknowledged silence. Alexandra dabbed her eyes.

"Sir Peter has my children, James. Somewhere in Saudi."

"And Faisal has my Andrew. But we're going to get them back." Lizzie was the one to give a disapproving look.

"How are you going to do that? The establishment is after you both, probably me as well. I'm sure it's only a matter of time until the police know we're here."

"Oh, the police already know that she's here," James said. "That's how we found you."

"So how do we sort this one, then?"

James stood back up.

"I suggest we go now. All of us. Publicly. That's our greatest protection, isn't it? To be as people out in the world. Where will these assassins hide amongst an adoring crowd? Well, adoring might be a tad strong. But a crowd nonetheless."

Lizzie did not look convinced. Alexandra had returned to self-commiseration, bringing even more sadness to the motel room.

"Once again, James," Lizzie said, arms folded. "How are we going to achieve this?"

"Well, there's an airport right here. Let's catch a flight."

Lisa hated other situation rooms that weren't her own. At MI5 HQ in Thames House, she was in command. She stood at the helm of the ship like Lord Nelson and directed operations as she saw fit. Coming into someone else's ops room was never as comfortable, particularly when Lisa's suspicion the operation was directed against her had only grown.

The Ministry of Defense bunker under Whitehall was as windowless and cheerless as she expected. The labyrinthine Second World War bomb shelter had been retrofitted with screens and hi-tech gizmos. Uniformed officers tapped away on screens outside of the glassed box conference room where Lisa sat, sipping burning tea from a takeaway cup while vehemently Pudgy argued with Sir Peter.

"Well maybe we should just return to K's plan," Pudgy said, glaring at Lisa. He dabbed the heat of the argument from his forehead. "Don't move forward with the killings at all. We can work on getting them into a voluntary exile."

"Maybe we should give this country over to traitors and usurpers!" Peter fizzed, but Lisa refused to be drawn in. She drank the tea and asked:

"Is all this equipment out there just for tracking the royals? Funny how you can't find them."

"We know where they are, K," Peter said, a vein popping in his forehead, "but the police are not cooperating and are not telling us where they are!" He slammed a fist down on the table. Lisa lifted her cup to protect it.

"Well, the police are not under my jurisdiction, Peter, that's the Home Office."

"No! This is a royal operation outside of parliament's purview. We are not involving the government. You're going to have to come up with a better solution."

Lisa shared a glance with Pudgy. He wanted to say much more with his eyes, but she cut him off by fishing a packet of sweetener from her coat and shaking it loudly.

"So, this operation has a name, does it?" Lisa ripped the packed open with her teeth and added it to the cup, stirring the muddy brown liquid with the tip of a pen. "We've had Operation Rex, Operation Regina, so what's this one, then? Operation Cold Blooded Murder?"

"Operation Fresh Start," Peter grumbled, staring at the unmarked map of London on their screen.

"Very Orwellian. But how many times are you going to make a mockery of our domestic security services before you give up on this *fresh start*?"

"I'm not the one making a mockery," he said, staring through the sealed glass box at the myriad of screens and monitors still unable to track the missing royals.

"Peter," Pudgy said, "she has a point. If we're seen to be turning a blind eye to open season on our royal family, then where will it stop? Politicians, business leaders; the world's assassins will be setting up shop all over London."

"And," Lisa cut in, "you told me I had until the coronation to convince them to leave."

"You do."

Lisa couldn't believe Peter had spoken without sarcasm. She glanced at Pudgy for some support, but he shrugged like a deli owner out of brisket.

"What do you say about the three assassination attempts until now, then?"

Peter turned back to them with the conceited stare of someone proud to be guilty.

"Nothing to do with us, eh, Pudgy? Who knows what those two have gotten themselves involved in. What with Alexandra's penchant for Mossad agents and James' desire for…well, anyone who'll have him, really."

"I've had enough of this," Lisa said, pushing away the tea that had gone from boiling to chilled in minutes. "A couple of philandering royals are no reason to activate the

Gaveston Protocols, and against a sitting monarch of all things. There's no way this is legal."

"Philandering royals are the very reason *to* activate the Protocols," Peter shot back. "They have one job. To procreate. One is diseased and the other has already muddied the bloodline. Who else is there? We can't reach over to a random lord in Hannover like in the old days."

"Muddied the blood line? Have you been smoking crack with eugenicists? You're ready to make Prince Hassan regent!"

"Gives us ten years to figure out another solution…or marry him off to another Swede."

"Jesus Christ!"

"Well, what would you suggest, K? Give our crown jewels over to a filthy Habsburg?"

"You know what, I don't really think Queen Victoria II died. She just had her brain transplanted into you, Peter. With the nineteenth century race science included."

The way Peter wore his self-righteous face had Lisa worried she wasn't so far from the truth. Lisa had not been around during the discussions to assassinate Prince Richard. That had been her predecessor, Dame Esmerelda, who'd paid for that decision with her life. No doubt Dame Esmerelda had weighed up the evidence, listened to reasoning, and given her objections, ultimately, Esmerelda's decision was not her own. The monarch was commander-in-chief, and the monarch had ordered her only son be killed. Lisa had been around enough politicians to know how the Overton Window of discourse went. Something unthinkable, once done, was no longer unthinkable. To kill an heir to the throne? A generation ago it had been done. Now it was the heir and the monarch. What would happen a generation from now? Lisa would stand for this no more.

"Sir Peter," she said, preparing to say words she had a feeling might go down in history. "I—"

"Quiet, woman! I told you until the coronation. But I am allowed make my own plans, am I not?"

"The Protocols have been signed, K," Pudgy agreed. "We must plan for the possibility that the King and Princess will not renounce their titles. We must plan for the defense, and the success, of the realm."

Lisa's ringing phone cut through the conversation. Pudgy and Peter reacted with horror at the breach in security.

"What?" Lisa said to them as she saw it was her office. "Do you really think these glorified Nintendo's actually do anything?" She unclipped her earing and answered, glad of the momentary distraction. "Yes, Dorothy?"

"Ma'am, I have the King on hold. He says it's urgent."

"I bet it is, put him through." Lisa wondered for a moment if to put him on speaker, but decided she would enjoy a slightly more underhanded approach. "Your Majesty," she said into the phone. Peter looked like he was about to implode. "We were just discussing the security arrangements for your coronation."

"Oh splendid," came King James' perennially deferential voice. She noticed it every time he spoke in any kind of official capacity. A sort of meekly held eagerness that was

absent when he spoke as a person. Prince Richard had not had such an impairment, that's why the people had loved the elusiveness of charisma. *"All ship shape, I hope. Sorry to be a bother, but I wonder if you could tell me where His Majesty's Armed Forces are holding on to my niece and nephew. I believe somewhere around Riyadh, no?"*

"Um, let me check that for you, Your Majesty." She covered the mouthpiece as Peter's forehead vein came within moments of aneurysm. "He wants to know where we're holding Hassan and Jasmine." Peter remained completely mum. He folded his arms at the very indignity of being asked. "Pudgy? The commander-in-chief is requesting information pertinent to the operation of *his* armed forces."

"Lisa, come on, I can't—"

"If the King," Lisa raised her voice so loud even the staff outside their glass box turned to look, "wishes to ride into battle on a horse or a Challenger Tank, that is his prerogative. If he asks his army to fight in a war, that is his right, and if he asks his commanders and officers for information to bring victory, that is our duty, and that is his order."

Pudgy looked defeated. In his very soul.

"The Riyadh Resort International. Fifteenth floor." Lisa's gaze did not relent despite Peter's protestations. "Room nineteen."

"Did you get that, Your Majesty?"

"Yes, I did, thank you ever so much. Well, I won't keep you." The phone went dead.

"What?" Pudgy said to Peter's unadulterated fury. "It's not like Princess Alexandra was on the phone, was it? They hate each other. There's nothing to worry about, the line of succession is fine."

"Oh look, boys," Lisa said, suddenly noticing the *breaking news* chyrons on a screen outside their glass box conference room rolling under footage of what looked like a number of royals walking across a tarmac to a waiting airplane. "Looks like we've found our missing king."

Peter shot like a rocket when he saw. He burst through the sliding doors yelling *turn that up* while Pudgy and Lisa slowly followed. Soon, a dozen of them were gathered around a screen, watching not only King James, but Princess Alexandra and Lizzie Windsor as well striding across the tarmac of Heathrow airport to a rumbling jumbo jet. The sight of Lizzie shoved a spike of concern through Lisa. But if she was with them, she was doubtless doing her job to get them to abdicate.

"Perhaps this is it," Lisa found herself saying. "Isn't this what you want, Peter? The royals in exile?"

"We have some more now on our breaking news story this hour," the anchor said over the video of the royals walking up steps toward the plane. *"His Majesty the King, accompanied by his sister Princess Alexandra and their cousin, Lizzie Windsor, have this hour boarded a plane for Saudi Arabia. We're still awaiting any details at all, actually, from the Palace, but we do know Princess Alexandra's husband, who she announced her separation from recently, has been made Crown Prince of the Middle Eastern Kingdom. There we can see the*

royals smiling and waving just before they board the plane. My, what a pleasant sight to see His Majesty and Her Royal Highness looking so…friendly."

"Stop that plane!" Peter roared, rushing around the bunker, throwing wheeled chairs into desks and bashing on keyboards to no avail. "Stop that fucking plane leaving our airspace right now!"

"Too late, sir," an attendant said. "It's already over Germany."

"We're just getting some video in direct from the plane carrying the royal family to Riyadh. This is a regularly scheduled flight, I might add. And it seems like King James and Princess Alexandra have seats in economy class. There we can see some images now of the royals laughing with passengers, helping the flight attendants serve drinks. And a lovely candid selfie from a passenger there of a broadly smiling James, Alexandra, and their cousin Lizzie with passengers. What a lovely sight. Here is some video recorded just moments ago of His Majesty the King."

"Alexandra and I just thought," James was saying from a tight economy seat, *"why do state visits have to be so expensive and complicated. We're all family, and of course our family have been over there in Saudi for some time, we thought we'd pay Alexandra's children a surprise little visit, have some tea with Faisal, it's been too long. and of course my own fiancé Andrew has been there in Riyadh as well, rather clandestinely I might add, but he's been there with Faisal helping him get himself set up now he's Crown Prince. There's no one better than Andrew at getting things done, you can quote me on that! But, yes, I think*

Saudi Arabia has had quite enough of my Andrew. After all, we do have a coronation to get fitted for."

It was Pudgy who laughed first. Peter was busy cursing the world. He shed his venom on Lisa as she smiled along with Pudgy. Vicious eyes flared her way like the penultimate scene before a villain's reckoning. Whether the depraved soul of a dead queen had possessed him, or Peter was simply determined of his own mind to destroy a dynasty, Lisa was very sure nothing was going to stop him. Unless she stopped him first.

"Where are you sneaking off to?" Pudgy asked Lisa as she headed for the door.

"To see the PM."

Chapter 18

ALEXANDRA WOULDN'T RECOMMEND A day trip to Saudi Arabia to anyone. Even for a royal's schedule, flying eight hours to Riyadh in economy class and then back again was pushing it. At least now they were on their way back in a private jet. Alexandra rested her eyes against the plush leather headrest, holding her daughter as she slept in the seat beside her, and listening to the soothing sounds of her son playing video games in the seat across from her. For all the joy of holding Hassan and Jasmine again, Alexandra couldn't shake the feeling she had dragged them out of relative safety, and was now flying them home into the belly of the beast.

In the end it hadn't even been a fight. More like a red-carpet welcome from everyone, except her husband. Well, ex-husband now. A courier had run up to them just moments before boarding the private jet as Faisal's Uncle Nasser had waved them off. He'd signed everything. The divorce was done. Legally, at least. James would have to approve. But the way James turned his face when she shared with him the good news as he and Andrew popped the first of several bottles of champagne suggested that wouldn't be a problem. James had even called the archbishop about excommunicating Faisal from the Church, although probably a moot point given Faisal was on the fast track to the Sultanate.

James' publicity stunt had done the job for all of them. The world's media was waiting with a red carpet when they landed at Riyadh. Along with a Saudi honor guard and several suits, plus Uncle Nasser, of this "new" Saudi Arabia that Andrew had apparently been helping Faisal build.

They'd barely finished Nasser's hastily-arranged tea in a gleaming government skyscraper high above the desert when Andrew had been rushed into the room. Apparently, Andrew had thought the Saudi police had come to arrest him, so he had fought them every step of the way until the gilded doors had opened onto Alexandra, Lizzie, James, and Uncle Nasser enjoying tea and scones.

But any tearful reunion was cut short, because the next moment the world's press was invited in, and the family was assaulted with a blaze of snapping photographers and whirring cameras.

"I believe the Crown Prince is on his way to a donor's conference," Andrew had told the assembled reporters, his hand casually upon James' thigh, *"but it's been a pleasure to have advised his team over the last few weeks. We've made some fantastic progress with urban planning, attracting investment and…legal reform, too. The Saudi government have committed to a process of women's rights and LGBTQ rights."*

"Step by step," a nervous Nasser had cut in. They'd been

ushered out quite quickly after that, Nasser afraid of any more consequential off-the-cuff remarks.

Her children arrived in a similar way to Andrew, ushered into a private departure lounge as they waited at the airport after their brief stay in Riyadh. With two children who'd spent the better part of their life ferried between homes and countries, neither was particularly bothered by being driven across desert sands in a British army convoy to be delivered, by order of His Majesty, straight into their mother's arms. Hassan was engrossed in his games console while Jasmine was quite happy watching cartoons on her portable device. They were happy to see their mother, of course, but more surprised about "Uncle James", who had hardly been a feature in their lives.

But James, to Alexandra's surprise, was a natural with his nephew and niece. He toured them around the small private jet as they boarded, took them to shake the captain's hand, and played for nearly an hour with Hassan on his games console while Andrew and Lizzie spoke quietly at the back of the plane over a bottle of champagne each.

Alexandra hugged the sleeping Jasmine tighter as the jet continued to carry them home. Those moments of instant ecstasy when she saw them, held them, and shepherded them away from Saudi Arabia, hopefully for the last time, had fallen into the pit of despair. Yes, they'd managed to pull off a heist, but her and her brother were still a wanted pair. She didn't buy James' assertion that fame itself would keep them safe. They needed to end this nonsense. If it was exile the authorities wanted, then now she had her kids back, exile she would consider. James, on the other hand, appeared to be going nowhere.

"The good thing about not having done much coronation planning," James was telling Lizzie just across the aisle, "is that no one knows what to expect. Will Andrew be alongside me? Will he not? What's the order, the singers, the ceremony? It's a week away and no one knows a thing!"

"Don't you think," Lizzie tried, "it might be an idea to postpone? Given the security situation."

"Yeah right," Andrew piped in from the window seat where Alexandra couldn't see. "We're doing this coronation even if it's the last thing we do."

They talked, while Alexandra closed her eyes and tried not to listen. They didn't so much talk as James and Andrew snapped back into their natural groove as Lizzie nodded along. That's what Alexandra had never had with Faisal, she realized. The end of her marriage barely a tertiary thought. No click. Conversation did not flow. Even in the early years, when Alexandra had thrust all of her pent-up sexual energy into her new husband, she admired him, idolized him perhaps, but she would never call them *friends*. Her brother and Andrew had that gay couple magic no straight man could replicate. They were not just friends but *equals*.

Hassan rushed back over to his uncles, desperate to show them something he'd accomplished in his game. In a moment, the three of them were stuck deep inside the console. That was gay couple magic. It didn't matter what words had been said or deeds done. They could walk out of orgies (as they probably had) hand in hand, giggling over things straight people would upend their lives about. Gay couple magic would have them sipping cocktails and playing video games after things straight couples would be filing for divorce from.

Lizzie let them be and slipped into the seat opposite Alex.

"Looks like the boys are having fun," Lizzie said, offering Alex a full glass which she took.

"They are. It's funny, Faisal would never. And he'd never let Hassan sit so close to James, that's for sure." They quietly admired the oddly close familial connection, one that felt so natural, yet had somehow been denied to each for so long. Alexandra knew it to be true of Lizzie as much as it was for her, too. "I wonder where it all came from, this animosity. Was it Faisal all this time?"

Lizzie rolled the champagne around her glass, sitting back like she was a vulture making lazy circles in the sky. Did Lizzie see her as a fellow vulture, or a carcass to be devoured?

"Did you know about Faisal and Andrew?" Lizzie's eyes narrowed as she spoke, staring with an understated indictment.

"Did I know what?" Alexandra asked the question of herself as much as Lizzie. Alexandra had studiously defended the line between suspicion and knowledge. These things she might wonder, but didn't want them to break through the barrier from heart to brain.

"Faisal knew that Andrew was with James…at Eton."

The plane did not fall from the sky. The engines did

not give way. Lightning did not strike nor did an asteroid rip through their wings. Alexandra felt each of those emotions, in turn, behind a fuzzy exterior that crested around her, like she'd touched a wet finger to a power cord. Faisal knew. He knew they were together back then. He knew, and so he had courted and married Alexandra for that very purpose of placing himself one step closer to power, and using Alexandra as his steppingstone.

It made sense, as if she'd found the missing chapter of a book she'd once read. What had been gray and unclear had now been colored in with sharp focus. Those whispered suggestions Faisal had shared with her at state occasions or family gatherings had been said not in jest or wonder, but with knowledge. Their first Christmas at Balmoral before they were married, Faisal had leaned across to Alexandra at the long dinner table. She'd thought he would whisper sweet nothings in her ear, but instead said: *Why does your brother bring his press secretary to a Christmas holiday?*

"Oh, I knew," Alexandra said. "I knew all about it. But let's not dig up ancient history." She smoothed down her clothes, layering up the walls that would protect her from the past. "How am I going to take care of these two?" Jasmine was still fast asleep, just as Alexandra remembered being seven and falling asleep pressed up against her father.

"I know how to protect them. Seamus."

"Seamus?"

"He's my half-brother. Saved James' life."

"That's right," James leaned across the aisle to say. "At

first glance you'd think he's a raging Irish Republican. But I trust him."

"There's a safe house," Lizzie said, severely serious. "A monastic community on the west coast of Ireland that Sir Peter and Lisa Mantis and the whole apparatus of the British state will never touch. It's protected by the CIA. JFK established it to smuggle weapons to the IRA. They'll be safe there, until—"

"Exactly. Until when? When does this end?"

"When we end it."

"Ms. Mantis?" the bespeckled secretary said as she appeared from the depths of the prime minister's residence. It was late, and she was clearly newly in with the new prime minister. The secretary did not stifle her yawn, but stretched and pulled her cardigan closer. Lisa noticed the paused reality TV show open on the phone clutched in her hands. A white earphone rested in one of her ears. Young, inexperienced, and straight from a PR agency. That was who Prime Minister Jason Keats staffed his government with.

Lisa lifted her handbag and followed the secretary down the dank corridor. Downing Street at night always carried the air of black and white and the nineteen-thirties. The warren of corridors rejected natural light, and the lamps were always turned off by the cleaners.

"May I take your…anorak?" the secretary asked. Lisa

frowned at the slight and clutched her deliciously expensive fur coat closer to her shoulders.

"No, you may not." The secretary pouted and nodded her head to the PM's door before turning away.

"Listen, darlin', you refer to me as 'K' at all times, do you hear me?"

"Whatever."

"Not *whatever*, but as 'K'. And if I get a lick of attitude from you again, I'll see that the pictures of you bobbing on whosoever's cock you sucked to get here will be front and center in the national papers, all right?"

The secretary's eyes widened. Lisa didn't have any evidence of the sort, but had made an educated guess. The young woman quickly opened the door for Lisa.

"'K' to see you, Prime Minister."

Lisa slid into the dark office where Jason Keats sat tieless behind a desk and a brittle lamp. She offered the young woman a crocodile smile.

"Thanks, love," Lisa said. Jason finally glanced up.

"Oh, yes, thank you, Tammy. That'll be all. Unless Ms. Mantis would like a drink?"

A flash of electricity passed between Lisa and the secretary.

"Prime minister," the young woman said, "it's security protocol to address the head of MI5 as 'K' at all times."

"Oh, right, of course, yes. Thank you, Tammy." She slunk away, but not before Lisa snapped her an encouraging wink. The young woman knew what side her bread was buttered on. "Drink, K?" Jason asked, heaving himself up from the table of files and tinkling glasses and bottles behind his desk.

"What does Sir Peter have on you, Prime Minister?"

"Are you sure I can't tempt you, K?" He ignored what she said and poured one for himself. "I think I'll have a whiskey."

"So, what is it? Sex, drugs, cash?"

"K, we barely know each other. And, anyway, aren't you supposed to be the head of intelligence?" He drank with a grin on his face. One Lisa did not like at all. She sat down across from him.

"In my experience, Prime Minister, the only ones who are good at hiding their...kompromat, are the gays."

"To the King!"

"So, what is it, Jason? Is the single man in Downing Street getting buggered on the side by Sir Peter?"

"What is your obsession with this man?"

"He's a threat to national security, Jason, and I'm this close to taking him out."

She saw the prime minister was ready to chuck another crass joke her way, but the harsh look on her face made him stop. He placed the glass down upon the papers and rested his elbows on the desk, leaning close into her as if spilling state secrets.

"Sir Peter has my approval for Operation Fresh Start."

"Hence my question, what does he have on you?"

"Lisa—" she bristled "—it is not unusual after a long and solid reign of the such we saw from the late queen, that a period of instability will follow. But instability is relative.

My predecessor sat behind this desk because Prince Faisal's dirty oil money was funneled into her bank accounts. You talk about kompromat, K, Princess Alexandra had buckets of it on Zia Wajid. Until poof! One day, little old James sniffs out the secret deal between his sister and the PM, and leverages the same kompromat to save his own skin and plunge this country into an expensive sibling tantrum. I hope you will agree this is hardly a sound way to make government policy."

"I'm not disagreeing."

"Historically speaking, our current predicament is little more than a natural rebalancing in relations between crown and parliament. The execution of Charles I, the Glorious Revolution, the story of our democracy is one of monarchy and the people keeping each other in check. And here we are again. Sir Peter has my full backing. Would I prefer them both to quietly vacate the stage? Of course. But we are dealing with not one but two threats to the realm. Hence the need for two bullets."

"You are leading a coup, Prime Minister, I hope you understand that."

"I did not start this process, K, but you can be damn sure I'm going to finish it." He stood up, their conversation over. "You were promised until the coronation, and I will ensure Sir Peter keeps that promise. But that is all. We will not crown another monarch, not for another decade or more."

"Until you can find a way to control Hassan, you mean?"

"Well…we'll see who will take the throne next. There's no rush, not after the tragic death of Prince Richard's only children."

Lisa heard what he'd said. *Only* children.

"Prime Minister," she held out her hand. "I have no doubt you are surrounded by those much smarter than you, I only hope you have the wisdom to listen."

"What a pleasant way to call me stupid."

"And I mean every word. Good night."

Andrew watched James from across the sitting room in Windsor Castle. The television played quietly in the background. Anything but the news. The King dabbed melted cheese from his chin. He always ate pasta like this. Individually, one spiral at a time. Andrew had finished his plate long before the last commercial break. Andrew missed this.

They sat as they often had at Windsor. Hidden away in a castle turret. The sitting room something out of a 1970s catalog. Frilly armchairs and floral wallpaper. It had been James' father's favorite place, Windsor. For a long time, it had been Andrew's favorite, too. Their Eton hideaway. The place of their first uninterrupted night together, when Andrew hadn't been forced to sneak out of James' room at an ungodly hour for fear of being caught by the schoolmaster. A place where they could hide from the world in plain sight, while Charles cooked them food and they chilled out with television and walks around the grounds.

"Is he still not finished yet?" Charles said, sweeping into the room in a Chinese silk patterned dressing gown. His hair—what was left of it—was wrapped up in a towel headdress, and he lathered moisturizer into his hands.

"I am now," James said, stuffing the last few pieces of pasta into his mouth so Charles could take the bowl. It was late. Charles had outwardly moaned about having to make food for them at such an hour, but clearly, he'd been overjoyed at Andrew's return. He showed his love though by complaining Andrew was too thin. Charles gathered up the dishes, the silk floating as he mothered around them, sending waves of a strange emotion through Andrew. That of being home.

"Oh! I have someone to see you," Charles said.

"Please no," James said. "I think we're done for the night." But Charles just smiled. He scurried off into the kitchen, while James and Andrew shared an awkward glance. They hadn't yet talked. They'd eaten, showered, talked to Charles, talked to some of the guards, and kissed, but they had not spoken about what had been, or what was to come.

Their sentence of silence was lifted, though, when Charles came back in through a different door, followed by an overexcited chocolate Labrador.

"Piers!" Andrew shouted as the dog leapt across tables and chairs and into Andrew's arms. "My God, you've grown!" Andrew was lapped by the dog he'd sorely missed, and who'd clearly missed him.

"The staff at Clarence House were complaining about

his constant whining," Charles said, picking imaginary dog hairs from his gown. "I suppose he missed his daddies."

Charles slipped out, leaving James without the distraction of food. Piers nuzzled into Andrew, his tail gradually slowing down from overexcitement to straightforward happiness.

"I guess he's glad you're back," James said from across the room. Piers lay across Andrew's lap, but stared straight at James.

"I think he's missed you, too." There was a sense of reluctance. A heavy sigh, as if James was tired of being hurt. "But I'm not going anywhere, not again." Andrew said it with defiance, his voice twisting at the end, threatening to open up into emotion. "Come and sit with us."

Piers' tail wagged hard again as James crossed the room and slipped onto the couch. Piers didn't know who to lick first, but it broke the unseen ice between them. Andrew offered a hand, sliding across Pier's fur. James took it. They sat still, holding hands over a dog, who presently stretched out between them.

"Andrew, I—"

"James, please. This was my fault. I…I freaked out. I got upset over a lot of stuff I had no right to. Samuel, he made me feel insecure, but for no reason. I don't care."

"He's gone."

Andrew saw James was serious. He hadn't expected that.

"You didn't need to do that."

"It doesn't matter. You didn't like it, and I should have

been more understanding of that. And more sensitive, about all that *stuff*. I let myself get carried away. But I'm getting rid of the dungeon first thing tomorrow. I don't need that, now that I have you."

"But James, it's not one or the other. You don't need to choose between me and you. That's you. That's part of you. Maybe we can use it together. At least that way I can make sure no one's trying to kill you."

It brought a smile from them both.

"I'd like it if we could use it together. And if there's anything you want...you just have to say. I saw what Faisal sent me. I don't want you to think you can't have what you want...what you need."

"Thank you, but I don't want that. I didn't at the time. Faisal was..."

"A manipulative bastard?"

"Yeah."

"I think we've all seen that now," James said, still holding tightly Andrew's hand. "Oh, I have something to show you." The dog lifted his head as James brought them over a box from the side of the room. He opened it carefully, bringing out plates, tea towels and biscuit tins and laying them out on the table. The light was dim, but Andrew could see it was a selection of coronation memorabilia.

"This is...us?" Andrew said, examining the biscuit tin along with a very intrigued snout tucked under his arm. The two of them were embossed on the tin. A picture from a recent state function Andrew hadn't even remembered. They were both on horseback, riding next to each other with broad smiles. James in his royal red regalia, and Andrew in a navy-blue admiral's uniform befitting his rank as prince. Andrew traced the words written in gold across the square biscuit tin that Piers was pawing, desperate to get inside. *The coronation of their majesties King James III and Prince Andrew.*

Not only on the biscuit tin, but also the mug on the coffee table had a picture of them both, this one in suits at their engagement party. A platter of plates with different shots of them through the years, from laughing at university to the more somber official portrait after their engagement. A lifetime of love summed up in a richly woven tea towel with both their names stitched on it.

"I hope you don't mind," James said, "but I spoke with the church whilst you were away. I'm afraid I had to give up on the idea of the church changing its stance on same sex marriage, but in return, they were willing to perform a joint coronation."

"James…" Andrew opened the tin and passed Piers a biscuit. "This is amazing, but you know what Lisa Mantis said. There are people out to get you. The whole state it seems. Are you sure we shouldn't just pack up this idea and go into exile? We could live together, somewhere quiet, somewhere alone. Leave this place and just live. Let Alexandra deal with it all, no? Give it to her if she really wants, or we can all fly away and leave it to…whoever."

"Andrew, I did a lot of thinking when you were away, and I learned I am me. Myself. James. For good and for bad. A king, a lover, a gay man, an HIV positive man, a submissive, the son of a man who is dead, the brother of a twin and half-brother of a sister, and most important of all, I am your fiancé. I'm all these things. If I run away from any of them, I'm not being me. Yes, it's scary. Yes, it's dangerous. And, yes, we might die. But, Andrew, if I am not me, and if you are not by my side, what's the point in being alive?"

"So, what are you saying?"

"I'm saying Andrew," James offered his hand, "let the haters hate. Take my hand, and let's make history."

Chapter 19

WELCOME BACK TO *BRITAIN TODAY* ON this historic coronation day of King James III and Prince Andrew. We're live from the press gallery outside Westminster Abbey where world leaders, and the world's press, have gathered to witness the coronation of the King. A day perhaps many of us didn't expect to happen, given recent events. But I'm joined once again by royal commentator Lord Hodes."

"Nice to be here again, Daisy, but, please, call me Bill. Yes, an historic day indeed. And as you said, one many of us were unsure how it would turn out. And even me, a grizzled old newspaper man from a different era, must sit back and see how much Britain has changed that we're here to witness the coronation of a gay king, and his partner."

"Well, indeed. Although we're told Prince Andrew's official title will be *loyal protector*, as opposed to, well, queen consort. But regardless, a coronation is always a time for celebration, and, we hope, unity, too. Few of us will remember the last coronation of Queen Victoria II some sixty years ago, but there seems to be a lot of unknowns and secrecy around this event. The traditional carriage ride from Buckingham Palace to Westminster Abbey was canceled given the recent security threats, but some have speculated about a last-minute change of plans. Are the royal twins still fighting over who's going to be walking down the aisle?"

"I think that time has passed, Daisy. We saw that recent state visit by both twins to Saudi Arabia, and of course Princess Alexandra is front and center in the crowd. We can see a picture of her there in the front row, sitting next to cousin Lizzie Windsor."

"Both looking resplendent, I might add. So, Bill, as a former newspaper man, do you think the press has perhaps made too much out of the royal family drama, given they all seem to be full of smiles today? Even at James' engagement party at the height of the canceled referendum campaign, the royal siblings looked quite comfortable together. Have we all made too much of these supposed tensions?"

Bill smiled at Daisy's question. He knew the world was watching him, sitting behind this desk set up in the press valley outside of Westminster.

"Well, Daisy, as a former newspaper man myself, and a father, all families have tensions. But few are subject to such scrutiny as the royals. I think it's a testament to James, Alexandra, and everyone who is close to them, that they've stuck together in recent months given all they've been through. Those horrendous assassination attempts have maybe reminded the royals that despite their differences, they're still one family."

"Very true, Bill. And I think we can see a member of

your family there among the guests, Lord Gregory, who, according to our order of service, is one of Prince Andrew's attendants for the ceremony. And we can see Lord Gregory marching quite quickly through the guests, I imagine going to assist Prince Andrew readying for his coronation today, too. But I'm just being informed the prime minister has been delayed, according to Number Ten, we don't quite know why, but we may have a delay to kick off. Let's watch and see what happens."

Lizzie sat close to the empty throne, within spitting distance. She was perched on the pew at the front of Westminster Abbey, sitting directly across from assorted religious leaders and dignitaries from across the Commonwealth. The aisle between them awaited the ascension of the new king, but they had been waiting for a while. The lustrous choir in flowing white robes continued their medley of warmups, singing everything on the set list twice, everything except their opening number: God Save the King.

Alexandra shimmied closer to Lizzie on the hard wooden pew, her jewels jingling, and adjusting the coronet on her head with silk white gloves from under the embroidered golden cape.

"People keep looking at me strangely," Alexandra whispered, covering her mouth with her gloved hand, more than aware a thousand lip reading experts were watching every move of her mouth from the TV cameras and drones hovering around.

"Probably wondering if you're going to slide up there instead of James," Lizzie whispered back.

"I'd better warn the choir, then." They shared a laugh, but it was from something akin to nervous exhaustion. People were milling around still. The official order to take their seats still not promulgated. "The PM isn't here," Alex continued, "and I don't think it's by chance."

Lizzie felt a chill sweep from the rafters, or from the royal guards with their swords, or from the endless flowing robes of the clergy which could hide all manner of deathly winds.

"Ladies," came the fork-tipped tongue of Sir Peter. He slithered alongside the pew, his back to where the cameras pointed down from the high ceilings. "Such a shame your children, our own royal heirs, have been unable to come and witness the coronation of their monarch. Highly suspect, one might say?"

"I suppose it's due to all this enhanced security," Alexandra said, quietly petrified Peter would make some comment and reveal he knew Hassan and Jasmine had been ensconced by Seamus on the far coast of Ireland. Alexandra had not taken them there herself. Merely waved goodbye to her children at the airport, being escorted by a gaggle of nuns to an IRA base on the promise of Lizzie's half-brother. She realized her kids were either going to hate religion, or love it.

"Still," Peter continued, his bony hands fingering the hymn book. "It does not bode well for the line of succession that two of its members are not here. Perhaps Parliament should take another look at who comes next?"

"Is there some reason you're hovering around here like a bad smell left by the archbishop?" Alexandra asked calmly.

"I have my place somewhere at the back. But I thought I would ask your royal highness if you might want to step in at the last minute, you know, should James continue to not show up."

"He's not here?"

"Would be a shame to waste a coronation. We'll print some tea towels and biscuit tins for you after. Oh, but your children wouldn't be here to see it. Never mind, I have the list somewhere. Who's next… Oh, Lizzie, what say you?"

"Fuck off, Peter," Lizzie cut in. "Don't believe him." Peter smiled with evil eyes before slithering away.

"Have they done something to James on his way here?" Alexandra whispered to Lizzie, forgetting to cover her face with a gloved hand. The world would be watching the stress on her face.

"They canceled the carriage ride because of security, I hope that wasn't a ruse as well."

Lizzie glanced around the waiting Abbey, heavy with anticipation. The world's eyes on them, and only growing more impatient. Nothing seemed close to starting. Lizzie figured she could safely slip out into the cloisters and sniff out what was really happening.

"I'll go and find out."

Andrew had been given a room to dress in that was traditionally used by the archbishop. It was directly behind the altar, so he could hear the choir echo through ancient stone walls, and imagine the crowds lining both sides of the aisle as two aides strapped his ceremonial sword into his navy blue and gold rimmed admiral's uniform. It had been decided by the master of ceremonies it might be inappropriate to give Andrew the dressing room traditionally used by the queen. Andrew didn't care, but had said the archbishop might make better use of the dress steamer in the queen's chambers.

One aide cleaned his sparkling riding boots while the other polished the already shining medals on his chest. The mirror reflected a dream, this uniform, this ceremony. But he couldn't ignore the danger lurking just beyond the ancient stone walls. They hadn't protected James in his basement dungeon. How could walls protect them now, when none of them knew what lay beyond, or who was trying to kill them.

The only door creaked open. Andrew jumped, precipitating a knock-on effect of surprise among the aides. He calmed the jangling medals as Greg slipped inside to Andrew's pleasant surprise.

"Greg!" The young man was almost unrecognizable in his black tails. "Don't you look handsome."

"I've nothing on you…Your Majesty." Greg bowed, but they both laughed.

"I'm still just an HRH for now. We've actually got to get through this coronation first."

"I'm sure it'll be a breeze. Anyway, I can see you're busy, I just came to wish you good luck."

"Thanks, man. But stay a minute. Seems to be delayed out there anyway."

"Yeah, the PM's still not arrived."

The aides swept away, dusting off Andrew's hat for the umpteenth time. The only place Andrew could sit with his sword was a small stool. Greg took a chair.

"Fuck knows how I'm supposed to sit in a throne with this get up," Andrew said, the sword clanking against the wooden stool.

"I'm sure it'll be worse for James."

"Yeah, he hasn't even practiced with the crown, he said. Too busy…well, coming and getting me back from Saudi."

"Just so you know," Greg said while looking down at his feet, "I hung out with James a few times while you were away. Nothing serious, just chilled with a bunch of others on his yacht and in Windsor. Nothing to worry about."

Greg wore the woolen smile of a sheepish yew led astray by the big bad wolf. Andrew wasn't sure if he'd ever considered the considerable age gap between them—a decade or more—but he suddenly felt a million years old next to this kid. Like an old man who should've known better than to corrupt a corruptible youth.

"I'm not worried," Andrew said, and meant it. "Thank you for keeping him company while I was away."

The door knocked again, and this time Samuel came through. He was dressed very much as an aide to the ceremony, not a guest, and for that Andrew was thankful. He would have made peace with reality if James had kept him around, but was infinitely glad James had asked him to move on.

"Your royal highness," Samuel bowed to Andrew, "my lord," to Greg. "It is time."

Sighing with the reality it was now or never, Andrew rose, and Greg offered a hug. It started soft and friendly, but turned hard. Greg pulled Andrew into him and held tight.

"You two are meant for each other," Greg whispered. "And you're our icons."

They parted with a smile.

"You're wise beyond your years, Greg. And for that, I'm sorry."

"I'm not," Greg replied emphatically. Samuel was impatient. Andrew followed him out of the dressing room with all his finery and clacking sword. They didn't go toward the nave of the Abbey, where the assembled masses awaited their arrival, but into a maze of back corridors. With the ancient brick and dark walls unlit by torches, it seemed they'd worked their way toward the crypt. A single wooden doorframe like a barrel splayed out waited ahead of them, Samuel gripped the rope handle.

"Are we going the right way?"

"Oh, yes." Samuel said. "I've just heard the PM has been delayed, so we should wait in here." Ancient hinges creaked open a pit of darkness.

"I think I should go back to where everyone else is."

Andrew turned away, his heart suddenly pounding. Nothing felt right. How would he get out of this maze? But there was no more time to think. Samuel's arms wrapped around Andrew's chest, trapping him from struggling for the sword. A moment later, a rag that stunk of gasoline covered his mouth and nose. He felt lightheaded immediately, but still with enough residual strength to reach up and knock away the cloth across his nose and mouth. As soon as he did that, though, Samuel's hand whacked toward his exposed neck, holding a syringe. It darted deep into the exposed flesh, and a searing chill pushed into his bloodstream. Instantly, Andrew felt his consciousness drift away.

"You're not going anywhere. Sir Peter's orders…"

"K!" An agent bounded through the clutch of intelligence officials tracking greater London from a makeshift tent on a Parliament Square Garden. This was not coronation security HQ; that operation was being run by forces hellbent on turning the coronation into a bloodbath. Lisa just didn't yet know how. "C, there you are." The agent breathlessly wiped sweat from his forehead. He'd just sprinted the several hundred feet and multiple cordons from the Abbey to their tent, as Lisa had asked him to do every fifteen minutes. "I have a visual on the King, he's still in the anteroom getting ready."

"Good," Lisa said, turning back to the bank of livestreams from across the Abbey, including inside James' dressing room. She was leaving nothing to chance. With three separate agents attached to James' royal protection officers, Coldstream Guards, and the police, she had multiple sets of eyes on the King at all times. Alexandra remained safely in her wooden pew, she could see from the livestream the princess sitting in her gloves and coronet, looking regally bored. But where was Lizzie?

"Richard!" Lisa yelled at a staffer; she was unsure which one. "I need eyes on Lizzie Windsor, now!" She probably shouldn't shout so loud when the world's press was camped about thirty feet away, their cameras trained on the unusual spectacle of a King being crowned under an air of reticence.

"Checking the feeds."

"Check faster."

"Ma'am, we've also lost eyes on Lizzie's agent."

"How did that happen!"

"Ma'am," another one ran up to her, holding a phone to her ear. "The PM's office is giving nothing away on his whereabouts."

"He's still not on his way?"

"Reading between the lines, I don't think he's coming at all."

Lisa leaned forward on the folding table, staring at the multitude of monitors stuffed into their compact tent. She'd assumed an accident would have befallen James en route to the coronation, that was the most likely scenario. So, she'd had him cancel the carriage ride, which Sir Peter had seemed unbothered by. Meaning they must be planning something during the coronation itself. And with the prime minister all but skipping the ceremony, could it mean the entire building would be under threat?

"Peter…" she said to herself. "What the hell are you playing at?"

Lizzie started to walk down the aisle of Westminster Abbey—away from the throne. She stuck to the side, nodding to the dignitaries she recognized or who recognized her, but her thoughts were only on getting eyes on James. She refused to glance up at the rafters of the Abbey, where extra layers of security would be watching, and Seamus, too. She didn't know how Lisa Mantis had pulled off bringing a convicted IRA terrorist inside the security cordon of Westminster Abbey, but it was supposed to be another failsafe against the unknown violence the state was preparing to perpetrate against any number of them.

"Lizzie," Peter's voice cut through her like a knife. "What are you doing back here in the cheap seats?" She didn't answer, but he rose from his pew and walked a pace behind her. "Strangest thing," he said with barely a whisper. "We found an Irishman running loose upstairs. Thankfully, he's in custody now, but you wouldn't know anything about that, would you?"

Lizzie spun around to face him. She opened her mouth

to speak, but no words came out. Across Peter's face was a maniacal grin. She said nothing. Heels clipped along the harlequin floor, away from the court jester who'd amassed so much power. Whatever this day would bring, if she had the opportunity, she would put a stake through Sir Peter's heart.

James, or where James was supposed to be waiting until the time came to coronate him, was well protected. Layers of soldiers in fatigues and berets menacingly pointed bayonets at Lizzie as she approached the corridor. A stressed woman with a clipboard and headset rushed over to her.

"Is it time?" the woman asked Lizzie.

"Oh, I don't know. I don't think so. I just came to see the King."

Lizzie warily eyed the double line of a dozen soldiers guarding the single door. More because it felt like a trap to keep James in, rather than a guard to keep the undesirables out. Lizzie was not too far removed from trying to bring down the monarchy herself to trust anyone who could get this close. She barely trusted her own conviction that she was as much at risk from the bout of regicide ready to spring forth. The clipboard woman nodded her through.

"We're so late anyway," she complained, "we might be quicker to have everyone come through here to swear allegiance to His Majesty." The woman yelled into her headset. "Where the hell is the prime minister?"

Lizzie stepped along the honor guard, man by man, gun by gun, toward the old wooden Abbey door. With

Seamus having been stolen away, Lizzie was afraid. It was a childish superstition, but knowing he was close, as well as armed, had given her some comfort. A name to shout when this day went pear-shaped. A hope to lean on that she might be saved from whatever fate Sir Peter had in store. With him gone, she walked the gauntlet of the soldiers alone. Unsure if they were friend, or foe, or firing squad. Lizzie reached out to grasp the ancient handle, her throat drier than the communion wafers waiting to be transubstantiated for James and his *loyal protector* Andrew. Lizzie had lost that battle; Andrew belonged to James. The least she could do was make sure James would be around to protect his *loyal protector*. The door budged an inch as she pushed, and a violent alarm cut through the air.

It rang so loud the soldiers seemed to think it was some kind of weapon. The clipboard woman rushed toward Lizzie, shouting: "What did you do?" Lizzie raised her hands and retreated a few steps back, sensible given the large number of guns now spinning around the corridor. Evidently, the alarm had started to cause chaos in the nave of the Abbey too, because beyond the corridor, people in their splendid finery were starting to evacuate.

The soldiers had the same idea. One kicked the door in, and several rushed in. Lizzie hung back, but she heard the shouts.

"Your Majesty, we must get you out of here."

"Get Andrew, now!" was his reply.

Lizzie was shoved back against the wall as some soldiers rushed away, and others bundled James into the corridor in his royal robes. Complete with everything to be coronated but the crown.

"Lizzie!" he said, trying to reach out despite the physical barrier of British Army uniforms surrounding him. "Is this it? Is Peter starting his putsch now?"

"I…don't know," was her honest response. The soldiers were trying to move him on, but he fought back the tide.

"Get yourself to safety," James shouted as his security protocol rushed him away and the clipboard woman descended into near hysterics. "And tell me the second you spot Andrew!"

Lizzie nodded just as James was swept away by the fatigued tide. The alarm was piercing, far stronger than any normal fire alarm, and far more suspicious, too. The running from inside of the Abbey was reaching stampede, and terrified shouts began to drift her way. Lizzie couldn't quite hear, and started to jog after the soldiers and the King. The voices were louder now, jumping between people's mouths like some incense candle had sparked a real fire deep inside the Abbey.

"It's a bomb!"

Chapter 20

SCENES OF CHAOS AT THE CORONATION,
Bill. Have you ever seen anything like it?"

"A bomb scare at a coronation? No, I can't say I
have, Daisy, but we're watching it here in real time."

The producers were snapping their fingers at both of
them, as presenter and guest were continually glancing away
from camera, looking back at the scene just behind them of
a hurried evacuation of Westminster Abbey. Bill and Daisy,
like all of the world's press, had a front seat to a thousand of
the world's most prominent people dressed in their royal
finery, being rushed from the Abbey portcullis, spilling into
the closed-off street and around the corner into Parliament
Square. Big Ben bonged in national ecstasy, celebrating the
scheduled moment when the crowned king should have
been marching out triumphantly to the adoring crowds now
being pushed even further back by mounted guards.

"Just to update our viewers," Daisy said, distracted both
by the enraged producer and her journalistic instinct to grab
a microphone and follow the Archbishop of Canterbury
running away with his skirts hiked up. "The coronation of

King James III has been thrown into chaos as a bomb scare has led to a full evacuation of Westminster Abbey. We're told the threat is real and specific, and…yes, yes. I am being told now that a man is in custody. This is coming from…direct from the prime minister's spokesman, I'm hearing. A thirty-six-year-old man who is known to authorities has been arrested. This individual has links to the IRA. Now we haven't verified this information, but it is coming straight from the prime minister's spokesman, that a thirty-six-year-old man who is known to be an active member of the Irish Republican Army was apprehended earlier inside Westminster Abbey. Bill, unbelievable scenes here at what was supposed to be a moment of national unity."

"Unbelievable indeed," Bill replied, quietly stunned at the brazen lies being spouted from all angles. It should have been murdered journalist Liv Finnegan sitting here, splicing through the nonsense and spin. The woman who wrote the suppressed book on how the royal family and British state had murdered Prince Richard to keep secret his first marriage, and two children, to an IRA operative, should be in Bill's seat. She should comment on all of this. Bill sucked in a deep breath, and smiled for the cameras, and channeled his inner Liv Finnegan. "I mean, firstly we have to ask why this information is coming from the spokesman of the prime minister, who doesn't have the highest-level security clearance, and not the operational command of the Metropolitan Police who are coordinating security today."

"Um…" Daisy said, alarmed at Bill's response. "Well,

maybe on an issue of such national importance, the PM has been leading the security response directly. Which probably why he's not here." She seemed proud of herself for putting one and one together, and still getting three.

"That would be a massive breach of protocol for the prime minister, who is not a security expert, and barely weeks into the job, to be directly leading a counter-terrorism operation. The PM should have been here two hours ago, so if he was aware of this threat, why did they not act sooner? Why are we seeing this anarchy behind us, when we could have had a more orderly evacuation."

"Maybe they only caught this IRA man now?"

"That's the other thing," Bill said, wagging his finger directly at Daisy like he used to do to his sub-editors. "It's beggars belief to imagine the IRA has either the operational capacity, or the political will, to even threaten a bomb scare at a coronation. Fifteen or twenty years ago, maybe, but not today."

"That's just what I'm being told, Bill."

"And you're doing a good job of repeating it, but there's something much more nefarious afoot here."

James had told the soldiers to leave him be and go help the elderly guests make the relatively arduous journey from the Abbey to the supposed safe zone at Parliament Square. The place was crowded with the guests, the choirs, and the staff of the national ceremony. James had whipped off the embroidered cape and pocketed some of the more ostentatious jewels he'd been adorned with, and stood in the center of the grassy square rapidly filling with those who should have been inside watching him have a crown placed on his head. A security booth was on one side, the world's press pushing up against a cordon on another, and a crate of bottled water had been dumped onto the ground by soldiers running around like they'd trained for this very moment.

An overheated and very dismayed archbishop had been left nearby, his escort running back into the Abbey which still whirred with the piercing threat. James snatched a bottle of water from the back and rushed up behind the elderly man.

"Here, drink this," he said, passing the bottle from behind.

"Oh, thank you, my boy." The archbishop drank with a shaking hand while James held his elbow. Then he spied who had given him the bottle, and water spat out of his mouth in shock. "Your Majesty, please—"

"Take it easy, Your Grace," James said, holding up the old man's arm so he could still drink. "We'll get that crown on my head very soon, I promise."

James desperately looked around for any sign of Andrew. It seemed only now those who had been deeper inside the church were coming out.

"Alex!" James shouted. He ran across the grass, dodging those who had already given up on going back inside and ruined their outfits by sitting on the ground. She was limping, helped by a policewoman and a soldier. "Alex, Jesus, are you all right?"

"Yes, I'll be fine." She pushed off from the others and leaned onto the crowd control barrier, a thin line that separated them from the media. James ignored them and offered her his arm which she took. "These damn heels are not made for running in."

"Did you see Andrew?"

"Oh no, not yet. His own security team will surely—"

"Lizzie!" James shouted, dropping his sister's hand. He ran toward her, getting closer to the beeping Abbey and the line of soldiers surrounding it. Lizzie was being urged to go closer to the relative safety of the square, and not stay too close to the Abbey, as others were being warned, too. But James ran into her and dragged her closer. "Did you see Andrew in there? Did he come out with you?"

"No, I didn't see him. But James, you have to get back. It's not safe in there. They say there's a bomb."

"Andrew!" James shouted, not caring who could hear him, and who was looking. "Andrew! Are you here?"

"Sir," a soldier said, holding him back from getting too close to the cordon. "You must get back to safety."

"Get your hands off me! Andrew!" James' heart was pounding. Of course, he would lose everything today. Of course, the fates would not let him be crowned next to the man he loved, the only thing he'd wanted all his life. "Andrew! I said, unhand me!"

"It's all right, let me handle this," came a soft, almost relaxed voice. It was Samuel, slipping up behind James and hooking his arm, shuffling him away from the soldiers. "I saw him, Your Majesty."

"Where? Where is he?"

"Come, away from the cameras." Samuel guided him several feet from the Abbey and the railings where journalists and TV crews did not scream questions, but simply watched the human tale unfold. "I saw him with Lord Gregory, Your Majesty. I was just coming to fetch Prince Andrew when Greg arrived. I told him this was not the time nor place, but he pushed into the room anyway and ordered us all out. I must confess I waited outside for a moment and I heard them together, Your Majesty. I heard them laugh and…well, it's not so polite, but Andrew seemed incredibly relieved to be with Lord Gregory once again."

James pushed Samuel away. He couldn't even register what this man was saying. Nor did he really care. Andrew could be balls-deep in Greg or Greg could be fisting Andrew with the royal scepter, James didn't care. He just wanted to know Andrew was safe.

Samuel tried again to grab James as he leapt toward the Abbey, but James shoved him away. It seemed like the last stragglers were being helped out of the portcullis. Troops were converging now, not willing to let James run through the gauntlet. James had opened his mouth and was just about to scream *Andrew* at the top of his lungs, when a violent, earth-shaking explosion ripped through the world and collapsed them all with shock.

James felt himself be thrown to the ground, as if kneecapped by an invisible force, and so had many others. Soldiers were shouting at each other and the dull, distant echo of a thousand screams ricocheted through Parliament Square. His hands scuffed and dirty from the ground he'd fallen onto, James wondered if he was underwater. The sounds of shouting were far and sodden, but his ears were ringing, and violently. He scratched at the ground, trying to find what was upright as the blue of the sky had disappeared. All he could see was gravelly smoke billowing from the Abbey, and the roaring heat of an open fire incinerating the thousand-year dynasty.

The explosion rumbled through the MI5 tent set up in Parliament Square overrun by refugees from the coronation, who were now running from the scene, toward Big Ben and the crowd-lined streets which had turned into chaos. Just like when she'd been a raw recruit in West Berlin and heard the sledgehammers break through the wall, it was time for Lisa to leave the bunker and get out into the action.

"Gun, now!" she shouted at the dozens of staffers so well trained they did not look up at the inferno outside, but remained at their stations. Someone rushed a handgun and holster toward her, and she strapped it on under her blazer. "Get the police doing crowd control out there before someone gets trampled to death. Get people off the streets and into parks and buildings." Lisa had already burst through the tent and into the hot cloud of burning ash billowing from the Abbey when she shouted the last order. "Tell Special Branch I'm taking over. Any decisions will come through me."

Lisa meant every word she said, and her team knew it, too, but running out into an active army operation she knew was orchestrated by the very state she was sworn to protect, things might not go so smoothly. Fortunately, most of the high-profile dignitaries and foreign leaders had or were being evacuated from the heat of Parliament Square. A cordon had been opened to the House of Commons where most of them were being led into.

"Keep them moving in there," she told the army commander directing the ambassadors of several major allies toward the Palace of Westminster, "and lock down the building. No one leaves parliament."

With the gun tucked into the back of her trousers, she rushed toward the most concerning scene of all. King James on the ground in a scuffed and disordered uniform, just feet from the press gallery with their cameras primed on the burning roof of Westminster Abbey. Both Princess Alexandra and Lizzie Windsor were trying to help James up while he was pushing them away.

"What's going on here?" Lisa shouted at the several soldiers unsure of how to deal with a wailing king.

"It's like we told him, ma'am," one soldier said to her, "even if there was anyone left in the building, it's too dangerous to go inside."

"There could be other bombs," the other agreed. "We're trying to evacuate the press from their stations here, but they don't want to go."

"James," Lisa kneeled down to the king, brushing through Lizzie and Alexandra. His arms covered his ears as he rocked from side to side, eyes shut against the chaos. "It's Lisa Mantis of MI5. Can you hear me?" She put a hand on his neck, and his eyes snapped open.

"Andrew!" James shouted. "Andrew's still in there and they won't let me in."

"All right, James, we're going to get him. But I need you to stand up for me. It's not safe this close to the building. Can you do that?"

"Ma'am," the soldier cut in again. "Like I said, the building is unsafe."

"And the second highest ranking royal in the realm is stuck in there," Lisa yelled back. "Why are you not running in to find him?"

The soldier looked shellshocked.

"That's our orders," he replied, folding his arms against any further inquiry. "No entry to the building under any circumstances."

Lisa turned away, making her disgust known. She knew exactly where those orders had come from. But she also held the only person who could overcome Sir Peter. She just needed to get him thinking straight.

"That's it, James, stand up for me. Now, tell me, why do you think Andrew is still inside?"

"He told me!" James yelled through tears, pointing at Samuel, a royal aide, who had been hovering ten feet back, leaning against a temporary wall set up for the press gallery. Samuel raised his hands as if about to be shot, standing between two *Britain Today* logos.

"I just told him what I saw, ma'am. Lord Gregory went

inside Prince Andrew's dressing room alone and sent us all out."

"What did I do?" came a voice from inside the press gallery Samuel was leaning against. Two people looked down at them from five feet up. The former *Gazette* editor Lisa had once arrested on trumped up treason charges, Bill Honnington, and *Britain Today* presenter Daisy Angus. But the young man who had spoken was just to one side of Bill, attached to a wired microphone and sitting at the desk as if he had been describing the scene to their program's viewers.

"Greg!" James shouted. Lisa held James back from running full force toward him, but Greg was climbing down from the makeshift stage. He still had a mic on and ran over toward James.

"It's like I was just saying to my dad now on the TV, Samuel's the one who came and took Andrew away."

"What?" Lisa said faster than James.

"Yeah. I was with Andrew talking as he was getting ready and just waiting for it all to start, and then Samuel came into the room, told Andrew it was time, and took him away. I dunno where they went."

From the corner of her eye, Lisa saw Samuel's face go white. He had been caught, and looked the part, too. Slowly, and then faster, he started to slink back toward the crowd.

"Arrest him!" Lisa shouted, pointing her gun at Samuel. He froze. The soldiers looked unsure of what to do, but Lisa wasn't talking to them. There was enough uniformed police around to seize on a command. Five officers held Samuel still and threw handcuffs on him. Lisa marched over and grabbed Samuel by the cuffs. "You lead them to Andrew, do you understand?" she said to him, plainly and clearly. James' face had already turned. Hope flooded his eyes, and he ran toward the army line. Two soldiers rushed to seize the handcuffed Samuel, and followed their king into the burning building. It took only a moment before Lizzie, Alexandra, and another two dozen of the armed forces had rushed back into the Abbey, shouting for *Andrew* at the top of their lungs.

"Well, well," Sir Peter said, sliding up beside Lisa. "Looks like you've sent the entire line of succession into a fiery pit of hell."

"What did you say? I can't hear you because of the explosion," she looked up at Peter who stared down at her with dismay. But, also, beyond him, to Bill Honnington, watching from his press stand. She gave him a wink. "Come over here," she shouted at Peter while helicopters roared overhead. She yanked his cuff toward the wall of the press stand. "What have you done?" she asked him. More heads were peering down from the makeshift *Britain Today* studio above, but Lisa, and Peter, were focused entirely on the burning Abbey and the royals within.

"What have I done?" Peter said, speaking louder as the helicopters buzzed across the blazing sky.

"You murdered Andrew and left his body to burn!" Lisa shouted, so everyone watching at home could hear.

"I did not!" Peter roared with anger, but quickly calmed himself. "Andrew is simply the bait. I'm just doing what her late majesty should have done a long time ago. Let this rotten seed wither and die so we can start afresh."

"Murdering Prince Richard wasn't enough?"

"Murder? My goodness, heaven forbid. We simply carried out the Gaveston Protocols against Prince Richard as lawfully allowed, just as we're doing with all these other threats to the succession. James, Alexandra, and their half-sister Lizzie, too. And all of it neatly pinned on her Irish Republican half-brother. A family affair if there ever was one. Anyway, Lisa, it's your signature on the Gaveston Protocols, not mine."

"I was outvoted by you, by the prime minister, even by the head of MI6. The Protocols passed, but I didn't sign."

"Either way, they were lawfully passed, and you have your copy, so what does it matter the manner of the death we deal them? Parliament beheaded Charles I, and this rotten crop will die by fire, or by bomb. Poetic, I suppose. Just as Guy Fawkes tried to blow up the king in Parliament, so we defenders of liberty blow up a corrupt core of Papist royals with bombs under Westminster Abbey."

"Under? Then why is the roof on fire?"

"Oh, that was just the distraction. I would move your people out, because in about five minutes," Peter looked at his shiny gold watch. "The next ones will collapse the building, and everyone left inside."

Lisa looked up. Not at the burning roof, not at the helicopters, not at the billowing plume of smoke rushing over central London. But only a few feet up, where Bill

Honnington, Daisy Angus, a TV camera and multiple production assistants, all staring down at them.

"What in the devil…" Peter looked up, then around, then turned and saw what he'd done. He didn't have time to offer a rebuttal or to say another word, because Lisa had clicked her fingers and the officers began to approach. Shouts from the press gallery rolled louder than the licking flames and the wailing sirens that screamed in the background. The police approached, but not fast enough. Peter leapt toward the burning church, running after the royals he'd tricked. A few police officers jogged toward the burning building, but jumped back when a violent crack of stone high in one of the Abbey's towers launched a rain of slate onto the ground.

"What do we do?" an officer asked Lisa, nervously calling the police away. The *nee-naw* of fire engines had finally made it through the cordons. Dozens of fire officers started to run toward the Abbey, laden with equipment. Lisa knew whatever she said would be pored over in an official enquiry. She might quietly wish that Peter would burn up in the building, but that wasn't the way things were done.

"There's a lot of people still inside. Let's get them all out."

Chapter 21

SMOKE BURNED JAMES' EYES. HE COULD barely see in front of him, let alone the handcuffed Samuel who was supposed to be leading them to Andrew. Behind them, soldiers were shouting orders, and more shouted back, telling them all to leave. There was smoke, and they were coughing, but the fire was still high in the ceiling. They had a little more time, a soldier had assured them. Just enough time to find Andrew, James prayed.

"It's this way," Lizzie called back, leading from the front where she kept Samuel close to her, beside an officer who held a gun. Alexandra was next with two more soldiers, then James and three men behind him. They worked through the nave where the pews had been scattered and smashed in the frantic exit from the building. High-heeled shoes and hats scattered and lay where they'd fluttered from the exodus. The Abbey spread out endlessly. A gigantic wound through time which opened to a waking nightmare, with the end constantly getting further away.

"Stop!" Lizzie shouted as they neared the sanctuary.

Their little band of coughing warriors held back. The throne was only feet away. It sat empty in the center of the altar, just waiting to be sat on. A terrifying crack came from above like a scream of thunder. They all looked up. A wooden beam had caught fire, which rapidly spread along the flags which draped from the ceiling.

"Everyone move!" cried a soldier, and just in time. Beams and burning British flags and royal standards collapsed from on high and crashed straight onto the empty throne. James darted to the side, jumping into concrete to avoid the collapsing roof. Fire roared close now, not just from high above. The throne itself caught fire, spitting up licks of red-hot flame as the flags and ensigns of the Commonwealth burned up around the charring wood. The velvet covers and cushions quickly sizzled.

James found himself on the hard ground once again, coughing up smoke that had nowhere to escape. Their group had split to avoid the falling beams which now kindled the flaming throne. He felt around, staying low to the ground.

"Lizzie? Alex? Is that you? Are you both all right?"

They were coughing, but okay, and helped each other off their sides and onto their feet, although remaining low because of the thick smoke now enveloping them.

"Where are the others?" Alexandra asked. James could not see, but he heard them. The soldiers and Samuel shouted from across the other side of the altar, but the burning beams would not let them pass.

"Quick!" Lizzie shouted to them both. "Andrew is supposed to be back here behind the cloisters."

They skidded across the polished floor fast becoming ashen. The pews where the choir had stood waiting to sing *God Save the King* stood empty as firewood. Lizzie knocked through a side door, bursting it open and they ran into a stone corridor mercifully free from smoke. She slammed the door shut, and they had a moment of respite from the chaos and flames.

"He was getting ready in the Archbishop's room," James said, trying to picture a mental map of the Abbey. There had barely been a single rehearsal for the coronation, just parts and pieces practiced in the last week. The route Andrew would take to the nave he didn't know.

"He won't still be there," Alexandra said, rushing along to the end of the corridor and away from the cloisters where the archbishop's room would be. "Greg said that guy came and took him away. I bet it was along here to the crypt."

"Why the crypt?" James asked, but they followed anyway.

"When Faisal and I were last here, for our anniversary blessing, I took a walk around the place. The crypt is like a maze, and there's only one way in… and no way out."

James ran ahead of Alex as Lizzie followed, darting through ever-narrowing passages that contracted as they ran. James twisted left and right as the darkness encroached. They were going down, deeper under the Abbey. The stones here were cold and damp. The place felt wrong. A catacomb of bones and chains, of endings and deaths. How would Andrew be here? What state would he be in?

"Andrew!" James saw the crumpled body in royal finery pooled on the dusty floor at the end of the passageway. Andrew had fallen, slumped against an old wooden door with a rope handle which only led further down to the crypt itself. Lizzie and Alexandra hung back while James skidded to the man he loved. Whom he would give everything to know he was all right. To be breathing. To see him smile again, or laugh, or be sad or still or joyous or bored. To watch him pick fights and slink into the bedroom with an apologetic face. To find him curled up in bed, mobile phone still in his hand while he quietly snored. To see his body twist out of the shower and wrap a towel around his shoulders first before drying himself off. To hear him sip the morning's first coffee, and crinkle the newspaper and dismiss every piece of food offered before hungrily diving in to eat. To see how his nose crinkled at surprising news, or how his lip folded when he concentrated. To smell his skin as he held James in a hug or his hair in the evening, or the warm breath that enveloped him like the sweetest-smelling smoke. To have Andrew once again was all he wanted. James was not ready for this to be the last time.

"He's breathing!" James shouted. "He's definitely breathing."

Alexandra folded Andrew onto his side, listening for a heartbeat while Lizzie nervously looked back at the way they came.

"Lay him in the recovery position," Alexandra said,

folding one of Andrew's legs up and his arm out. "His heartbeat is strong. Might be a sedative."

"Are we going to drag him out?" Lizzie asked. James had never seen her look so afraid. "Because I think someone's coming."

Someone was. The footsteps were getting louder. Heavy slams against ancient stones. But not in the ordered rote of soldier's boots. These footsteps were scattered, singular, and furious.

Peter panted around the corner, his face sodden, clothes singed. Lizzie retreated to the wall. James stood in front of Andrew's still-unconscious body, protecting him and his sister who was unbuttoning the high collar.

"Well," Peter said, finding his breath. "Here we are. The bastard royals."

"What did you do to him?" James screamed, voice cracking into a hoarse cry.

"Christ, James!" Peter yelled back. "You're the king and all you care about is your bloody—"

"Don't talk about him!"

James went flush with rage. He saw only red. Only violence. Only the endless hunger of a cannibalistic institution, with no end to murderous schemes. He didn't feel it, but James' boots were thrusting him forward, arms outstretched, he grabbed Peter by the collar and whacked him against the wall.

"James!" Alexandra yelled while Lizzie weaved between them to break them apart. Alexandra pulled James from behind. He unhanded Peter, but wasn't quite sure why.

Alexandra took him back to Andrew while Lizzie stepped forward.

"We need to get him medical attention."

"Oh, shut up, you dumb bitch." Peter shoved her right in the throat. Lizzie fumbled back and fell against the wall, stunned. "None of us are going anywhere."

James saw two options, to fight Peter or run deeper into the crypt through the wooden door. He threw himself toward it and it swung violently open, but was lodged against something and cracked at the top. As the low, distant light crept in, he saw the crates. Piled so high they blocked the door from opening more than a foot.

"You've heard of the Gunpowder Plot, Your Majesty?" Peter asked, a sly grin dripping from his weathered face. "I'm not a papist, but you can think of this a little like that. I am Guy Fawkes, and I am going to restore the monarchy back to glory." His face twisted in hate as he stepped closer to James, who was now dangerously behind Alexandra and the unconscious Andrew. "You half bloods and homosexuals have denigrated our throne for long enough with your grubby little hands and disgusting perversions. Our queen, you don't even deserve the honor of being called her grandchildren. She sacrificed. She fought."

"She killed our father!" Alexandra yelled from the floor. Her hands protectively around Andrew's head. Peter was coming closer, his body contorted like a dead spirit was aching to get out and suck their souls.

"She killed a traitor," Peter spat. "Your so-called father

was nothing but a low-life, philandering, Catholic-fucking, ungrateful—"

Peter stopped talking. His eyes roared wide. He didn't know why. He looked around and quickly realized he couldn't breathe. A thin blue ribbon was being held around his throat, pressed in hard by Lizzie. Her determined face peaked out from behind his shoulder. He tried to turn, she squeezed tighter. He tried to lift his hands, but his face went red. Then purple. Then blue. Desperate wheezing sounds gasped from his fading face. His lips bitter blue, almost the color of the silk noose being ever more tightened around his throat. Harder, harder. His eyes sparked red. Bloodshot, bursting. More desperate clawing, but it wasn't even close. A second or an age passed. But finally, finally, in the depths of the crypt of Westminster Abbey, with a ton of explosives primed to go off at any moment that they did not know, the lifeless body of Sir Peter, trusted private secretary of the late Queen Victoria II, dropped to the stony floor, as lifeless as a sack of potatoes.

Lizzie remained standing in place, the body at her feet. James and Alexandra both stared not at her, but the emergency service personnel rushing in behind. Firefighters and soldiers in masks and oxygen tanks. They stepped aside for two helmeted figures with a stretcher who rushed straight for Andrew. Two more came forward for Peter, too, but then Lisa Mantis stepped around the corner.

She wore no mask, no protective gear. She seized up the situation in a second while Andrew was carefully lifted onto the stretcher and people were trying their hardest to get masks onto James, Lizzie and Alexandra.

"Dynamite!" James said for want of anything else to say. He pointed to the broken door.

"I know," Lisa said. "This place is going to blow in minutes." She seemed unbothered and peered down at Peter's dead body. "Leave this one here," she ordered. "Let's go."

Lisa had left Peter's body to the inferno with little more than a shrug, but Westminster Abbey was on fire, and it was time to run. Beyond the tight-knit crypt were the firefighters in their space age gear who had to move in single file, the rest of the burning Abbey was a hum of frantic activity. Gas-masked workers rushed out jewels, cushions, candelabras, and silver communion cups. Anything that could be rescued before the roof finally caved in.

"Everyone out!" Lisa yelled, again and again, up and down the nave, grabbing soldiers by the scruff of their collars and kicking them toward the exit. "There's more bombs."

People took their orders, grabbing what they could and running as yet more fiery beams crashed into the altar, now devoid of the relics. James ran as close to Andrew's stretcher as he could, wanting nothing more than to get out. As they departed the smoky interior for the flashing lights and wailing sirens of the outside, bomb disposal robots were being sent in from armored squads where the press gallery had sat. But the paramedics with Andrew on a stretcher kept running, straight toward the relative distance of Parliament Square.

The green grass had been well trampled, but already cleared of the coronation guests. But no one had moved on the world's media, who were decamped just across the barrier on the far side, snapping pictures and video of a figure being brought from the smoldering Westminster Abbey. Yelling and shouts, James didn't listen, nor did he want to hear. He didn't care that the press knocked down one of the crowd control barriers in their excitement when they saw James jogging alongside the stretcher. He didn't pay any attention to the couple of photographers falling over themselves to snatch a perfect shot of the king bent over his fiancé against the backdrop of Westminster Abbey ablaze.

James only cared that Andrew's eyes had flickered open. James burst into an endless smile. Streaked with tears, but a smile nonetheless, his hands cupped around Andrew's exhausted face. In only the time it took for Andrew to glance up at the raging fire and the stream of soldiers pushing the cordon even further back, he knew what was happening.

"You…saved me," Andrew said, his voice a faint, croaky whisper on the breeze. James shook as he tried to shush him, but Andrew was strong enough to find James' fingers, and clasp them tightly.

"No…you saved me."

They kissed. Not for the last time, but the first of many more.

One year later

"Well, Bill, here we are again," Daisy said, grinning straight to the camera. Bill offered the exasperated grin the audience apparently loved from Britain's new darlings of breakfast television.

"That's right, Daisy. *Britain Today* is coming to you live from the royal wedding of King James and Prince Andrew. We're camped here in the press gallery outside the once magnificent Westminster Abbey." Bill turned away from the camera to glance behind him. A rehearsed move, but one that brought a solemn moment of mourning to the once-magnificent monument to the monarchy which now stood as little more than an edifice of an open-air construction site.

"The church was deconsecrated last year by the Archbishop following the awful events of the coronation, but at least it gets around the Anglican Church's continuing ban on same-sex marriages within their churches."

"Not a day for politics, Daisy," Bill said with a smile and a wink, as was written on the teleprompter. "But I echo your sentiments. Because today is a day about love. The love between our sovereign, King James III, and Prince Andrew, the Duke of Cornwall, crowned alongside His Majesty and in his own right last year in that hastily arranged ceremony at Lambeth Palace."

"We're waiting for the guests to start arriving to this wonderful open-air venue with the sun streaming down, and of course pass judgment on the fashions," Daisy paused for Bill's cue.

"I'll be the judge of that," he said with a chuckle.

"Let's take a look at the love story of King James and Prince Andrew, friends from childhood, and soon to be spouses for life."

They both glanced down at the screen pointing up from the desk as it played a montage of footage of the couple, from their days at Eton, through university and then James' career as a professional playboy throughout his twenties. The entire production staff of *Britain Today* had worked for weeks to edit out the countless women James and Andrew were almost always pictured with.

Daisy leaned into Bill as makeup artists rushed to their sides, dabbing blush and fluffing her.

"Hard to believe," she said as her cheeks were dabbed with a brush. "They only fell in love after Katyn died."

Bill wanted to laugh out loud. He'd almost forgotten the official record of events most people stunningly seemed to believe.

"I think they've been fucking since high school," Bill said, flicking through his papers. Daisy snarled in surprise.

"You can't prove that."

"I nearly did."

"When?"

"When I was editor of *the Gazette*. Would've been the scoop of the century."

"Well why didn't you publish it?"

Bill paused. There was so much he could say, but the stopwatch on the pre-recorded reel was ticking down with only seconds until they were back on air. And somehow, he didn't hate the official version of their love story.

"Buy me a drink one day and I might tell you all about it." Bill grinned at Daisy's shock, as they went live once again.

"What a hat!" Daisy said as they entered the third hour of their live coverage of the royal wedding. On their screen they watched the scenes of the filled-up chairs laid out in ordinary rows along the scarred floor. The ruined walls and piles of rubble in a half-state of rebuilding had been decked out with flower wreaths and decorations sent in from primary schools across the Commonwealth. James and Andrew had invited children to make decorations for the royal wedding, along with home-made flags and cakes for their own street parties. The once-magnificent stone and marble replaced with colorful paper rings and streamers, with an endless motif of rainbow.

"And that's...who is that heavily pregnant woman, Daisy? The one who's just sat down at the front next to the King Mother, Princess Alice."

"Jenna Thompson, that's the royal couple's surrogate. She's twenty-seven weeks I believe, now."

"My goodness, she's huge."

"That's what happens with twins," Daisy said as they watched her on the screen chatting to Princess Alice who'd chosen to wear white to her son's wedding. "And it's more likely with IVF as well. They took sperm from Prince

Andrew, and the eggs were donated by James' *relation* Lizzie Windsor." Daisy used the word delicately given the rumors sparked before Sir Peter's death that Lizzie Windsor was actually the half-sister of James and Alexandra. Bill had quietly confirmed to them the truth. "And there we see Lizzie Windsor on screen now, or should I say *Princess* Elizabeth, after her recent elevation by the King."

"We can see Princess Elizabeth looking absolutely beautiful, I might add Daisy, in her role as maid of honor wearing cream Vera Wang, I'm being told."

"Oh, come on now, Bill, you know a Vera Wang when you see one."

"And she's talking there with Queen Alexandra, who took over her temporary duties as Queen Regent last night in a statement released by Buckingham Palace. The King's twin sister will act as Queen Regent while His Majesty and Prince Andrew enjoy their honeymoon, and then for the duration of King James' paternity leave."

"That's right, Bill, and they better make the most of that honeymoon because caring for twins is quite the challenge for any new parents. Although, so is acting as monarch for the next year to eighteen months, but Queen Alexandra will be assisted by Princess Elizabeth in carrying out those royal duties."

"Quite the turnaround from a few years ago, isn't it?" Bill said, employing some of his famous frankness the viewers of *Britain Today* couldn't get enough of. "I mean a few years ago, these four were at each other's throats, and now here they are, all sharing the throne."

"Yes, yes, lovely sentiment, Bill, but I've just spotted your son there in the crowd. Lord Gregory is looking mighty handsome, I must say, but who is that eye candy on his arm? Does Gregory have a new boyfriend you've not told us about?"

"Daisy, this kid has boyfriends that even I don't know about!" Bill peered at the screen. This one he did actually recognize. A young theater actor who Bill quite liked because he addressed him as *your lordship*. Bill was the Marquess of Essex, after all. "If I'm not mistaken, that's the lad playing in the West End just now. He keeps leaving makeup stains on my towels when he comes back to ours after a show."

Daisy chuckled. The guests were taking their seats, and Bill fished out the order of service as the ceremony was about to start.

"So, to all our viewers at home, now, as they say, is when things start to get interesting. To open the wedding service, the London Gay Men's Chorus are just coming up to the front now to sing the national anthem, *God Save the…*" Bill trailed off. The order of service didn't say, it just had *national anthem* written on it.

"Wait," Daisy asked. "If Alexandra is acting as Queen Regent from now and for the next eighteen months, but King James is still present, and getting married, then which version does the choir sing? *God Save the King*, or *God Save the Queen*?"

"Good question, Daisy, I guess we're about to find out."

The End.

About Harry F. Rey

Harry F. Rey is a Pushcart-nominated author and lover of gay themed stories with a powerful punch.

Alongside The Line of Succession series, he is the author of the gay rom-com All The Lovers, also available from Deep Desires Press.

His other works include the queer sci-fi series The Galactic Captains, the WWII-era gay historical novel Why in Paris? and Six Days in Jerusalem. His work has also been featured in anthologies including Not Meant for Each Other from Lost Boys Press and Queer Life, Queer Love from Muswell Press.

Website: https://harryfredrey.wixsite.com/harryfrey

More by Harry F. Rey

The Line of Succession
The Line of Succession 2: Acts of Treason
The Line of Succession 3: Interregnum
The Line of Succession 4: Rex v. Regina
The Line of Succession 5: Royal Prerogative
The Line of Succession 6: God Save The…?

All The Lovers

Also from Deep Desires Press

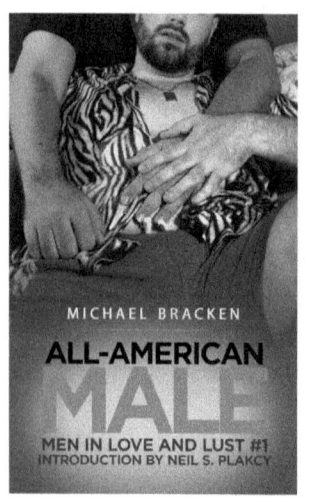

All-American Male
Men in Love and Lust #1
Michael Bracken

When college student Bernie is dragged to a Christmas party where he knows nobody, the last thing he expects is to be naked and between the thighs of the sexiest man he's ever met.

While older men aren't usually his thing, there's something about Professor Maeyer that gets Bernie going in ways he hasn't felt for a long time. So, when the party ends and everyone's gone home and it's just Bernie and Professor Maeyer, he gets a deeper education, the kind that can't be taught in class, the kind that can only be taught in the bedroom.

Bernie's about to learn just how much Professor Maeyer can blow his mind (and his load).

"Learning Curve" is just one of nineteen scorching hot and smutty-as-hell stories in this sweaty, throbbing, pounding collection of gay erotica from Michael Bracken, acclaimed author of erotic short fiction.

Available now in ebook and paperback

Also from Deep Desires Press

All-The Lovers
Harry F. Rey

Welcome to Leeds, 2007. Welcome to drag before Drag Race *and hook-ups before Grindr. Welcome to 19-year-old Nick's oh-so-complicated love life. Welcome to* All The Lovers.

Still hung up on ex-boyfriend Shawn, Nick tries, tries, and repeatedly fails to find a meaningful connection in a parochial gay society still defined by closets and cruising. With fabulous best friend Mylo and straight-laced flatmate Jenna by his side, Nick's journey to self-discovery forces him to confront not only his own demons, but those of all his lovers as well.

All The Lovers is a sexy, hilarious, and eye-opening chronicle of Nick—a working class teenager from the North of England exploring love and sex in a pre-Grindr world.

Available now in ebook and paperback

Also from Deep Desires Press

When Things Happen Together
Jordan Clayden-Lewis

Two travelers on the ultimate Australian road trip. Two numbers that will change their lives forever.

Thomas is in need of a change. Being an aspiring artist from London, he hopes a working holiday in sunny Australia will be the muse he's been waiting for. But it isn't Australia's vast landscapes that are his source of inspiration...

After a string of unromantic dates, Thomas meets Bruce, a handsome Irish traveler with alluring almond eyes. The more time the pair spend together, however, the more they start seeing the numbers 1122 everywhere.

Are the numbers just a coincidence, or is something greater at play? Is Bruce really who he says he is, or is there more to him than he's letting on?

A story about seizing the moment, finding a sense of home, and embracing love when it comes knocking.

Available now in ebook and paperback

www.ingramcontent.com/pod-product-compliance
Lightning Source LLC
Chambersburg PA
CBHW052004020726
47501CB00004B/992